TATE

LIGHTHOUSE SECURITY INVESTIGATIONS

MARYANN JORDAN

Cover by: Graphics by Stacy

ISBN ebook: 978-1-947214-60-6

ISBN print: 978-1-947214-61-3

❀ Created with Vellum

Ravaged. That was the only word Tate could think of to describe everything about this day. As part of the Honor Guard at the funeral of a fallen service member and fellow SEAL, he felt ravaged. Considering the funeral was for his best friend since childhood, he felt ravaged.

Looking across the flag-draped coffin toward Nathan's parents clinging to each other, their faces were ravaged. And when he captured and held the gaze of Nathan's sister, Nora, the woman he planned on marrying, he saw nothing but raw, ravaged emotion pouring from her.

The service was soon over, the salute was given, the flag folded and presented. He sucked in a ragged breath, reminding himself to breathe even though his chest ached with each inhalation. The idea of passing out almost brought a smile, thinking that Nathan would have found it hilarious for Tate to faint at a funeral. With a last glance back toward the now-bare coffin, the idea that Nathan would never laugh again ravaged him.

The funeral had been hard enough to get through, but he felt choked in the crowded house full of mourners. If one more person came up to him to thank him for his service or tell him that they remembered he and Nathan had always been together, he was not sure he'd be able to handle it.

One look at Nora's pale face while standing in her living room gave evidence that she felt the same. Without speaking, he simply linked fingers with her, and they walked out together. He assisted her up into his truck, having no destination in mind. Dark clouds were beginning to roll overhead, adding to the silent, somber mood.

After a while, he finally drove to the Double T, his family's ranch, and parked outside the barn. Filled with memories of the three of them throughout their youth, at that moment it was the only place he wanted to be. A storm had been brewing all day, dark clouds moving in, lightning in the distance, and the winds started to whip fat raindrops against the front of the truck. He climbed down from the driver's side and raced around to her door. Cognizant of the heels she wore, he scooped her into his arms and carried her into the barn before setting her feet to the ground. He glanced down, wondering if being there was upsetting, but for the first time that day, she looked as though she could breathe. She took his hand, linked fingers with him, and walked to the ladder leading to the hayloft.

Climbing close behind her, his feet had landed on the wooden floor just as she kicked her shoes off. They walked together to the wide opening and stared out toward the mountains in the distance. By now, the storm had descended all around them. With rain pelting the tin roof and the winds howling, they turned and faced each other, drawn by the magnet that had always existed between them.

They moved slowly at first, hands simply grasping each other's shoulders as the distance between their bodies closed. He bent and kissed her lightly, but her fingers tightened, and she clung to him, the kiss taking on an intensity he had not planned for but they both needed.

Clothes were soon tossed, his uniform heedlessly dumped onto the hay. Their hands roamed wildly, noses bumped as tongues thrust, and lips devoured each other. The need to bury their shared grief in each other's bodies overtook all other thoughts.

Kneeling when they were completely naked, she soon slid to her back, her breasts beckoning, arms lifted and legs spread in need and invitation. Dating for years, this was not the first time they'd had sex, nor the hayloft been their hideaway, but he could not remember ever needing her body quite so desperately. When he finally plunged into her warm sex as her arms and legs clung to him, he could no longer tell where he ended and she began.

Lightning speared through the dark and the following thunder shook the barn. She surprised him when she pushed against one shoulder, and he rolled to his back, his cock still deep inside. She leaned forward, her honey-blonde hair creating a curtain as her hands clutched his shoulders. Her eyes squeezed shut and her breasts bounced as she rode his cock, lifting and plunging with a ferocity that he knew mirrored his own.

She threw her head back, crying out her release, and shame hit him at the realization he had not taken care of her needs, having concentrated more on his own. She fell forward, her breasts tightly pressed against his chest, and he flipped her so that she was once again on her back. She continued to cling to him, her eyes now open and pinned straight to his. He lifted one of her legs so that he could drive his cock deeper.

Finally, he shuddered as his orgasm sent shockwaves throughout his body. Continuing to pump until every last drop was drained, he barely managed to fall to the side, pulling her close as he dragged aching breaths deep into his lungs.

The only thought in his mind had been to forget, but as she held his gaze, memories came rushing back. The three of them racing around the ranch as kids. The first time he'd looked at her as a woman one summer when she pranced around the swimming hole in a bikini. The promises he and Nathan made when they joined the Navy. Especially the last promise... the one that said he'd take care of Nora.

As they dressed, he held her close, kissing her forehead. He wanted to ask if she was okay, but one look at her still-grief-stricken face and he knew the loss of her brother was almost more than she could bear. If he could take away her pain, he would have. His SEAL training had prepared him for everything—except how to make this better for her.

2

TEN YEARS LATER

They're missing it all.

Casting his gaze upon the other occupants in the business class section of the plane, Tate did not see one other person looking out their window. Snoozing. Reading. Working on their computers. Ordering their next drink. But no one was paying attention to the ever-changing vista below.

He shifted in his seat, glad his long legs had extra room, then leaned over to stare out his window and continue his perusal of the ground from his 30,000 feet elevation.

Flat plains and rolling hills. Green grass and scrub brush. Thick forests and craggy peaks. The occasional city could be seen in the distance, but below, houses and barns nestled amongst acres of wheat on farms or at the edge of massive cattle ranches. Roads weaved between small towns, the thread that connected everyone below.

The man across from him flipped up the visor on his

window, leaned over and peered down, then immediately turned back to his computer, his expression never changing, dismissing the view below.

But for Tate, the wide-open spaces below settled deep inside, bringing back memories of home. The place where he was born and raised, taught love of family and love of the land. Where he was taught pride in hard work and the reward of good fun.

Home was saddling his favorite horse and riding the ranch, keeping an eye on the cattle that grazed in the pastures near the base of the hills. Home was also hours spent on the massive tractor, plowing, planting, and then harvesting the hay. Home was learning how to hunt and fish with his granddad.

Home was Sunday mornings, sitting in the family pew of the little white church in the nearby town, listening to the preacher and singing hymns. It was a Sunday dinner that his grandma, mom, and sister prepared that would feed the whole family, some of the farmhands that lived nearby, and anyone from church that his dad recognized needed a good meal and good company.

Home was the county fair each summer where his mom's apple pie almost always took home the blue ribbon and everyone was begging for grandma's apple butter recipe.

Home was where he grew into his large hands and feet, finally filling out the gangly body of his early-teen years. Reaching six feet, five inches, he'd packed on muscle with his mom's good cooking and the hard, daily ranch work.

Home was high school baseball games, where he knew everyone in the stands and they cheered for each kid like they were their own. Home was long bus rides to get to school, but he didn't mind because he could stare out the window at the land all around with his friends at his side.

He scrubbed his hand over his chin, smiling as more memories flooded his mind. Home was also tearing up dirt roads in pickup trucks as a teenager, the rougher the terrain, the better. Home was sneaking his first cigarette and beer behind the barn and hiking up the mountains behind the family ranch with his best friend, Nathan.

Home also brought back memories of Nathan's sister, the beautiful girl he loved when he was young and full of ideas about the life he wanted to lead. The girl he was sure he'd marry one day. Settle on part of the ranch. Build a house. Raise a family.

A sigh left his lips as his thoughts turned.

Home was also time spent alone in the mountains, sitting on a rock outcropping and surveying the expanse of land, wondering what else was out there in the world. Excitement. Adventure. Big cities. Big oceans. Ports of call. And when the call to duty sounded, he and Nathan joined the Navy, but his dreams of the future were always of hearth and home. Those ideas were what kept him grounded when missions took him around the world and danger lurked in the shadows. *What would I have done differently if I knew what was hiding in the shadows? Dreams change, and the young become less idealistic, forging new paths and new places to lay our heads.*

A former SEAL now employed as a Keeper for Lighthouse Security Investigations, he made his new home in Maine but still loved being able to travel the world. A few weeks ago, he was in French Guiana on a rescue mission and had just finished a security detail in Texas. He enjoyed his post-military life, especially being able to take this detour to celebrate his mom's birthday by returning to his childhood home for a visit.

As the plane began its descent into the Denver airport, he smiled as the ground rose to touch the wheels of the plane and the pilot executed a smooth landing. His fellow business class passengers were checking their phones and watches, putting away their computers, and pulling out their itineraries for the next leg of their journey.

For him, it would be a quick flight on a much smaller plane to Rawlins, Wyoming.

Thirty minutes later, he was back in the air, once more staring out the window at the familiar landscape below of forests and mountains, grassland and scrub brush. This time, the smaller plane flew closer to the ground and the cars and trucks on the little roads were easily visible. Less than two hours later, he walked through the small airport, out into the bright sunshine.

Home for a few days. Minutes later, with his duffel bag in one hand, he grinned at the sight of another high school friend, now brother-in-law, Thomas. Dropping his bag, he clasped Thomas' hand in his before pulling him in for a back-slapping greeting. Thomas was not as tall as Tate but muscular with a ready smile and friendly demeanor.

"Jesus, man, my sister must be feeding you well." Tate popped Thomas on the stomach, laughing as the other man jumped away, rubbing his midsection.

"Fuck, Tate. Working the ranch, I've got no time to get fat." Grinning, he wiggled his eyebrows. "But then, Caroline learned how to cook at your mama's knee, so she always takes good care of me."

"Hell, I can't wait to taste their cooking again." Tate reached down and grabbed his bag, hefting the large duffel. Years of hauling heavy loads as a young man and then as a SEAL enabled him to shoulder the heavy bag as though it were weightless. Walking alongside Thomas, he easily spied the family ranch pickup truck, faded blue with the logo for Double T Ranch on the side, dirt on the tires, and dust covering the back. "I see Dad's still got the pickup running."

Thomas chuckled, shaking his head as they both climbed inside. "One of the reasons your dad's ranch makes money is that he doesn't waste it on stupid shit. As long as a truck, tractor, or any piece of machinery can run, he keeps it going."

Right on cue as he turned the switch, the old truck fired to life and, spinning the steering wheel with a practiced hand, Thomas pulled out of the parking lot and onto the road. They quickly left any semblance of civilization behind. The family ranch was about thirty miles south of Rawlins and they drove on a two-lane highway, cutting through the hills and valleys.

Thomas kept up a running monologue about the

ranch, his kids, and any gossip about people Tate used to know. Settling back in the seat, Tate listened with enjoyment, not surprised to find that many of his high school friends were now running their family ranches or businesses. Boys he played ball with were now married with kids, much like Thomas. Girls he had flirted with were now moms. Some of the boys and girls he knew had left for college or jobs elsewhere, but many of the farms had been passed down through the generations.

Tate always winced when he thought about his grandfather's reaction to him leaving high school and joining the Navy. It had been his grandfather's dream that he would stay in Wyoming and continue to run the ranch with his father. At one time, that had been his dream also. *Thank God for Caroline and Thomas.* His father accepted that his heart had been set on becoming a SEAL, and Tate had been able to leave with little guilt, knowing that his older sister Caroline was marrying her sweetheart who was eager to work the ranch.

They passed the outskirts of the little town and he swung his head around. His gaze snagged on a little strip mall shopping center that used to be nothing more than a local grocery. "Whoa," he murmured under his breath. Reading the businesses, his voice raised. "Nail salon. Day spa. Cell phone store. Coffee shop. A Chinese restaurant!"

Nodding his head with vigor, Thomas grinned. "Hell, we've got pizza, a brewery, Mexican, Chinese. Of course, there are more steak and barbecue places than you can shake your fist at." He glanced to the side and added, "Sometimes, after church on Sunday, we'll stop and have a meal out."

He jerked his head around again, this time staring at Thomas. *What the fuck?* "Since when did Mom quit cooking a big Sunday dinner?"

Thomas shrugged his beefy shoulders, turning onto another—and smaller—two-lane road. "She still cooks, but we don't have as many ranch hands as we used to. She says that sometimes it's just nice to sit down in a restaurant and let them do all the fixing."

"I know changes make sense, but... hell, somehow, I still think of this place as it was when we were kids."

"I know you didn't see it 'cause it was on the other side of Rawlins, but we've now got a new medical center. Your mom finally convinced your dad to go in for a full checkup since he didn't have to go very far."

Before he had a chance to ask more about the family, Thomas turned off the road and onto a lane underneath a sign declaring Double T Ranch. The drive was paved, but dust kicked up all around, nonetheless. Without thinking, his gaze peered through the windshield, ignoring the pastures to either side as he strained to see the familiar house that rose from the side of a hill. The massive barn was off to the left, but it was the house that held his attention.

Two stories made of wood and stone nestled amongst the trees his great-grandfather had planted. Massive windows filled the front, offering the residents an unparalleled view of the ranch with snow-capped mountains in the distance. A wide porch extended from the side, steps leading down to a large stone patio, complete with benches and chairs surrounding a firepit. The flowerbeds were all dormant, but shrubs lined the patio and walkways.

Memories hit again, of family and friends gathered for barbeques, his mom bustling around with platters as his dad manned the grill. After everyone left or turned in for the night, he and Nathan used to lean back in the Adirondack chairs, drink a beer, and look at the stars, dreaming of a life outside of Wyoming.

By the time Thomas pulled the truck to a stop in front of the house, the screen door had opened. Out rushed his niece, two nephews, his sister, Caroline, and his mom, Susan. The children rushed down the front steps, bypassing their dad on the way to greet Tate. Swinging his niece into his arms, he ruffled the hair of his two nephews, shocked at how much they had grown since he last saw them. Caroline stepped forward to kiss Thomas before moving into Tate's arms. Her long dark hair was shorter, now swinging just above her shoulders, but her eyes sparkled as they always did when she looked up at him.

"You were always pretty, Sis, but every time I see you, you look more and more like Mom."

She smiled up at him, accepting the compliment. "And you look just like Dad." Her hand reached up and she touched her finger right to his temple. "Hmmm, is that a little gray I see?"

"I don't know what you're talking about." He laughed, but the reality was that each morning when he looked into the mirror, he spied the few grey hairs. With his niece still in his arms, he left his sister's side and jogged up the steps to the porch and right into his mom's arms. "Beautiful as ever, Mom."

"I can't believe you've finally taken a weekend off to come to visit! And for my birthday!"

"I'm glad it worked out." He passed his niece off to Thomas so that he could wrap both arms around his mother, kissing the top of her head.

Her eyes searched his, her arms wrapped around him. "When do you have to go back?"

"I know it's short, but I can only stay two nights for now. Then I need to get back home for another job."

"Mace certainly keeps you busy." Shrugging, she smiled. "But I know it's what you love and that's all any parent wants... for their child to be happy." She patted his cheek and then nodded toward the barn. "Go on down. I know your dad's anxious to see you."

As the others went into the house, he jogged down the steps and along the path leading to the barn. His mom was right... Mace kept all his employees busy. A former Special Forces and CIA Special Operator, Mace Hanover had created Lighthouse Security Investigations when he left the service. Hiring SEALs, Deltas, Rangers, Special Forces, Air Force Ops, and CIA Ops, he'd created an elite security team.

It was no secret Tate's mom would have loved for him to return to the farm, but she also understood that was not his calling.

The massive wooden structure rose before him, its green-painted tin gambrel roof a beacon even from the road. The hayloft doors were partially opened, allowing the breeze to blow through. He grinned, remembering the countless bales of hay he and Nathan hauled to the loft. Nathan's dad had been the grocery store manager, not a business that Nathan was interested in. So, his best friend would spend many afternoons and most summer days at the Double T Ranch.

Most of their hay was stored in the massive round bales, but the smaller square bales had been placed in the hayloft to use for the horses. A flash of the hayloft being used for a very different reason by he and Nora flew through his mind.

Pushing that aside, he moved through the wide, open doors of the barn, stopped to touch the wooden frame, and remembered the solid feel and the scent of horses, hay, feed, and sweat from a long day.

ATVs had now replaced some of the horses they used for checking on the ranch, and his mom had a golf cart for getting back and forth from the orchard.

But his father still loved to ride, and at the sight of his silver-haired dad tossing hay into the stalls with the horses, he grinned. *Some things don't change.*

Frank Tate. He had been given his father's name and as a child was called Frankie. When he was in high school, his friends just called him Tate and going by his last name stuck. It was solidified when in the Navy. But, staring at his father now, he knew he would always be Frankie to his parents.

His father still stood over six feet tall, hard muscles built from years of ranching. He turned at the sound of

Tate walking into the barn, and his hazel eyes twinkled as a smile spread across his face. "Son!"

Walking straight into his dad's strong embrace, the two men hugged and back-slapped. "Good to see you, Dad."

"Help me toss a few more bales around, and we'll head to the house. Got a small party planned for your mom tomorrow, and she's tickled pink that you were able to be here."

With the two of them breaking open the small bales and spreading them around, the task was quickly accomplished, and they headed out of the barn toward the house. Going through the back door, they entered a large mudroom, essential for a working ranch. Washing his hands at one of the sinks, he looked over his shoulder as his dad pulled off his boots and shoved his feet into slippers before scrubbing his hands and arms as well. They dropped the dirty towels into the hamper provided. Leaving the mudroom, they moved through the pantry and into the large kitchen where his mom and sister were setting out platters of fried chicken, potato salad, and green beans.

His mom looked up as the men walked in, her smile wide. His dad bent to kiss her upturned cheek before she ordered, "Serve yourself and then have a seat. I'm gonna pull the peach cobbler out of the oven."

Tate inwardly chuckled when he saw everyone follow his mom's instructions. She ruled the roost when it came to mealtimes. Thinking back, Mom had been in charge of mealtimes, homework, athletic schedules, Sunday church attendance, proper etiquette—

"What are you waiting for?"

Her voice cut through his musings and he laughed out loud. "Sorry, Mom. Gathering wool, I guess."

The lines radiating from her eyes deepened as she smiled. "Being home brings back memories, doesn't it?"

"Oh, yeah." Settling at the table, he sat between his nephews and across from Thomas, Caroline, and his niece, with his parents at the ends. He ate his fill, the food tasting better than any he'd had at a restaurant. The conversation was lively around the table as he caught up with the ranch and local news, and his nephews peppered him with questions about the places he'd traveled. He caught the long looks of concern that Caroline settled upon her oldest son who, at ten years old, already had an eye for traveling the world. *That one will never stay on the ranch.* When that thought hit him, he glanced toward his mom and wondered when she knew that he was destined to leave Wyoming.

After dinner, the family spilled into the expansive den. The comfortable sofas with cushions meant for lounging held most of them. His father reclined in his Lazy-Boy while his mom rocked in the old rocker that she'd inherited from her parents. A game was on the TV, but the sound was low, the adults still talking. His dad and Thomas talked about the ranch, interspersing their discussion with questions for Tate.

Caroline took the kids upstairs for their baths and to get ready for bed. His mom followed soon after. His dad moved to the sideboard and poured three whiskeys. Handing one to Thomas and one to Tate, he lifted his tumbler into the air. "To the past. To the future. To family."

Tate took a hearty swallow of the peaty brew, the amber liquid burning as it went down, his father's words ringing in his ears.

3

That night, after everyone had retired, unable to sleep, he wandered the house. Walking silently from room to room, he was flooded with good memories. He gazed at the pictures on the wall of the den, the small frames cataloging several lifetimes. An old photograph of his father as a child, standing in front of what would now be considered an antique tractor. Pictures of he and Caroline on horseback. Caroline and Thomas' wedding. Photographs of he and Nathan, arms around each other as they stood on the baseball field. Moving along the wall, his gaze landed on a picture of his and Nathan's graduation from Navy boot camp, his smile wide as he was surrounded by his family.

And there, tucked under his arm, was her. Nathan's sister. *Nora*. Long, honey-blonde hair. Dark brown eyes he swore he could stare into for hours. Cute curves that hinted of what they would become as she matured. Smiling a slightly-crooked smile that always made him want to kiss her. *God, we were young, and the world spread out before us like a present ready to be opened.*

Soon after, he had his first deployment and within a year had been accepted into the training that would take over another year. As a young, brash man, cocksure and ready to take on the world, he had convinced Nathan to do the same, and while they were assigned to different teams, they were both stationed out of Virginia. Downtime was spent together just like when they were kids. *I thought we were unstoppable. God, I was so wrong.*

Sighing, he turned from the wall of memories and climbed back up the stairs, hoping to eventually find sleep. Passing by the hall bathroom, he noticed a faint light coming from the crack of the unclosed door. His sister's voice carried gently through the silent house.

"I'm sorry, I would've told you sooner, but we weren't sure he was going to be able to come. I know you were hoping to see Mom tomorrow, but Tate will still be here. I think his flight leaves early Sunday afternoon, so if you want to come by Sunday evening, that would be great."

Brow furrowed, he wondered who Caroline was talking to so late at night. *And why do my plans make a difference to anyone?* Not normally one to eavesdrop, he should have passed by the door and gone into his bedroom, but curiosity held him in place.

"Yeah, I know. I'm sorry, too, Nora."

Nora? He blinked in surprise. He used to wonder if there would come a time when he could see her or say her name and not have the stabbing pain from the knowledge that he fucked up royally.

A heavy sigh left his lips as it always did when he thought of Nathan. There were other friends and fellow servicemen and women who did not make it back, but it was Nathan's death that had rocked his world.

Hours after he and Nora tried to bury their grief in each other's bodies, he'd prepared to fly back to Virginia to rejoin his team, standing underneath the huge ash tree, saying goodbye to her. Looking back, he could not remember when he'd decided to break up with her. Was it when she'd turned her tear-filled eyes up to him, begging him to come home safely to her? Was it when he'd thought of the promises he had once made to Nathan that he would never hurt her? Was it after they'd spent that night holding each other, finding comfort, and burying the pain when they made love in the barn? *Who the hell knows? All that matters is that I did, thinking it was the best thing to do.*

Two months later, with a cowardly email, he ended things. *It seemed like the smart play at the time... a way to keep her safe in case I didn't come back.* He lifted his hand and gently rubbed his chest over his heart. *Ten fucking years ago... God, I was a moron.*

She had stayed close to his family but managed to never be around when he was home. He understood that Nora would have been hurt, but years later, she continued to avoid him at all costs.

"We'll see you Sunday evening. Goodbye, Nora."

Now, shocked that his sister felt the need to be clandestine while talking to her, he stayed planted in the hall, his hands on his hips, surprising Caroline as she came out of the bathroom. Eyes wide, she started to drop her phone into her robe pocket, but he shook his head.

"Seriously, Caroline? You don't have to hide talking to Nora from me. Believe me, I know she doesn't want to be here when I'm here. I just hoped in time it would get better and we could at least talk."

His sister's eyes now narrowed. *Shit, I've woken the dragon.* Like his mother, Caroline's gentle personality soothed everyone in almost every situation. But, when angry, it was best to watch out.

Her finger jabbed into his chest as she whispered harshly, "You're the one who left, Tate. I don't blame you... it was your calling. But we all thought that Nora was going to be part of this family, connected to you and us. You're the one who walked away. But just because you've moved on doesn't mean she feels the same."

"I haven't forgotten her. She's the one who refuses to come around when I'm here."

Caroline leaned back, drawing herself up to her full height, and held his gaze. Something moved through her expression, but in the dark hallway, he could not define what he saw.

"Being around you is painful for her, Tate." He opened his mouth to respond, but with a quick shake of her head, she continued, "It's not my place to explain why. You moved on because that was your choice, and she moved on because she had no choice. But that doesn't mean she wasn't gutted."

"Hell, Caroline. You're the one who told me she was dating someone seriously again several years ago."

"That was six years ago. It was a mistake. I knew the guy wasn't right for her, and she finally figured that out. But if you think that also didn't have something to do with you, then you'd be wrong."

His chest deflated with a heaving breath, and he stared at his sister, wondering what the fuck she was referring to.

She heaved a great sigh and reached out to place her hand on his arm, giving a little squeeze. "Don't worry about it, Tate. Let's all enjoy your weekend here. We see you so rarely, I don't want it marred." She lifted on her toes and kissed his cheek before slipping back into the master bedroom.

He stood in the hall for a long moment, his emotions swirling as much as his mind. Finally, he turned, then stopped and looked back toward Caroline's closed door. *Why are Caroline and Thomas in the master bedroom?* His father's snores came from the smaller bedroom across the hall. His head jerked back and forth between the two doors, but no answer to his question could be discerned.

Walking into his bedroom, he climbed into bed, new questions stabbing at him. *Why is Mom no longer cooking big Sunday dinners? Why has Dad gotten rid of many of the horses? And how close is my family to Nora that she planned on spending Mom's birthday here at the ranch?*

As the questions whirled, he was not surprised when sleep still did not come. But most of all, it was thoughts of Nora that filled his mind. *Sis only had it half-right. It was my choice to leave, knowing that my life as a SEAL would keep me away for years. But my heart never really moved on.*

Saturday morning dawned sunny and cool, and Tate looked around the kitchen carefully to see if he could discern differences in how the ranch was run. Thomas had eaten breakfast early and headed out to check on the cattle. Caroline had taken care of the children and was already working on the food for the birthday celebration. His father was lingering over a cup of coffee at the table, something Tate had never seen him do before.

Turning to his dad, he asked, "What can I help you with today? You've got me all day long and Mom's party isn't until this evening. What can I do?" It did not escape his notice that his parents and Caroline shared a look.

His father drained his cup and stood. "Let's ride out over some of the fields."

He wasn't surprised when his father chose one of the ATVs, and soon they were bumping over dirt paths, leaving behind many of the pastures as they rose steadily in altitude, climbing the hills leading to the mountains around the ranch. Finally stopping at an outcropping of rocks that overlooked their spread, his father shut down the engine and leaned back in his seat.

They sat quietly, observing the beauty of the land while listening to birds chirping in the trees. The sunshine warmed where the cool breeze blew. The expansive sky only had a few clouds passing overhead, creating shadows on the land below.

"I grew up on this ranch. So did my father. I raised my two children here. I love this land only second to the love I have for God and my family."

As his father continued speaking, the niggling of unease that had crept through Tate earlier now flared into concern.

"At one time, I thought I'd pass this land to you, but you had another path in life to choose. I was shocked when you first started talking about the Navy, but your mother helped me realize that we all have a road we must walk. I've known Thomas since he was a boy and was proud when he married Caroline. He's a good husband, a good father, and a good rancher."

"Dad, I've got to tell you that you're making me nervous."

His dad chuckled, swinging his gaze from the valley before them to Tate. "Your mom always said I needed to just spit things out and not beat around the bush. I brought you up here to let you know that your mom and I are going to make some changes. We're slowly turning more and more of the ranch administration over to Thomas and Caroline. He's got good ideas and a good crew of men that now work for him. "

The heaviness in his chest eased, and he nodded. "I can understand you wanting to take things a little easy, Dad."

"It's more than that, Tate. Your mom and I are planning to build a smaller house on the property but down the road. A place where we don't have to worry about maintenance, and we can shut the door and travel whenever we want to."

Unable to hold back the gasp that rushed from his lungs, Tate's mouth dropped open. *Move? What the fuck?* "Why would you need to move? I noticed that Caroline and Thomas already have the master bedroom! Are they pushing you out of your own—"

"Son, I taught you to think about your words before you say them," his dad said, his eyes narrowed. "You know good and well they're not pushing us out. Yes, we could just keep living in the house and consider retirement and travel when we wanted, but that's not fair to them. They need to make this place their own. We're only gonna be a couple of miles away, and I figure we'll be over here a lot. But for this place to become Caroline and Thomas' home and ranch, your mom and I need to step back. They don't like it, but it's what we feel we should do."

Slumping in his seat, he shook his head slowly, his father's words making sense, and yet, seeming unbelievable. "Dad, you said it yourself… you've been on this ranch your whole life."

"Our new house will still be on this land… just not right next to the big house." He twisted around to hold Tate's gaze and lifted his brow. "And you think I've never wanted to see anywhere else?"

Tate stared dumbly at his father, unable to think of anything to say. His father chuckled again and reached over to pat him on the knee.

"Oh, we're not leaving this area," he assured. "We're going to be right down the road, probably over here just about every other day, if I had to guess. But your mother and I have got a few places we'd like to visit and the time just seems right." His smile widened and he added, "We're even planning to go on a cruise in a few weeks."

"Jesus, Dad, I don't even know what to say. I mean... on one hand, I want to say congratulations because I think anyone who's worked as hard as you and Mom deserve a break. On the other hand, I guess I'm just shocked because I never imagined you being anywhere except right here."

"I just want to make sure that you understand that you're not getting left out. Your grandfather sold a lot of acres many years ago, and I've sold a few more. Thomas and I agreed on downsizing so that the ranch was manageable and yet still profitable. But that money from the land sales went straight into investments and is doing fine. All that is earmarked for you."

Shaking his head, he argued, "No, no. I've got my own money. You don't have to do this."

"It's part of the legacy that goes to you, Son. The land will go to Caroline and your grandfather's money will go to you. But don't worry, your mom and I plan on doing a lot of living and a lot of traveling. Hell, without having to take care of the ranch all the time, we might make it over to Maine to visit you."

Clapping his father on the shoulder, he nodded. "I'd be proud to have you any time, Dad. My house is right on the water and the fishing is good."

"That's what I'm talking about!"

They sat quietly for another moment, their gazes

drifting over the pastures down below, the scrub brush along the trails, and the thick trees behind them leading up to the mountains. The past mingled with the future, but Tate's mind stumbled between the two. Children growing up and leaving home seemed natural. Parents wanting to do the same? Not so much.

He glanced to the side and noticed the lines etched in his father's face appeared deeper, while at the same time he seemed at peace.

"It's God's country," his father said. "But your mom and I are looking forward to some new adventures."

Starting the ATV again, his dad drove back down the hills while Tate's mind still swirled with the news. It would seem strange to think of his parents not being in the big house, and yet the idea that they were excited about what the future would bring crossed over to him. By the time they arrived back at the barn, he could say he was happy for his parents but knew it would take a while for the changes to settle deep inside.

While the rest of the family went about their day getting ready for Susan's birthday, he borrowed one of the ranch trucks and drove back through town to the small cemetery behind the church his parents and grandparents had attended. Parking near the front, he smiled, looking up at the brick building, the white steeple rising toward the vast blue sky.

He grinned, memories of sitting with his family when he was young, listening to the minister preach. He remembered church socials where he and Nathan would dart between the tables, seeing who could eat the most food. And whenever Nathan crossed his mind, thoughts of Nora were not far behind. Two years younger, she was determined to keep up with both of them, and often had.

Climbing from the truck, he walked past a few other vehicles in the parking lot, knowing the church staff was still at work. A chill was in the air, the breeze starting to whip about as he walked toward the back of the church and through the metal gate leading to the cemetery.

His feet stumbled to a halt as he looked ahead and saw a lone figure standing in front of a group of headstones. He didn't need to see the names on the stones to know the identity of the mourner. Nora. His heart thumped, threatening to pound out of his chest. He battled the desire to stalk straight toward her, demanding that she talk to him. Working to control his breathing, he kept his gaze pinned on her.

Indecision filled him, an emotion he rarely felt. Caroline's words from the previous evening scored through him, and as much as he wanted to walk over and greet Nora, he didn't want to cause her any pain. Every nuance was noted, each paired with a memory. Her honey-blonde hair stood out in stark relief against the dark jacket she clutched around her. He remembered her hair flying behind her as they rode horses over the ranch. He also remembered his fingers dragging through the silky strands when they shared their first kiss.

Her face was pale, but he remembered how tanned she used to become every summer, working and playing in the sun. From where he stood, it appeared she was wearing her nursing scrubs and he imagined the thin cotton pants provided little warmth.

If she were anywhere else besides Nathan's gravesite he would have approached, but here, in this place of grieving, he forced his body to lock in place. Giving her privacy, he turned and leaned back against the sun-warmed brick wall that surrounded the cemetery, tilting his face toward the sky and closing his eyes for a few minutes, allowing the memories to flow over him.

Hearing a slight noise, he looked over and saw that Nora had turned and her gaze was pinned on him. Pushing away from the wall, he faced her but did not move closer. As much as he wanted to approach, his feet stayed rooted to the ground. He was too far away to discern her expression, but she quickly turned and began weaving through the headstones, heading back to the parking lot. With her head down, staring at her feet as she walked toward the far gate, she never looked back.

He reached up and rubbed his chest as a dull ache settled deep inside and he found it hard to breathe. With her now gone, he mimicked her actions by weaving through the headstones toward the grouping that was so familiar. At one time, there had only been a single gravesite that he visited... Nathan's. Now, Nathan's grandparents' headstones flanked him on one side, and his parents' graves were on the other. It seemed strange to think that Nathan's stone wasn't solitary but was joined by all the others in his family. But then, of course, that meant that Nora was now alone.

Kneeling at the grave, he sighed. Reaching out, his

fingertips landed on the icy cold marble, longing for that connection. "I fucked up, Nathan. I was supposed to take care of her and thought I was. But I fucked up and I've got no idea how to fix it." He sighed again, but no more words came. He didn't ask for forgiveness, but instead, continued to allow the cold to seep inside.

He wasn't with his friend when he died, but he'd been with others his unit lost. They all ripped deep inside, but nothing quite like the loss of Nathan. A lump formed in his throat, threatening to choke him as it always did. Squeezing his eyes tightly shut, he battled the sting then finally allowed the tears to slide down his cheek. He swiped at his nose before scrubbing his palm over his face, wiping away the visible traces of his grief. Nothing would erase the grief buried deep inside, but that was fine. That emotion he could wrap around like a blanket, taking comfort in its familiarity.

After a few more silent moments, he stood, and with a last gaze downward, turned and headed back to his truck.

The rest of the weekend was spent with family. It was as though everyone was trying very hard to pretend that life was normal when in reality he wondered if things would ever be the same. The family celebrated his mom's birthday and caught up on each other's lives with Tate offering stories of a few of the places he had visited and listening as his mother described the cruise they were going to take.

When the next day dawned, the family piled into the huge family van for the drive to the airport. He hugged his parents after obtaining promises that they would come to visit. He shook Thomas' hand warmly, having already taken a moment the previous day to let him know that he was pleased to see the ranch in such good hands. He kissed his sister and promised that he would come back to visit soon, then swung his niece around in the air, kissing her in the middle of giggles. With final goodbyes to his nephews, he walked through security, his enjoyment of his weekend mixed with the sense that times were changing.

Whether he was ready for the changes are not… they were coming.

4

Tate parked outside LSI, waving toward the man on the riding lawnmower. Horace Tiddle had been hired by Mace years ago to help maintain the buildings and surrounding grounds. There was no need for the location to be secret, but Mace liked his privacy, and the lighthouse sat at the end of a long, wooded lane with a private entrance. Thick, green grass surrounded the buildings leading to the rocky coastline where the Atlantic Ocean waves crashed rhythmically against the stones and boulders.

Stepping inside the house, he moved straight into the kitchen and smiled at Horace's wife, Marge. Horace, a former SEAL and CIA Op, now had the look of a grandfatherly seadog. Marge, another former CIA Op, could easily be mistaken for a grandmotherly Drill Sergeant. She took care of the Keepers while running a tight ship.

The scent of apple muffins wafted through the air, and he grinned. "Did you use my mom's recipe?"

"Absolutely," Marge assured. "I know when to bow down to greatness, and your mom's apple recipes are the best."

Taking a bite of a muffin, he nodded. "Just as good as Mom's." Winking as Marge smiled in pride, he grabbed the basket to take down to the compound's workspace. Once through the various levels of security at the back of the house and the base of the house, he exited the elevator into the cavernous main room of Lighthouse Security Investigations. The room, sealed and environmentally protected, held computer equipment, stations where the Keepers manned keyboards, and large screens. Specialized printers, processors with high-speed connections, servers, and other computer equipment filled much of the room, circling around the massive table in the center.

A hall led to locker rooms, workout room, and equipment storage, eventually leading through more security and into caves leading to the rocky coast.

Passing by two desks, he smiled at Sylvie, Mace's beautiful wife and LSI's ever-efficient office manager. Stopping at the second desk, he hefted his hip on to the corner and smiled at Babs. "You ready to tie the knot and shackle yourself to Drew for life?"

The athletic woman with a purple streak through her dark hair looked up at him and winked. "For better or worse… but I confess, I'm hoping for better."

"I am too, Babs." Drew, another Keeper, and Babs had danced around each other for several years, finally giving in to the attraction they both felt. Their relationship had not had an easy path, but everyone at LSI was happy about their upcoming wedding.

"By the way," she began. "How was your parents' cruise?"

"A helluva lot better than yours was." Babs had discovered she became seasick on a cruise she had taken last summer. Getting off the ship had not proven to be any better when she ran into modern-day pirates and Drew had to fly in to help. His parents, on the other hand, had discovered they loved cruising in the Caribbean. "They enjoyed it so much, they're planning on taking another cruise to Alaska in the spring."

"Hell, man. When your parents decided to take some time to travel, they really decided to go."

He looked over at one of his best friends, Blake, and nodded. "You got that right." He set the basket of muffins on the back counter next to the large coffee maker. Dumping sugar and creamer into his huge mug, he headed to the table and settled in with the others.

Once everyone arrived, Mace began. "We've got several security contracts right now, most of which can be done here. Cobb is on a detail in El Paso, Texas, and probably won't get finished for another couple of weeks but is flying in for Drew and Babs' wedding this weekend. Walker is still in Washington DC, finishing a detail with the head of the Senate Intelligence Committee, but will also come back for the wedding. Rank will head to D.C. after the wedding to meet with our liaison at the FBI."

"Aww, it looks like our wedding is going to get the team back together again," Drew quipped. He twisted around and wiggled his eyebrows at Babs. "Aren't we the popular ones?"

She rolled her eyes and shook her head, her lips curving into a smile.

"We just want to see you get all dressed up, then fall apart and cry like a baby when you see her walking down the aisle," Blake said. "I can see you tearing up right now." Blake clutched his heart with one hand and wiped a fake tear with the other.

Drew flipped him off, but they all laughed, knowing Blake was exactly right.

Taciturn Mace fought a grin, then closed the folder in front of him. "Everyone's got their security detail assignments on their tablets. If you need any help, see Josh. After lunch, anyone who's game can join me for a run and swim. It's bracing outside, but I figure you SEALs will be right at home."

A few goodhearted shouts were called out, the natural camaraderie mixed with competition among the various former servicemen always at play.

Later that afternoon, he found his rhythm as he ran along the path through the woods. Lost in thought, he was still aware of Blake coming up behind them.

"You gonna spill?"

Moving slightly to the left so that Blake and he could run side-by-side on the path, he asked, "Spill?"

"You've had something on your mind this past month ever since you got back from your parents' ranch. Is it all the changes they're making?"

They ran silently side-by-side for a moment, Tate trying to decide how much he wanted to say. He snorted at the thought of sharing his thoughts but figured Blake might understand. "Gotta admit, it's weird thinking of my parents not being on the ranch every day. I know it's the only life they've led, and they've loved it... I just never thought about them wanting to do anything else. Now, they call me from a trip they're on and I can hear how much fun they're having."

"My dad's still working, but my mom retired right after my sister had kids. I figured she'd get bored out of her mind, but she's loving being a grandma. I guess we all have a hard time seeing our parents wanting to live their own lives."

"When you put it like that, it seems ridiculous. I mean, my parents completely supported my decision to join the Navy and become a SEAL instead of run the ranch. You'd think that I'd support their lives as well."

Their footsteps continued to pound along the path through the woods that ran near the coast. The sound of waves crashing on the rocks below could be heard.

"Anything else that's got you inside your head?"

"What are you? My fuckin' psychiatrist?" he bit back, a grin on his face.

"Hell yeah, if it gets your head back in the game. Personally, I think it's the old girlfriend that's got you tied up in knots."

"Yeah, maybe." He shrugged as they rounded the bend in the path and ran closer to the coastline. "I admit my sister said some things that have stayed with me. My reasons for breaking up with her at the time were sound, and I figured she'd get on with her life. I didn't keep up with her because, I guess, in truth, I didn't want to see how she was moving on with her life. But my sister indicated that things for Nora haven't been what I thought they were."

"You think there's a chance for the two of you again?"

"I don't see how. Maybe if I'd pulled my head outta my ass years ago. But now? I'd give anything just for a decent conversation with her. I think that's what gets me the most, is that we never really had a chance to... to... hell, I don't know."

"Have closure."

Feet stumbling, he swung his head to the side. "Closure? Jesus, you are like my fuckin' psychiatrist."

"I'm being serious, man. That's what you call it when you don't have a chance to tie up all the loose ends."

Watching Blake grin, he groaned. "Fuck. With a bunch of you all getting engaged and married, you're going to give the rest of us a complex that we don't have our shit together."

"Fine, then I can just keep using my psychiatrist skills." Blake quipped.

Flipping him off, Tate veered down the rocky shore and dove into the water. The cold slapped at him, dislodging the tangled emotions running through his mind. With the view of the lighthouse up ahead, his strong strokes sent him toward his goal. *Focus... just stay focused on the job. That's all that's important.*

That evening, he sat on the back deck of his home. After

Mace had hired him, he'd lived in an apartment until he could find just the right property. The older house was a cottage-style saltbox two-story home. In good shape, he was pleased with the wood floors, huge brick fireplace, and windows that overlooked the water.

He often swam or kayaked to his heart's content in the bay outside his property that led straight to the ocean. The kitchen and bathrooms were not modern, but the bones of the house were good, and it stood solid against the winter.

It had been important to put down roots after years of wandering the world with one deployment or mission after another, longing for what his parents had. *But it's fuckin' lonely. A beautiful view... but fuckin' lonely.*

In the past month since he had returned from the family visit in Wyoming, he thought often about Nora. His sister's words had played over and over, making him wonder if Nora still had feelings for him. *Nora is beautiful, smart, a sweetheart. Why has no one snapped her up?* He remembered Caroline's comment about Nora's former boyfriend.

"That was six years ago. It was a mistake. I knew the guy wasn't right for her, and she finally figured that out. But if you think that didn't have something to do with you, then you'd be wrong."

Taking another swig from the longneck beer in his hand, he grimaced as he so often did when certain memories passed through his mind. It had seemed easy to be involved with a girl back home when he first joined the Navy, but becoming a SEAL was an altogether different feeling. Out of contact during missions. Unable to let her know where he was or what he was doing. Needing to be ready at a whim, but he also saw the toll it took on the ones back home. And then Nathan's death. Breaking up with Nora seemed like the noble thing to do. *Damn near broke my heart, but it gave her the freedom to love a man who'd give her a home. What a fuckin' pussy I was.* Now, based on his sister's words, he wondered if that had been a mistake.

Tate felt the vibration of his phone in his pocket during the wedding ceremony, glad that he had turned it to silent. Ignoring the incoming call, he smiled as Drew and Babs exchanged their vows. He'd thought nothing would replace the closeness he felt with his SEAL brothers, but Mace had accomplished the same brother-hood and sense of family with the Keepers. Drew and Babs had been through a lot on their way to finding each other.

The sun was shining, sparkling off the water crashing below the lighthouse. Drew's family was present, but the Keepers were all the family that Babs had or needed. Against her typical badass persona, she wore a beautiful gown and as she walked toward the front, he'd never seen Drew grin so widely. And if he wasn't mistaken, a tear formed in Drew's eye.

He'd been present for the weddings of Mace and Sylvie, Rank and Helena, Walker and Sara. But as he lifted his hand and pressed against his chest, he knew this wedding felt different. And it would be stupid to pretend he didn't know why.

Nora.

If life had been different, Nora would already be his wife. They would've gotten married at the same little church his parents and grandparents had. *Hell, we would have already had kids by now.* That thought stung, and he pressed his fingertips against his chest a little harder. Not wanting to analyze his thoughts any more at the moment, he was relieved when the ceremony was over and Drew swooped Babs into his arms, giving Tate a chance to cheer loudly instead of think about his own missed opportunities.

Later, having made his way through the tables loaded with food in the large dining room, he looked for an empty place to sit. Moving to one of the tables, he smiled at those already there. "Hey, darlin'," he greeted. He placed a kiss on Julie and Helena's cheeks before offering a chin lift to Walker and Rank.

"So, when are we going to get to see you stand up there blubbering as your beloved walks to you?" Julie asked, her smile wide.

"Until I find a woman like you, probably never." The quip fell easily from his lips, the twinge in his heart hidden behind his laughter. Feeling a light touch on his arm, he turned to the other side.

Sara, Blake's fiancée, held his gaze with a concerned look on her face. Leaning closer, she whispered, "I worry about you, Tate. I can't think of anyone who deserves a good woman more than you."

He smiled, her concern warming. Having helped

with Sara's rescue—and having had his life saved by her when she grabbed a gun to shoot someone sneaking up on them—they shared a closeness. "Save your worry for that ornery cuss you're engaged to."

"Hey! I'm not ornery!" Blake argued. "Or at least I won't be as soon as I get Sara to say 'I do'."

"How's the wedding planning going?" Helena asked.

His phone vibrated again and saved him from having to listen to more wedding planning. He murmured his apologies as he slid from the table. He walked to the side and pulled it from his pocket. Seeing his mother's message for him to call immediately, he dialed her number as he stepped away from the gathering.

"Mom? What's up—"

"Oh, Frankie, it's your father."

His feet stumbled as he continued to make his way outside, his heart pounding. "Dad? What's wrong with Dad?"

"We're at the medical center. He was having chest pains and Thomas got us here faster than if we waited on an ambulance. The doctor says he's going to be fine, Frankie. He says it wasn't a heart attack, but he's got some blockage and they're going to put in a stent."

"Mom, I'll be there just as soon as I can. I gotta get home and grab a bag and get to the airport as soon as I get a flight. I'll text you and let you know my flight number."

"Oh, honey, you don't have to rush here. I just wanted you to know—"

"I'm not about to wait here. I'll be there just as soon

as I can get there, and tell Thomas he doesn't need to meet me. I'll get a rental car and come directly to the medical center."

He heard the sigh of relief and softened his voice. "Mom, he's a fighter. He's going to be fine."

She sniffed and choked, "I... I know. I just... can't..."

"Mom, he's gonna be fine. Now, you go be strong for him until I get there, okay?" He knew his mom needed something to focus on and he was sure he'd said the right words when her voice grew stronger.

"You're right. Yes... I'll go sit with him for a while, and travel safe, Frankie. I love you."

"Love you, too, Mom."

Disconnecting, he stayed for a few seconds, letting the cool air blow over him as he gathered his wits. Mission planning fell into place, giving him something he could gratefully hang onto. Call the airline. Get home and pack. Get to the airport.

Turning, he headed inside and walked swiftly over to Blake and Sara. Seeing alertness in Blake's eyes, he leaned in. "Got a call from my mom. She said my dad went into the hospital with chest pain. The docs told him that it's not too bad, but he's going to have a stent put in."

Blake grabbed him by the shoulders and held his gaze. "What you need from us?"

Shrugging, he said, "I probably won't be gone more than a couple of days. I'll let Mace and Sylvie know, but I wanted to make sure to touch base with you as well."

"Keep us up on what's happening."

Sara stepped closer, her arms encircling his waist to wrap him in a hug. "I'll be praying for your family."

His friends' concern moved through him, and he offered a chin lift before turning toward Mace. With hasty explanations and goodbyes to the rest of the Keepers, he jogged to his truck parked in the front of the lighthouse.

5

Stepping off the elevator onto the third floor of the hospital, Tate's gaze shot to the sign on the wall indicating room numbers. Turning to the left, he walked past a small waiting room and a nurses' station before stopping outside of room 315. The door was open, but he hesitated, throwing his hand onto the cold metal doorframe, steeling himself. *He's fine. It was not a heart attack.*

Straightening, he sucked in a ragged, cleansing breath before letting it out slowly. Squaring his shoulders, he lifted his chin, and with a purposeful stride, he walked into the room and smiled at the man in the hospital bed. Now, his big, robust father with a grumpy expression on his face sat wrapped in a light blue hospital gown. *Nothing says I-am-no-longer-in-charge like a hospital gown.*

As his father turned his sharp, hazel-eyed gaze up to Tate, it struck him once more how much he looked like his dad. His mother always said so, but children generally don't see the resemblance until they get older. Now, at thirty-three, when Tate looked in the mirror, he could easily see his father staring back. "You're looking good, Dad."

His father grumbled, earning a reproachful glare from his mom before she beamed her smile toward Tate. "Sweetie, I'm so glad you're here!"

"There was no reason for you to call him," Frank groused. "It's a procedure, not a heart attack."

Susan drew Tate into a hug before twisting her head and staring at Frank. "If you don't stop being such a grump, I'm going to ask the doctor to give you a happy shot while he's got you in there doing the procedure." She looked back up at Tate and shook her head. "Regardless of what your father says, I know he's thrilled that you're here."

They had little time before the nurses came to take Frank for his procedure. Tate leaned over and clasped his father's hand, bending to pull him in for a hug at the same time. "See you soon, Dad. Kick some ass… you've got more traveling to do," he whispered. He felt his dad chuckle against his chest and smiled. His mom blew him a kiss as she walked along with the nurses when his dad was rolled down the hall toward the elevator.

Caroline had already been in to see their dad earlier that morning before she headed back to the ranch. Thomas was used to taking care of everything back home, so Tate knew the ranch was fine. As promised, he sent a text to Caroline letting her know that their dad had just been taken for his angioplasty. Promising to let her know as soon as he heard anything, he settled into the hospital chair in the corner, shifting around in an attempt to find a comfortable position. Finally giving up on that pursuit, he leaned his head back and closed his eyes.

The soft pad of rubber footsteps caused his eyes to jerk open, his SEAL training allowing him to sleep while still being aware of his surroundings. A nurse had walked into the room, her back to him, and moved directly to the whiteboard on the wall. Her dark blue scrub pants did little to hide the perfect ass presented to him. Her thick blonde hair, the color of wheat at harvest, was pulled back in a low ponytail, the ends curling as they reached the middle of her back. She lifted her hand and erased the previous nurse's name on the assignment board. His heart pounded as he watched the letters now forming underneath her hand. Short. Simple. And oh, so fuckin' familiar. **Nora**

Nora. Memories of high school kisses under the bleachers, whispered promises of forever in the back of his pickup truck, horseback rides over his family's ranch as they talked of growing up, getting married, and one day owning the family land moved through his mind. She knew he wanted to be in the Navy, his goal to become a SEAL. She vowed to wait for him, and it seemed so easy at the time to let her make that promise, not knowing what his future held. *Jesus... young fuckin' fools.*

Before he had a chance to speak, she turned and gasped as her dark brown eyes landed on him, her hand now jerking over her heart. Her mouth opened and closed several times, but no words came forth.

He took to his feet, observing her head tilt back as he now towered over her and her eyes stayed pinned to his, a myriad of emotions pouring over her face. Shock. Surprise. Maybe a flash of anger. And if he was not mistaken... pain. He stepped forward a foot, her eyes still wide. "Nora."

She blinked and whatever emotions she had felt and shown were shuttered as a curtain dropped. Now, in their place was a professionally cool nurse. "Oh... I... I didn't realize any family was in here." Her hands fluttered before clasping together in front of her. "Um... hello."

Thrilled that she had not fled the room, he smiled. "I'm glad to have a chance to see you. You look wonderful."

Her gaze shot to the side, and she swallowed heavily several times. "Yes... well, um... I'll be back to check on your father later."

He glanced at the clock on the wall. "I don't know when he'll get back down here. Can you stay for a few minutes?"

Giving her head a quick shake, she lifted her gaze to him. "I have other patients to check on. But he should be in recovery soon and once they bring him down, I'll come back in."

He took another step forward, but she skirted around him and out the door faster than he thought she could move. A heavy sigh billowed from his lungs, and with his hands on his hips, he dropped his head to stare at his boots.

And just like that, she walked away. Fuckin' hell. Just like

I did ten years ago.

Nora Stiles escaped to the small staff restroom behind the nurses' station. She grabbed hold of the sink, her knuckles white. With her eyes squeezed shut, she fought to catch her breath. A grimace crossed her face, and she jerked her head up to stare at her reflection in the mirror. *Get a grip! You knew this was going to happen sometime. It's been years... he moved on. There's nothing special about him. He's just a relative of a patient. Just a man.*

Unfortunately, her self-talk did little to make her feel better. After all, lying to herself rarely did. *Okay, so he's not just a man. He's Tate.*

She had seen him a few times over the past ten years but always at a distance. Coming out of the feed store with his dad. Balancing one of Caroline's kids on his shoulders at the 4th of July parade. Carrying some of his mom's prize-winning pies to the fair. And each time, she watched him from afar. People coming up to shake his hand, congratulating him on his military service. It still sliced through her that Nathan was not with him, accepting the same congratulations. *How often did I think I could do that too? Walk up, smile, say hello.* But each time, her heart had ached at the very sight of him, and she scurried away like a frightened mouse.

A noise from the hall caught her attention and she jerked her body into action, now embarrassed that she had fled the room. Grabbing several paper towels, she held them under the water and then patted her neck.

The cold on her skin shocked her back into focus. Sucking in a deep breath, she let it out slowly, determined to go back out and finish her shift.

With renewed determination, she threw open the door and walked out, nearly running into one of the doctors. Coming to a quick halt, she slapped a smile on her face before heading to the nurses' station. An hour later, she watched as Frank was rolled down the hall toward his room. She rushed over and greeted him, pulling Susan in for a hug. "I'm so glad I got to see you."

"I hoped you were going to be Frank's nurse today," Susan said.

It did not escape Nora's notice that Susan was staring intently at her. Offering a slight smile which she hoped hid her churning emotions, she said, "Everything went fine with his procedure, but the doctor wants to keep him overnight just to make sure. Let's get him settled."

Once in the hospital room, her professionalism kicked in, and she checked his stats and performed the tasks necessary to make sure Frank was comfortable while she did her best to ignore Tate's presence—unsuccessfully. *How can Tate's presence fill the entire room?* As though the years of separation had never occurred, she could feel his presence even when she was not looking at him. A tangible thread had always connected them.

"Frank," Susan said as she leaned over her husband. "Look at who your nurse is."

Turning toward his bed, she smiled as his eyes blinked open and confusion morphed into recognition.

"Nora, good to see you."

"And you too, Frank. Everything went fine, and you're just in the hospital overnight for observation. I think the doctor is going to have you and Susan ready for your next cruise soon."

She continued small talk as she completed her duties, then, as soon as she could, she escaped out the door once more, avoiding eye contact with Tate.

An hour later, finished with her rounds and charts, she walked down the stairs to the cafeteria. She had caught a glimpse of Tate leaving his dad's room a few minutes earlier and heaved a sigh of relief. *Good, that's good. Of course, it's good.* She stopped at the bottom of the stairs, glad no one was around so that she could lean her head against the door and tap her forehead on the wood without being seen. Standing straight, she mentally dislodged the past from her mind and strode into the hall.

The hospital was new, and while small, it offered an excellent cafeteria. Choosing her food, she opted for a quiet booth in the corner. Sliding as far as she could go, wanting a few quiet moments to herself, she pulled out her phone to continue reading the latest e-book she had downloaded.

A tray suddenly plopped onto the table next to hers, and she jumped in surprise. Her gaze jerked up just as a large body settled next to hers, effectively trapping her in the booth. Her breath heaved as she stared agog when Tate offered her a wide smile.

"Wh... what are you doing?"

"What a coincidence, finding you having lunch at the same time I was hungry. And in a nice little corner booth where we can chat, won't be disturbed, and you can't escape."

"You can't just sit here like this and trap me in the booth! Are you crazy?"

"Nora, I've been called many things in my life. Probably most of them I deserved. But so far, crazy is not one of them."

She opened her mouth to argue, but he continued talking, his voice now softer. "Nora, you avoid me every time I visit, and I get it, I really do. I'd just love to have a chance to talk."

She made the mistake of twisting slightly in her seat and now faced him fully as he turned her way. His eyes drew her in, achingly mesmerizing. She felt the familiar pain in her chest and knew that heartache was real. *Why? Why does it still hurt so bad? And why is he doing this now?*

"Come on, Nora. It's been ten years. Surely we can talk by now."

Sitting up straighter, she forced her lips into a tight smile, refusing to let him see the pain that she'd buried for so long. "You're right. It has been ten years. Quite honestly, it's been so long and our lives are so separate, I can't imagine that we have anything to talk about." She turned back to her sandwich, determined to force down a bite.

"We used to have a lot to talk about. As I remember, we talked about anything and everything."

"Yes, Tate. *Used* to. *Talked.* Past tense. Years ago." She noticed he had not picked up his sandwich, his attention focused on her. *Just keep chewing. Just chew, swallow, and for goodness' sake, don't choke.*

"If you hadn't avoided me every time I came home, it wouldn't have been so many years ago."

"You made that choice, Tate."

"I didn't make the choice to avoid each other forever," he argued in return.

"Why are you doing this?" she huffed. "I'm sure anything important that's happened in the last ten years, Caroline's already told you."

He twisted further, his arm now resting on the back of the booth behind her, his torso fully facing her. "I'd rather hear about you from *you*."

She closed her eyes for a few seconds, her mind in turmoil. *Done. I'm so fuckin' done with avoiding.* Plopping her sandwich unceremoniously back into her plate, she turned to hold his gaze once again, this time lifting her eyebrows. "So, what shall we talk about? Caroline has mentioned you're no longer a SEAL."

His brow furrowed as he gave his head a quick shake. "I didn't mean for us to talk about me—"

"Hey, just trying to make conversation. If you're not interested…"

A heavy sigh left his lungs before his top teeth landed on his bottom lip. A gesture her eyes focused on, wishing it wasn't as attractive as it was.

"No, no, I *am* interested." Turning more fully toward her, he acquiesced. "I retired from the SEALs about five years ago. Did some missions for a special agency for a couple of years. The last two years I've been employed with a private security firm based out of Maine."

Not having any idea what kind of work that entailed, she battled the urge to ask if it was dangerous. "Um... do you... um... like it? The work you do?"

"Yeah, I do. The military was great, but I like working for a private company now."

She nodded, unable to think of anything else to ask. Looking back down at her now-unappetizing sandwich, she grabbed her water, taking a long sip.

"And you?"

Her gaze jerked to his face, but the intense look in his whiskey-colored eyes caused her to shift her attention back to her plate. Lifting her shoulders in a slight shrug, she replied, "Not many changes around here. I'm obviously a nurse at the hospital."

She jumped as his large hand landed on her forearm, the heat searing from his touch. She tensed, fighting the desire to jerk her hand away mixed with the desire to lean into his warmth.

"I was out of contact for long periods of time when I was on missions, but Caroline told me about your dad and then your mom—"

"Yes, well... um..." Tears pricked the back of her eyes, and desperate to keep them from falling, she swallowed deeply. *I haven't cried in a long time... why does he still have this effect on me?*

A wince crossed his face, hitting his brow. "I'm sorry, Nora. I was gone on a... a mission. *Missions,* actually. I didn't get word from Caroline until much later for either of them. I... I'm sorry."

She nodded rapidly while pressing her lips tightly together. Finally, clearing her throat, she managed to whisper, "Well, there was nothing you could have done." She forced her gaze back to his face, a tremulous smile on her lips. "It doesn't matter. I'm... I'm fine. I've got a good job. I've got good friends. I've got a small apartment that's all mine. And your family has done an amazing job over the years of stepping in and making sure I was never alone." Even as the words left her mouth, she knew they were a lie. *Oh, yes, I'm very much alone.*

Sparing him a glance, he appeared to be struggling but remained quiet. She noticed everything about him, just like so many years before. The crease in his brow when he was thinking hard about something. The way his gaze held hers when she spoke, making her feel as though she had his full attention. Now, she also noticed the crinkles emanating from his eyes and the few flecks of silver at the hair closest to his temple. Whatever she had imagined, it did not appear his life had been carefree. She gripped her fingers together, fighting the urge to reach up and touch the stubble covering his jaw. Looking back at her plate, she sucked in a ragged breath.

Please just eat your lunch, Tate. Eat, make small talk about the weather, and then leave. At least give me that. Just then, her hospital phone rang, and she quickly answered. Listening, she made a shooing motion with her hand. "Move, move, move. I've got to get back up... a new patient has arrived, and they need me to see to it." Grateful that he shifted out of the booth, she leaned over to grab her tray.

"No, Nora. You go on, I'll toss this out."

With a quick nod, she turned and hurried out of the cafeteria, the bizarre conversation they just had still playing over in her mind. Shaking, she entered the empty elevator and leaned back against the wall. She dropped her chin and stared at her shoes, her body quivering as she tried to make sense of the whirl of emotions.

Whispering into the empty elevator, she said, "Oh, Tate. The truth is that for me, you were *the one*. What sucks is that I was not *the one* for you." Wiping an errant tear that was sliding down her cheek, she squeezed her eyes tightly shut. As the elevator came to a stop, she stood straighter and sucked in a deep, cleansing breath before exiting. Forcing a practiced smile onto her face, she attempted to push thoughts of Tate to the back of her mind and walked swiftly to her next patient.

6

Tate plopped back down into the booth after Nora left. He found it hard to suck in enough oxygen, as though he'd just finished a mountain run in full uniform, carrying a pack. *Jesus, I'm wiped.*

It had been so easy over the years to think that breaking up with her had been the right thing to do. He had needed to focus on his next mission. Not having his head on straight when in the middle of an assignment could get himself or his teammates killed. Some fellow teammates, both as a SEAL and when he worked for CIA Special Ops, were married, but he'd always wondered how they managed to handle the pressures of the job and the pressures of a family.

Now, all he could see in his mind was the hurt in her eyes, the tremor in her voice, and the rapid flutter of her pulse at the base of her neck. For all her bravado, her pain was real. And the realization of that hurt like a bitch.

Leaning back in the booth, he pushed his tray away,

no longer able to stomach the idea of food. *What a cocked up, fucked up mess.*

A sound close by startled him, and he looked up to see his mother sliding into the seat across from him, a cup of coffee in her hand. A soft smile eased across her lips as her eyes searched his face.

"Your father's taking a nap, so I thought I'd grab a cup. I saw you with Nora, and I thought I'd let you two chat."

A snort erupted as he shook his head. "It was hardly a chat. More like avoidance on her part followed by incredibly awkward conversation."

She nodded and sighed. "Nora's held things in for a very long time. Things have eased up for her in the last couple of years, but for a long time after you left, it seemed like one thing after another kept happening to steal her happiness."

"Caroline's told me some, but I really wanted to talk to Nora. I want to reconnect, but she shuts me down so quickly."

"The breakup was devastating to her, Frankie. I know it wasn't easy on you either, but she was here, right in the middle of all her memories. She lost her brother and then you. And while you were still alive, thank God, you took yourself from her when she was vulnerable. You were gone for a long time, and I don't think she ever found any closure. I've often thought that if she could have had a chance to talk to you... or yell at you... or cry at you... whatever she needed to do to get it off her chest then she would be better. I've always felt that her unresolved feelings were holding her back.

Almost as though they hold power over her until she can let them go."

They were silent for a moment as an ache settled deep in his chest. "It was ten years ago, Mom. You know it wasn't like everything was perfect for me. I didn't break up with her because she would drag me down or because I didn't love her anymore. I broke up with her so that she could have a life without worrying about me."

Cocking her head to the side, she tucked a strand of wispy hair behind her ear. "You never gave her a chance to make that decision on her own. It was as though you decided what was best for her, and by breaking up, you took away her choice." She lifted her cup, blowing across the surface of the liquid before sipping. Setting the cup down on the table, she licked her lips before holding his gaze again. "Son, I'm curious… you've been out of the service for several years, and while I'm sure you date, you're still single. Why do you think that is?"

The air felt thick in the small cafeteria, and Tate felt raw as he sucked in a deep breath. Unlike some men who never discussed their feelings, he had no problem trying to understand what was going on in his head. It was what was going on in his heart that was more difficult. Finally, shaking his head, he said, "Honestly, Mom? I've never found anyone that really seemed like they got me."

She remained silent but kept her gaze on him.

"It's hard to connect with someone who has no idea what ranch life is like. Or growing up near a tiny town. Or being grateful when you're out riding on horse trails and can get a signal on your phone so you can listen to your favorite country station."

That last comment brought out a smile from Susan as she shook her head slowly. "It used to drive your father crazy that you'd use up all your data listening to Garth Brooks."

A chuckle erupted from deep within him and some of the tension eased from his chest. "I think, in the back of my mind, I always thought I might return and find Nora happily waiting for me." He slowly shook his head, dropping his chin. "God, that was stupid."

Nodding, Susan agreed. "Yes, that was stupid. No woman should have to sit around for ten years and wait for a man who didn't put in the effort to maintain a relationship."

He jerked back, his hand pressed dramatically to his chest. "Wow, Mom, just give it to me, why don't you?"

"I will!" She laughed, quirking an eyebrow, then sobered. "Frankie, if you expected her to sit at home while you went off to war, you were born in the wrong era. But what's sad is that I know she would have done that if you'd kept your original promise to come back to her. When you broke up with Nora, you gave up the right to think that she might still be here for you."

"Caroline told me she was dating someone a couple of years ago," he argued back. "I don't see a ring on her finger now." He watched as pain slashed through his mom's face before she quickly hid the emotion. Brow furrowed once again, he asked, "Why do I get the feeling there's more to that situation than I know?"

Lifting her cup, Susan took the last sips of her

coffee. Scooting out of the booth, she stood, holding Tate's gaze. "That, my dear, is something only Nora can tell you. Who knows? Maybe one day she will." Grabbing her purse, she said, "I'm going to head up and see if your dad's awake. I'll see you in a little bit." She started to walk away and then stopped, looking over her shoulder at him. "You know, some love stories do end in a happily ever after."

Watching his mother walk out of the cafeteria, he sighed. *Yeah, but I stopped believing in fairytales a long time ago.*

Nora finished washing the few dishes from her early dinner. After pouring a glass of wine, she rounded the counter that separated the kitchen and living room. Her apartment was tiny, but she had little inclination for finding something larger.

It was not long after her father died that she moved back into her childhood house to stay with her mom. Her grandmother's arthritis worsened, and she moved in as well. Nursing at the hospital during the day and caring for her mom and grandmother at night, the added upkeep on the large house was overwhelming. When they both died within a year of each other, Nora was ready to sell.

"Are you sure you know what you're doing? Surely you don't want to sell your family home!" Well-meaning friends and curious acquaintances were certain she was reacting to being alone and not making a sound deci-

sion. Thank God that Caroline understood. Nora had never been tied to things, only people. Rambling around the big, empty house would not bring her family back. She held their memories inside her heart but longed for a place to lay her head that would not constantly remind her of being alone.

Now, her small apartment gave her just what she needed. The large living room window faced the west, and she watched the sunset over the range of mountains in the distance. It was the view that sold her on the apartment. When the building manager first showed it to her, it was one evening after her shift at the hospital, and as they stepped inside, the brilliant sky of the sunset shone through the window. She had been instantly filled with the memories of her and Tate watching the setting sun from somewhere on the Double T Ranch.

She sipped her wine, settling on the sofa with her back to one of the arms and her legs stretched out over the cushions. It was impossible to not think of being so close to Tate today, so she didn't try, allowing the memories to wash over her in waves.

Time had not diminished his looks. Quite the contrary, maturity had aged him well. His jaw was square. His body muscular. His eyes were just as hazel but had lost the youthful twinkle, now a little more wary. She closed her eyes and the vision of his face so close to hers in the hospital cafeteria was all she could see. So close she could've leaned forward a few inches and kissed him.

A knock on her door jerked her out of her musings. Eyes wide, she rushed to look out of the peephole. Her breath left her lungs in a rush as she saw Caroline standing outside. Throwing open the door, she attempted a casual expression on her face but should have known her best friend saw right through her. "Hey, come on in."

"Hoping I was my brother?" Caroline stepped over the threshold and offered a hug.

"What? No... no. Why on earth would I think that?"

"Mom mentioned that the two of you were talking in the hospital today."

She should have known nothing went unnoticed in a small town. "I thought you were going out with your family?"

"We did go to dinner, but Thomas and I had driven separately since I was at the hospital with Dad. He took the kids back to the ranch, and I told him I wanted to stop by and check on you."

"Caroline, I'm fine. I always love seeing you, but there was no reason to check on me." She walked to the kitchen counter and lifted the bottle. "Wine?"

"No, thanks. I had some with dinner and I'm driving. I'll take some water."

She poured a glass of cold water from the refrigerator and handed it to Caroline. The two women settled on opposite sides of the sofa, their glasses in their hands. They sat in easy silence for a moment, but she knew her friend was dying to ask. "I can hear the questions bouncing around your head, so I'll put you out of your misery. Yes, I talked to Tate today. No, we didn't talk for long, and quite frankly, we didn't say anything of any importance."

Caroline sighed heavily but remained quiet, sipping her water. The silence continued between them, now blanketing the room.

"I wish you would tell him. If for no other reason than so he'd know why you avoid him."

The conversation had taken place numerous times over the past years, but her response was always the same. "What purpose would it serve? If I wasn't willing to trap him to me years ago for a reason, why would I want him to pity me now?"

Each time, she'd responded the same way. Caroline would hold her gaze with a tearful one of her own and nod slowly. Only this time, instead of just sipping her water quietly, Caroline continued. "He's different on this trip."

"His dad is in the hospital. Of course, he's different."

"No, it's not just that. It was even when he came home a couple of months ago. His life is more stable now. He loves his job as a security specialist but mentioned how he could pick and choose his assignments. He seems calmer, less intense. I know the changes in the ranch threw him, but he seems genuinely happy with Mom and Dad's new life. He's even completely cool about me and Thomas running the ranch."

Taking another sip of wine, Nora glanced out the window, seeing the sun dip beyond the mountains, blanketing the room in deepening shadows. She reached up and turned on the lamp next to the couch, casting a glow over them as she set her wine glass on the table. Turning back to her best friend, she warmed under Caroline's concern and care. "I'm glad for him. Really, I am. I'm glad that he's now in a job where he feels more control, and certainly less danger. I'm glad that he's happy his parents are going to enjoy their retirement. And I'm glad that he recognizes that you and Thomas are the right people to manage the family ranch." She reached across the space and placed her hand on Caroline's arm, giving a little squeeze. "Honestly, I am glad for all that. I just don't see what any of it has to do with me."

Caroline set her glass on the coffee table before twisting her body fully toward Nora. Reaching over, she grasped both of Nora's hands in her own. "What this has to do with you is who you're meant to be with. Honey, I don't want to hurt you, but the truth is nothing is tying you to this little town anymore. As much as I wish your parents were still here for you, they're not. You've got a job that would allow you to work anywhere you wanted. Maybe it all comes down to timing."

Her heart lurched, threatening to pound out of her chest. Tilting her head slightly to the side, her brows lowered. "Timing?"

"Maybe it was never a question of *who* you were supposed to be with… just *when* you were supposed to be with them."

She opened her mouth, then snapped it closed. While Caroline's words played around in her head, she watched her friend pick up the empty glasses and take them to the sink. Jumping to her feet, she met Caroline at the door, wrapping her arms around her. As the two friends hugged, she whispered, "Thank you."

Pulling back, Caroline blinked away the tears. "Nora, I have no idea what the right thing to do is, but I know closing yourself off all alone here in this little apartment, in this little town, will never get you closer to finding love."

She locked the door after Caroline left, then walked over to the wide picture window. The view was now cloaked in darkness, but her mind was not on the mountains—it was in the past. *Maybe Caroline is right... if he knew, he'd finally understand why my heart still aches.*

7

"I heard from one of the nurses in the ER, who heard from one of the pharmacy techs, who heard from her cousin who's a radiologist, that once his huge house gets built, he's going to get a divorce."

"I don't think that's right! My nephew is a plumber, and he's been over at the new house and says that the wife is over there all the time."

"Yeah? Huh, I heard he's got a piece on the side. Don't know who, but someone said—"

"She could take him to the cleaners in a divorce settlement. You know, the poor wife who puts her husband through medical school and then he tries to dump her later. I don't think that flies anymore!"

"Well, as popular as he is with the board, I don't think he'll have any problem becoming the new Chief of Staff—"

Rolling her eyes, Nora walked past the nurses' station, ignoring the gossip, as usual. She didn't bother looking to the side, knowing that they would be rolling their eyes at her also. She hated gossip, finding it petty and often hurtful. She hadn't heard who they were talking about but figured the ears of some poor doctor in the hospital were burning from the chatter.

"Nora!" Seeing Dr. Hawkins walking down the hall, she noticed the nurses immediately stopped their gossiping. Hoping he wanted to see her about Frank's discharge, she met the cardiologist with a smile.

"I'm glad I caught you before you went into Frank's room. Overnight, he spiked a low fever. It's now under control, but I don't want to discharge him today. I want him to have twenty-four hours here with no fever before we send him home."

While it was not unusual for anyone to have a low-grade fever after a procedure, concern for Frank speared through her.

Before she had a chance to question further, Dr. Hawkins continued. "I've already talked to Frank and Susan. She's on board, wanting to make sure he's good to go home tomorrow. Frank?" Chuckling, he said, "Well, you can imagine that another day in the hospital is making Frank unhappy. Just figured I'd warn you."

She nodded, not having any problem imagining the grumpy patient she was getting ready to see. Slapping a smile on her face, she stepped into Frank's room. Once again, not only was Susan there, but Tate was, also. Maintaining professionalism, she reiterated to Frank and Susan that Dr. Hawkins only wanted to make sure everything was fine before discharging him.

Patting his leg, she said, "You know, we're lucky to have a cardiologist here at the medical center. He wants to make sure you'll go home in the best condition possible." Ignoring his grumbling, she added, "Hey, this just means I get to keep checking on you a little longer."

Recording his normal temperature and blood pressure into the computer, she turned to find Tate's gaze on her. A hesitant wariness was in his eyes—almost as though he was uncertain how to greet her after their lunch yesterday. Determined not to let her smile drop, she inclined her head toward him and murmured, "Good morning." His smile was immediate, his hazel eyes once more taking on the sparkle she had fallen in love with as a child.

Swallowing past her nerves, she turned to walk out of the room, aware that he followed close behind. She felt his hand on her shoulder, and she stopped, closing her eyes for a few seconds as her heart pounded wildly before turning around to peer up at him.

"I want to thank you for taking such good care of Dad."

"You don't have to thank me, Tate. I could say it's my job, but it's really my honor. Your parents have been very... um..." Her words halted, suddenly uncertain.

"Very...?" he prodded.

She hefted her shoulders in a little shrug and continued, "Very good to me."

"Would we be able to have lunch together again today?"

After avoiding Tate for almost ten years when he came back to town, it seemed strange to consider his invitation. "I'm afraid we're short-staffed today, and I'm covering for another nurse."

"That hardly seems fair." His brow furrowed as he scowled.

"And how many meals did you have to miss when you were a SEAL?"

Pretending to pout, he shook his head. "You don't play fair." She didn't reply, and he continued to press. "Well, if not lunch, will you have a chance to grab coffee?"

Nodding, she glanced at her watch. "I can take a break in two hours. I'll be down in the cafeteria for a cup of coffee."

"Then I'll see you in two hours." He offered a chin lift and his grin made her insides flip-flop once again as he turned and went back into his dad's room.

An hour later, she turned the corner and watched as Dr. Hawkins hurried down the hall, a woman in a pencil skirt and heels, her arms full of papers, rushing next to him. He turned and made eye contact with Nora, an expression of relief on his face. "Nora, could you do me a favor? Ms. Pendleton is here to drop off some drawings for the house my wife and I are working on, but I've just been called to the ER." He thrust a key into her hand and added, "Could you please open my office for her and then make sure to lock it as soon as she drops these files on my desk?"

"Of course, I was going to be walking right past your office anyway."

He hurried to the door leading to the stairs and disappeared. Turning to Ms. Pendleton, she said, "His office is right down here." She unlocked his office and opened the door, stepping inside. Seeing the notebook stuffed with drawings, fabric swatches, and paint chips, it dawned on her that Dr. Hawkins must be the source of the early morning gossip.

"Do you think I should leave these on his desk or over here on the table?" Ms. Pendleton asked.

Glancing around his office, she could see that his laptop and several medical files covered the top of his desk whereas a table to the side only had a few boxes. "I'm unsure what he wants you to do, but I have to admit I don't think his desk is the best place since there are medical records there."

Ms. Pendleton nodded and moved to the table, setting her notebooks down and spreading them out. She picked up one of the cardboard boxes and looked over at Nora. "Should I move the boxes out of the way?"

Reaching over, she plucked the box from the woman's hands and said, "Ma'am, I really can't say, but I wouldn't move anything if possible. I think it's best to leave Dr. Hawkins' office the way we found it."

Mrs. Pendleton nodded, a tight smile on her face, and left her work on the table. Thanking Nora, she walked out of the room, and Nora moved to the table to replace the box. Uncertain exactly where Dr. Hawkins had it, she glanced at the other boxes before setting it on top. Recognizing a medical supply company name on the box, she set it next to the others. Stepping out of the office, she closed the door and locked it. Pocketing his key, she hurried back to her next patient.

Ready for a break, she gratefully headed to the cafeteria. She walked straight to the coffee kiosk as though that was the only thing on her mind while surreptitiously looking around to see if Tate was already there. Not seeing him, she got in line.

"Oh, my God, look what just walked in!"

"Honey, I've been looking at him for the last two days. His dad's up on the third floor and I keep hoping his dad will have to stay in the hospital longer just so I can keep staring."

Without turning around, Nora knew exactly who the two employees standing behind her were talking about. It's not that there weren't handsome men in Rawlins, but Tate would make any woman look twice. But hearing one joke that they hoped his father had to stay longer set her teeth on edge. Twisting around, she bit out, "Keep your opinions to yourself! Talking like that about a patient is horrible, not to mention completely unprofessional!"

Before either woman had a chance to retort, her gaze looked behind them, seeing Tate approach. She could feel the heat of a blush sting her cheeks. Ignoring all others, he walked straight to her.

"Hey, Nora. Sorry I'm late."

"You're not. I was... um... early."

Not wanting to look at the faces of the women behind her, she was glad she was next to order. Getting two coffees, she handed one to Tate and they moved over to the sugar and creamer station.

"Hey, are you okay?" he asked as they walked to a table.

Blinking, she jerked as she took a sip of too-hot coffee. "Yeah, it's just a busy day. On top of that, I some-times get tired of working in a small hospital in this little town where gossip is the biggest way to pass the time. If there's nothing new to talk about, then people make up stuff."

He glanced to the side where the women were staring at the two of them. "Is this uncomfortable for you? Me sitting here with you?"

She shook her head. "No. At least not because of them. If they weren't gossiping about you, they'd make up something about someone else."

"So, you're not uncomfortable because of them but you're still uncomfortable?"

Shifting in her seat, she nibbled on her bottom lips. "Wow, you've got a lot of questions, don't you?"

"I just want to know how you're doing," he said, leaning closer.

She stared at her coffee, feeling the need to look anywhere except at his face. *Looking at him used to be my favorite thing, but for so long now, it's the last thing I wanted to do.* Finally, she lifted her gaze, immediately drawn in by his eyes. "I'm fine, Tate. Really. I confess that it's weird, considering that I've now seen you more in the past two days after doing my best to avoid you for a very long time." He opened his mouth, but she jumped in, not giving him a chance to speak. "I can't explain it, certainly not now. Anyway, baby steps, I guess."

Glancing at her watch, she sighed again. "I'm sorry, I really do have to run. I've got to get back up on the floor, and I have Dr. Hawkins' office key that I need to return. But Frank is doing well, and I don't see why he can't go home tomorrow."

She stood, and he stood with her. "The least I can do

is walk back upstairs with you," he said. "Even if it's just a moment, I'll take it."

Uncertain what to do with that little tidbit of information, she simply nodded. Leaving him at his dad's room, she hurried back to the nurses' station, ignoring the speculative looks the other nurses were giving her. *Frank will be discharged tomorrow, and Tate will soon go back to his life in Maine. Whatever these last two days of chats may have accomplished, we're still worlds apart.*

That evening, Tate sat alone on the front porch of the ranch house. Caroline and Thomas had taken the kids to dinner, and his mother had not yet returned from the hospital. A huge slice of his mom's apple pie had been consumed. The fork and empty plate sat on the porch next to him, and a longneck beer bottle dangled in his hands. Country music played in the background from his phone, and he tilted his chair back, resting his feet on the rail.

The sun was setting over the western range, painting the sky ablaze with color. How many nights when he was on a mission would he watch the sunset and imagine his family back home on the ranch? And how many of those same nights did he think about Nora? *Hell, most of them.*

When he broke up with Nora, he had been on the other side of the world. Ready, but anxious for an upcoming mission that was as dangerous as it was adrenaline-inducing. He tried to remember what he was thinking when he sent the email. He knew she would be upset but somehow thought that would be better than waiting for him, never knowing when or if he might return. Caroline had almost immediately responded, laying him out for his cruel and selfish behavior. She gave him pause, but when Nora never tried to contact him, he figured that Caroline exaggerated Nora's distress.

His trips back to Wyoming were sporadic while he was still with the SEALs. The first trip home, he was anxious to reconnect, but Nora refused to come around or answer his calls. On the next couple of visits, she managed to always be working. After he left the SEALs and was on missions with the CIA Special Ops, he only made it home once in several years. On that trip, he spied her at dinner with another man. It made sense—after all, she was a beautiful and smart woman. What shocked him was the jolt straight to his heart.

He lifted his hand and tugged at the chain around his neck. A small, handcrafted silver medallion hung on the chain with the initials T and N intertwined. Nora had gifted that to him when he left for the Navy. Unable to wear it when in uniform, it stayed with his possessions and was the first thing he slid over his head when he became a civilian.

What I told Mom was right... I was stupid to think she might still be here for me. Sighing heavily, he lifted the bottle, swallowing the cold beer.

"What if time doesn't do what it's supposed to do? What if I never get over you?"

The music of Lady A sounded over the airwaves and

he dropped his feet to the porch floor, his beer bottle barely dangling between his fingers. *Jesus, I thought time would make it all better.* His breath caught in his lungs as reality crashed over him. His voice carried out into the wide-open space. "She was the one. *The one.* And I fuckin' pushed her away."

His feet slammed down onto the boards of the porch as he stood suddenly, a new mission on his mind.

8

As she powered off her e-reader, Nora glanced at the clock, surprised to see that it was only eight o'clock. A knock on her door had her jump to her feet. She peered through the peephole, this time stunned to see Tate standing in the breezeway outside her door. Sucking in a quick breath, she glanced down at what she was wearing.

With a grimace plastered on her face, she threw open the door, not missing his wide-eyed perusal as he dropped his gaze from her head to her toes and back up again. She knew what he was observing... hair piled messily on top of her head with a chopstick holding it in place, flannel pajama bottoms in a bright plaid, paired with a long-sleeve, slouchy, baby blue T-shirt, and thick gray socks.

Not giving him a chance to comment on her appearance, she tilted her head to the side. "Yes?"

Blinking, he offered a smile. "I'm sorry to come by

unannounced, Nora. I just thought that maybe we could continue our conversation from earlier."

Now, it was her turn to widen her eyes in surprise. "Continue our conversation?"

A gust of wind blew through the breezeway, and she shivered. Fairly certain that her nipples were poking through her shirt, she refused to look down to check. Keeping her focus on Tate, she caught his gaze drop to her chest and then quickly go back to her eyes. She shivered again and grimaced. "Well, come on... don't just stand there and let the cold air in."

Part of her hoped he would decline, but he smiled wider and stepped forward, causing her to scramble out of his way. Closing the door behind him, she stood with her arms wrapped around her waist, uncertain of what to say or do.

He turned, his eyes warm, and said, "Yes, I'd like to continue our conversation. I know it's presumptuous to come over so late at night, but I just didn't want to wait any longer."

She felt foolish as they continued to stand. Waving her hand toward the sofa, she said, "Would you like to have a seat?"

He moved quickly and sat on one end of the sofa, looking up at her expectantly. She walked over to the chair and plopped down, unceremoniously tucking her feet up under her hips. A grin played about his lips as though he recognized her avoidance tactic.

Sighing deeply, she schooled her expression and held his gaze. "Okay, what do you want to talk about?"

"Us."

Unable to hide her surprise, she blinked. "Uh... us?"

"Yes. Some things need to be said. Things that should've been said a long time ago, but I was too chicken shit or too stupid to say them."

He was still staring at her, but she had no idea what to say to his comment. Sucking in her lips, she waited.

He leaned forward and placed his forearms on his knees, his hands clasped in front of him. "Nora, I know you never understood this, but when I broke up with you, I truly thought I was doing it for you."

"For me?"

"Yes."

Her breath left her lungs in an angry rush, and she threw her hands up to the side. "For me? Are you kidding me? How on earth did you rationalize in your mind that breaking my heart was for me?"

His expression no longer held certainty as regret seemed to move through his eyes. "You had just lost your brother."

She snorted and rolled her eyes in an ineffective attempt to keep his words from piercing her heart. "Oh, I remember that very well, Tate. I also remember how the night of his funeral we helped each other grieve by promising our love... as we *made* love."

He winced and shook his head. "Hell, Nathan was my best friend, and I'd promised him that if anything ever happened, I'd make sure you were okay." As though mimicking her actions, he unclasped his hands and lifted his palms upward. "I knew I was going back into missions that were dangerous and had no idea if I was coming home. I didn't want you to have to go through the agony of burying me also."

"Are you crazy? Tate, I lost you when you walked away. Maybe I didn't bury you, but I might as well have. I was in love with you. You made the decision that I'd be better off without you just because you *might* not come back?"

His breath seemed to catch in his lungs. "I see that now... that I decided for both of us, and it was wrong. That's what I wanted to tell you. When I broke up with you, all I could think of was that it was a way to protect you. It seemed noble at the time to offer you a chance to have a normal life."

"Why do you think I've avoided you the times you came home? Just seeing you, knowing that you walked away from what we had gutted me. Every single time it gutted me." She fell back against the cushion, winded from the emotions slicing through her. Dropping her chin to her chest, she shook her head slowly, licking her dry lips.

They sat in silence for a moment before she gathered the strength to lift her head and hold his gaze. "Everything went to hell, and I was all alone. You sent me a Dear Jane email and for reasons I won't elaborate on, I didn't handle that well and ended up losing almost a year of my nursing training while I got my shit together."

He visibly winced, but she powered through, her voice hard and rough, foreign to her own ears. "I managed to get my degree, but instead of getting out of Wyoming and traveling together the way we planned, I ended up staying here where I had a support system. When I finally matured enough that I could have done something else, my father had a heart attack and died."

Another wince crossed his face, hitting his brow, this time managing to break into her tirade. "I'm sorry, Nora. I was gone on a... a mission. I didn't get word from Caroline until much later."

Still on a roll, she jerked her hand up, palm facing him, and ignored his apology. "Mom's health grew worse and she was unable to keep her job. I gave up my apartment and moved back in with her to help. I love... *loved* my mom, but I was nursing all day and then came home and nursed in the evenings. I'm not stupid enough to think that your job as a SEAL was all fun and games, but I assure you my life back here was not either. But no matter how much I helped care for her, it was better than losing her, which I did in the same year. So, I was twenty-six years old and very much alone."

Lifting an eyebrow, she shook her head slowly. "I was so stupid, Tate. Sharing your grief when we buried Nathan, then sleeping with you that night gave me hope that we might still have a future. You have no idea how much I still regret that night when the next morning you were gone in every sense of the word. And when I say regret... I can't begin to express the repercussions from that night." She squeezed her eyes tightly shut, blocking out the images as she blew out her breath.

His hand landed on her knee, his fingertips digging in slightly as he squeezed. "I know I keep saying this, Nora, but I never meant to hurt you. I knew that night was a mistake—"

She jerked as though slapped, her eyes snapping open, wide with pain.

"No, no, that's not what I meant," he rushed. "I just mean that I had one night for bereavement leave and then I had to get back to my team. I never meant to hurt you. Leaving you alone that next morning gutted me, too. I wanted to stay by your side but had no choice."

An icy coldness filled her chest. "Don't worry, I wasn't always alone. I finally began dating, but I'm afraid I wasn't woman enough for him, and so, after two years of dating, he broke it off." Giving an exaggerated shrug, she added, "Caroline never cared for him, so I suppose in the end she was right."

He lifted his hand as though to place it on her arm, and she shifted back. His face contorted, but his eyes continued to hold her gaze. "I'm sorry, Nora. So fucking sorry. You're right. I thought I was doing the proper thing and being brave, but now I realize it was a chicken-shit way out. But, please, can we talk? Can we, can we... I don't know, can we just talk?"

Even with his apology, her anger ratcheted up and tears clung to her lashes. Wrapping her arms around her waist, she lifted her chin and held his gaze. "To what purpose?"

"Because I'm no longer willing to *not* have you in my life. I thought about you all the time. I agonized. I wanted to pick up the phone and call you to tell you I'd made a mistake. I wanted to email you and say that I'd been a moron and we needed to stay in each other's lives. But there was always another mission. I needed to focus or the men around me could die."

At that, she shivered, thoughts of Nathan slamming into her. The agony of her brother's death had never really left, only stayed further in the background for longer periods of time.

"When I finally got out, the first thing I wanted to do was find you and tell you that I was sorry. But every time I was back home, you practically ran from me. I knew I'd hurt you, but as time passed, I couldn't understand why you wouldn't even get near me."

She jumped to her feet, struggling to suck in air as his words pelted her. "Because when you left, I lost everything! Everything!"

He took to his feet as well, stepping closer. Her palms landed on his chest and she pushed, her face contorting with the tears now streaming down her cheeks.

"I know you thought you lost me, Nora, but I'm still here. You didn't lose everything."

Her heart squeezed, and she wondered if it was possible to have a heart attack from so much pain. Chin quivering, she held his gaze. *Does he think he wants it? Fine, maybe it's time.* "Oh, Tate," she said, her voice dropping an octave, ice hanging on her words. "I did lose everything. I lost our baby."

His mouth dropped open, no sound coming forth as he stared in stunned silence.

She walked on wooden legs toward the front door, throwing it open wide. With the sweep of her hand, she uttered one final word. "Leave." Part of her was glad that he actually walked out with no argument, and the other part felt abandoned once more.

Her heart squeezed, but no more tears fell. Over the years, she had cried less and less, slowly accepting her life and her past. Staring at the now-closed door, she wondered if she should have remained silent instead of burdening Tate with the knowledge that they could have had a baby. Turning out the lights in the apartment as she made her way to the small bedroom, she moved into the bathroom and completed her nightly routine on automatic pilot.

It was when she lay in bed with the dark of the night closing in on her that she decided she had done the right thing. He wanted to know why I avoided him for these past years. *Finally, he knows my pain.*

Nora's words had slammed into Tate, taking him by surprise. Trained to react in any situation, all his skills fled him as he stumbled out of her apartment. He'd wanted to refuse to leave, force her to tell him everything, but it was obvious she was holding together by a thread. The urge to hold and comfort her was strong, but the news that she had been pregnant had left him reeling. *God, it must've happened the night of Nathan's funeral.*

He closed his eyes, but the image of Nora's tear-stained, agonized face was impressed onto the backs of his eyelids. At that moment, he was certain he would never get that image out of his mind. *Nathan, if you were here, you'd kick my ass. I promised to protect her and failed spectacularly.*

Somehow, he made it to his vehicle and drove to the ranch. Unheeding of placing one foot in front of the other, he made it inside, barely keeping his emotions together when a voice from the living room startled his feet to a halt.

"You went to see Nora."

He turned slowly and saw his mother sitting by herself in the living room, wrapped in her comfortable robe. Her face radiated sadness and the creases seemed deeper.

"You knew, didn't you?" As soon as the question was asked, he could see the answer in her eyes.

She opened and closed her mouth several times, then finally sighed. "Yes. Not... well, I didn't know for a long time, and by the time I found out, there was no reason to bring it up to you. Plus, it was always Nora's story to tell. But Caroline was with her when Nora miscarried, so she wasn't completely alone. I'm sorry, sweetheart. I truly am."

He stood rooted to the floor, his heart aching. "At least it explains why she hasn't been able to tolerate the sight of me for years."

Susan stood and walked to him, reaching out to place her hand on his arm. "I don't think it was the sight of you she was running from, but more like seeing you brought back memories that were hard for her. It just seemed like she kept getting hit one time after another. Nathan died. You broke up with her. She found out she was pregnant and miscarried. Then her dad... then her grandmother and mom."

"Jesus, how did she keep going?"

"We stepped in as best we could. We tried to be there for her. She's a strong woman, but she closed herself off as a means of protection."

He held her gaze for a long moment, his breath catching in his throat. "I was going to be a father. Jesus Christ, Mom. I don't know what to do with all of this."

"I don't know what to tell you, honey. I don't know how to ease this burden for you."

She stepped forward and wrapped her arms around his waist, and he tucked her in tightly, both receiving and giving love. She finally pulled away and said, "As much as you're hurting, I'm glad you know. I never liked knowing something about you that I couldn't share. I also never liked that Nora held in her pain for so long. It's good that she shared it with you."

"I don't know. I'm not sure that she sees me as someone she wants to be around. It's more like she told me to finally get me to leave."

"And will you?" Before he had a chance to ask her meaning, she jumped in. "I know you have to go back to Maine... that's where your life is now. But do you see yourself giving up on Nora completely? Placing her in the past and closing the door on the feelings you always had for her."

The quiet night gave him few answers, but he slowly shook his head. "I can't see walking away from her now. It makes me want to comfort her, not just because of our shared loss but because I want her in my life."

Susan squeezed his waist before stepping back, sighing. "I'm heading to bed. Your father's coming home tomorrow, and I need to be ready for him."

Just as she reached the bottom of the steps, he called out to her. "Mom, I'd already vowed to break through the wall she's put between us. Now, I'm even more determined to do so. I can't change the past, but I can offer a future."

Susan smiled gently and nodded. "I think that's perfect."

He lay in bed for hours, unable to find sleep. Thoughts of a grieving, pregnant Nora continually ran through his mind. *When she realized she was pregnant, was she excited? Eager to tell me? Waiting till the next time I came home?*

The dark silence of the night crept over him. *I was going to be a father.* Sitting up in bed, he ground the heels of his hands into his eyes, attempting to quell the tears he felt building.

Finally flopping back onto the mattress, he stared at the ceiling until sleep finally crept into the edges of his consciousness. What he'd told his mother was true, but now, the idea reverberated through his being. *I can't change the past, but we will have a future.*

9

"You're doing amazing, Frank."

Nora smiled down at the man who had been like a surrogate father to her for years. Surprised she was able to drag herself from the bed that morning and show up for work, she hoped her makeup tricks for covering dark under-eye circles worked to hide her pain.

Tate's visit the night before had dredged up emotions she'd thought long buried, keeping her awake far into the night. Feelings of loss, grief, heartbreak. Working in a hospital she knew that these emotions were common. She had to face illness and death, accidents and old age, pain and suffering every day. To be a successful nurse, she channeled her empathy toward her patients while maintaining an emotional distance that allowed her to complete the technical aspects of her profession.

After Tate left her apartment, numbness had set in. The tears that fell were not so much for her losses as they were for her loneliness. It was strange being the last living member of her family, having lost each of them too early. Most days she filled her time with her job and had been so adopted by Tate's family that she could push back the emotional shadows that crept around the edges of her life.

She had never spoken of the miscarriage to Susan or Frank. Caroline was the only one to know her secret at the time. She had not even told her parents, wanting Tate to hear it from her first.

Part of her hated the way the words came rushing out to him the night before, with no preamble, no preparation. But once they were spoken, there was no pulling them back in. After he left, she even wondered if it had been worth staying silent for all those years, holding the pain in, letting it eat away at her a bit at a time. Strangely, by the time she awoke this morning, her breathing was easier with all her secrets now out, no longer choking her with the need to remain silent.

Continuing to check Frank's blood pressure, she reiterated, "You're in great shape and everything looks wonderful."

Frank looked up at Nora and smiled. "So, do you think I'll be discharged?"

"I'll leave that up to Dr. Hawkins, and he'll be here in just a few minutes. I thought he might have already been in here since he gets to the hospital so early each morning. He was on his way in, but I noticed he got a call at the nurses' station."

"I hope I can get out. I promise to be a good patient. After all, I've got more trips with Susan planned."

Finishing his chart on the computer, she walked

over and stood next to his bed, staring at an older version of Tate. Same hazel eyes. Same square jaw. "I think it's wonderful what you two are doing. When Caroline first told me, I was so surprised. I guess I never imagined you and Susan being anywhere except working the ranch. I'm sure it must be hard to decide when to retire when you own and work the land."

He reached out and patted her hand and nodded. "I was born and raised on that ranch, and it's still in my blood. But I've still got some years left in me to see some places I never had a chance to see. I'll always come back to this area... it'll always be our home. But I wanted to give Caroline and Thomas a chance to make it their own home, and they can do that better without me and Susan right in the same house with them."

She smiled and started to turn away when his hand clenched slightly on hers. Looking down, she waited to see if there was something he wanted.

"What about you, darlin'?"

"Me?"

"When are you going to start moving forward and following your heart?"

She snorted. "Let's not worry about my heart. After all, you're in the hospital for *your* heart."

Hearing a noise, she looked over her shoulder expecting the doctor to walk in, seeing Tate and his mom instead. Susan immediately moved to Frank, and suddenly Nora couldn't think of anything she was supposed to do. She had no idea how or if he'd processed the bombshell she'd dropped on him last night. Her breath held in her lungs as he stepped closer, his eyes locked on hers. His mouth moved, but she was focused on his eyes as his gaze roved over her face. Blinking, she jerked. "I'm sorry?"

"I reminded you to breathe."

Her breath left her lungs in a rush, and she felt the hot burn of a blush move over her face. "Of course, I'm breathing," she snapped.

"Glad to hear it. It wouldn't do for the nurse to pass out onto the floor, now would it?"

Still uncertain how to act around Tate and unable to sense his thoughts, she ducked her chin and turned back toward Frank, eyes widening as she observed him and Susan smiling at her. "Well, I need to go. I'm sure Dr. Hawkins will be in soon and talk to you about your discharge." Stepping closer, she patted Frank's arm again. "I am glad that you're doing so well."

"Susan and I'll be at the ranch. I figure sitting on the front porch watching my grandkids run around like monkeys will be the best place for me to convalesce. You just might have to come to check on me while I recuperate."

She winced at the reminder of grandchildren, but with Tate standing so close to her, she simply nodded. Turning, she looked up to see him staring intently at her, pain now in his gaze. Walking out into the hall, he stilled her steps with a hand placed on her arm.

"It's just hit me, Nora, that you've had to watch my parents with Caroline's kids, always reminded of your loss." His fingertips curved in gently, warmth moving through his touch. His brow was furrowed with anguish. "I'm so sorry."

For the first time, instead of feeling like crying, she wanted to comfort. She lifted her hand and placed it on his, giving a little squeeze. He shifted his fingers so they were linked with hers. "Thank you." Those two words seemed too simplistic for the emotions moving between them but were all she could think of at that moment and appeared to be what he needed.

Inclining her head toward Frank's room, she said, "Go be with your dad. We can talk later." A relieved smile spread across his face, reminding her once again how handsome he was. Slipping her hand from his, she turned and walked down the hall. Blowing out a breath, it hit her that the exchange had not taken more than a moment and yet had not gutted her. *Maybe I can do this... be near Tate without getting my heart trampled again.*

"Nora, I was just looking for you," Dr. Hawkins said, interrupting her thoughts. "We've got a special case coming in and I'm making a change in the nursing assignments."

Turning toward him, she smiled at the efficient senior doctor. Giving him her attention, she waited.

"The Police Chief called to say that a prisoner is being brought in. He didn't give me any details other than he has a severe laceration that had been treated but now appears infected. An armed guard will be with him. They've requested that he be seen in a private room, not go through the ER. We've got several empty rooms at the end of this hall near the service elevator. I'd like to keep the traffic in and out of his room to a minimum."

"I understand. Do you know when he's coming in? I've got Frank Tate being discharged this afternoon."

"I'm going to have Jeanette take over for your other patients until the prisoner is out of here."

Hiding her surprise, she replied, "Okay, Dr. Hawkins. I'll finish up my notes and should be ready when he comes in."

He glanced to the side, before leaning closer and lowering his voice. "These situations make me a little nervous, but that's one of the reasons I chose you. You're levelheaded, avoid gossip, and I know you'll put the patient first regardless of his situation." With a quick nod, he turned and walked down the hall.

"Everything okay?"

Whirling around, she jumped, seeing Tate close by, not having heard him approach. "Yes, yes. I'm... uh... I'm fine."

He opened his mouth as though to speak again, his eyes moving from her face to Dr. Hawkins' retreat down the hall before landing on her again. "This isn't the time or place to get into everything we need to talk about, but if you need anything, just let me know. I mean that, Nora. Anything."

He stepped closer, and her head leaned back to continue holding his gaze. His presence seemed to surround her, filling her with warmth instead of hot anger or cold indifference. "Okay," she whispered, suddenly not sure what she was agreeing to. Stepping backward, feeling the need for breathing room between them, she said, "I've got to get back to work. Goodbye, Tate."

Once at the nurses' station, she glanced in his direction, but he had disappeared into his father's room.

Sucking in a deep breath, she let it out slowly. She still had no idea how he was handling her news from the previous evening and knew they had much more to say to each other, *But it finally feels good to let go of the secret... at least part of it.*

With Tate filling her mind, Nora had little time to wonder about her new patient. She waited by the service elevator, stepping back when the doors opened and the gurney was rolled out. Three uniformed guards flanked the patient, and she turned, waving them toward the room directly across the hall. It was not until two male hospital nursing aides shifted the patient into the bed and she heard the metallic clink of the handcuff onto the bed rail that she got a good look at her patient.

He was older than she'd anticipated as evidenced by the amount of gray streaking through his brown hair, deep crinkles emitting from his eyes, and leathery skin. He was slender, and his muscles were lean and appeared strong. One arm was bandaged from his wrist to above his elbow. She leaned closer, the blood pressure cuff in her hand, but he slapped out with his good hand, knocking the cuff down. Startled, she had no time to react before she was pushed back and one of the guards handcuffed the patient's other hand to the bed rail.

"I'm sorry, Miss," the prisoner grunted, his voice depicting one who'd probably had a two-pack a day smoking habit for years. "I'm in a lot of pain." He leaned to the side and coughed before grimacing as he tried to catch his breath.

"Mr. Carlson, my name is Nora, and I'll be your nurse. I'm going to place the automatic blood pressure cuff on your upper arm and then I can leave it. The cuff will inflate every fifteen minutes and record your blood pressure. And the pulse oximeter will measure the oxygen level in your blood. Right now, can you tell me on a scale from one to ten what your pain level is?"

"When I'm not moving my arm or coughing, it's probably about a four or five. When I move, it shoots up to about a nine."

She typed his stats into the computer and nodded. "Okay, I'm going to step outside to see what tests the doctor wants to order. I'll be back as soon as I can."

She was familiar with family members sometimes trying to crowd around a patient, but this was the first time she had to move amongst large law enforcement officers. The only one she recognized was Billy Perkins who worked for the sheriff's department. Offering him a quick nod, she scooted past the others and into the hall, not surprised when Billy followed her.

"Hey, Nora, you doin' okay with this?"

"I'll treat him just like any other patient, Billy."

His face scrunched as he shook his head. "I understand what you're saying, but you need to have your wits about you. The sheriff brought him in from the county jail. He wasn't picked up in town, so I didn't know anything about him until this morning." Tilting his head toward the room, he said, "The deputy in there told me about him, and I want to make sure to give you the same warning."

She glanced behind him and could see a few nurses looking their way from the nursing station. "I know Dr. Hawkins wanted to keep this quiet, but there's no way in a gossipy little hospital anyone can keep a secret. Come on. Let's step over here where we can have a little more privacy."

She walked to the end of the hall, still near the door to Mr. Carlson's room, and leaned close to Billy. "What do you think I need to know? I mean, I know he's a prisoner, but he looks pretty harmless."

"From what the deputy from the jail told me, David Carlson lives up in the hills somewhere. Thinks the government is out to get him, so he's built his own hideout."

Sucking in her lips, she shook her head slowly. "Okay, but that's not illegal."

"No, but stockpiling weapons and running drugs are."

Her eyes jerked open wide, and she said, "Seriously?"

"Oh, hell yeah. They now think he's the one suspected of running a meth lab somewhere in the area. They've been after him for a while, but it wasn't until he got pulled over for having a brake light out that they finally got him. From what I understand, his truck was filled with drugs. Believe me when I tell you he is one seriously wanted man who's going to go to prison for a long time."

Dr. Hawkins walked down the hall, glancing at Billy before his gaze landed on Nora. "You ready?"

Plastering a smile on her face, she nodded. With a quick goodbye whispered toward Billy, she followed the doctor into Mr. Carlson's room.

"Hello, Frank, I'm Jeanette."

Tate glanced up as an older nurse came into the room then looked toward the door to see if Nora was following. He stood to the side as Jeanette checked on his dad, wondering why Nora had not come back into the room. Even though she had not run from him this morning, a niggle of doubt slithered through him that she might be avoiding him once again.

Stepping just outside the door, he looked up and down the hall. A police officer was standing at the very end near the window. Shifting slightly, Tate was able to see the officer talking to Nora. Her attention was held rapt by whatever the officer was telling her. The same doctor who had been in to see his dad now walked toward the end of the hall, spoke to Nora, and they quickly disappeared into the last room.

His Spidey senses at full alarm, he looked down as Jeanette was walking out of his dad's room. "What's going on down there?"

Jeanette looked back and forth quickly, her eyes round. Leaning closer, she whispered, "A prisoner from the county jail was brought in. I don't know anything about him, but I can tell you that he came up on the service elevator and not through the ER, and he's got deputies guarding him in there."

What the fuck is Nora doing down there?

"One of the nurses on the floor overheard Dr. Hawkins, the Senior Physician of the hospital, assign just one nurse to the prisoner's care. He wants to keep the gossip down." A chuckle slipped out and she added, "With so many police and guards down there, why he thought they could keep this a secret, I'll never know."

She hurried out of the room, and after a quick glance toward his father, satisfied his mother had things well in hand, he stalked down the hall. As he neared the door, the police officer leaning against the doorframe saw him coming and shifted quickly to his feet.

"You're Frankie Tate, right?" Without giving him a chance to reply, the officer grinned widely. "I'm Billy Perkins. We were in school at about the same time, although I think I was a year or two behind you."

Fighting the urge to plow Billy out of the way, he stopped and smiled in return, careful to plant himself so that he could see Nora just inside the room.

"I heard your dad was in here. Hope he's doing okay."

Nodding, he said, "Thanks, Billy. I see you've become a deputy."

"I've been with the sheriff's department for a while. Man, I can't believe it's you. Your dad always talked about you being in the military and now working for a hotshot security specialist. Hell, I've been right here in Rawlins my whole life and you've traveled the world."

Surreptitiously keeping an eye on Nora, he smiled in return toward Billy. "Don't let that impress you. I've been to a lot of places that I would never want to go back to and often thought the sunsets here were better than anywhere."

"You can say that again. I'm married and have two kids and wouldn't want to raise them anywhere else." Billy turned and glanced into the room, then looked back at Tate and lowered his voice. "Got a prisoner in there. We think he's a big-time drug manufacturer who got busted just for having a broken brake light on his car."

And I'm not carrying a fuckin' firearm. Choking back a sigh, he asked, "So, what's he in here for?"

Hefting his shoulders in a shrug, Billy said, "I just got called in when they arrived at the hospital today. From what I can tell, he busted up his arm when they tried to arrest him. The jail has a nurse, but no doctor—"

"Tate? What are you doing here?"

He had watched Nora coming out of the room, catching her eyes only when Billy shifted out of the way. "I saw Billy down here and thought I'd come to find out how he was doing."

Her eyes narrowed, and he knew she was not fooled by his casual answer. She stepped out of the way as Billy walked back inside the room. "I swear, the police are worse gossipers than the nurses."

"How secure is the prisoner?"

Hands on her hips, she glared up at him. "I'm not going to discuss another patient with you, Tate."

"Not asking for anything personal, Nora. I just want to make sure of your safety. How secure is he?"

Hesitating, she pinched her lips tight, then finally huffed. "He's handcuffed to the bed rails. I'm perfectly safe. Geez, I can barely get to the patient through the guards." She glanced down the hall then back to his face quickly. "Is everything okay with your dad?"

"He's fine. Mom and Caroline are with him and he's getting ready to be discharged. I was curious why you got switched out and then saw Billy down here."

Cocking her head to the side, she said, "And you just had to find out what was going on, didn't you?"

"Guilty," he said with a grin. Glancing back into the room, he said, "I'm going to be nearby for the rest of your shift. I know you've got lots of people around, but I want to make sure you stay safe."

She opened her mouth and he was sure she was going to protest, but then she surprised him. Shrugging, she said, "Okay."

He battled the urge to lean down and take her lips in a kiss. *Slow... I need to take this slow. I fucked it up years ago and don't want to do that again.*

She held his gaze for just a moment, confusion in her eyes as she stared. "Look, Tate, about last night—"

"Not now, Nora."

"But it wasn't fair for me to just drop that—"

"Not now, babe. We have plenty of time to talk later, but right here isn't the time or place." He reached out and placed his hand on her arm, squeezing slightly. "Yeah?"

Her head jerked in a nod. "I'll see you later." Turning, she walked back into the prisoner's room.

Moving to a quiet corner near the waiting room past the nurses' station, he pulled out his phone, calling LSI. "Josh? Need a favor. There was a man arrested recently in Carbon County, Wyoming. He was carrying drugs. He's now been transported to the Rawlins Medical Center. I need a name and anything you can find on him." Chuckling, he said, "Yeah, my dad is doing fine. But this is right down the hall, and I want to know what I might be dealing with."

Disconnecting, he looked down the hall, wishing Nora was in his sight.

10

"Talk to me." Tate, seeing the caller was Josh, had picked up his phone on the first ring. *Ten minutes... good man, Josh... no wasting time.* He stepped out of his dad's room and once again moved toward the waiting room near the visitor elevators.

"David Joshua Carlson. Fifty-nine years old. Born in Oklahoma. His parents were barely of legal age, living in a commune. Mid-1960's, love, sex, rock 'n' roll, as well as drugs. His dad died from a heroin overdose when David was about five. Looks like mom left him at the commune with others to take care of him more often than she was there. Arrested several times for solicitation and drugs. She finally died of an overdose by the time he was twenty. I did some digging on the commune, and while they didn't have a lot of trouble with the law, they did gain notoriety when an investigative journalist lived amongst them for a while. It seems they eventually went from free love to fearing government takeovers. Mostly stockpiling weapons, food, and drugs for an eventual siege."

With his gaze pointed down toward his boots, he rested his free hand on his hip while he absorbed Josh's information. "Recent activity?"

"Employment history is sketchy. Looks like he was a rambling man, according to his tax records. Started out in construction and eventually fell into long-haul trucking between Texas and Montana. He was married at one time to Betty Frieder, but he was arrested several times for drug distribution. Did a few minor stints in prison, and that was it. Betty and David had two kids, but she divorced him ten years ago. She and her kids live in Fort Collins, Colorado, not far from where you're at. Gotta tell you, in the last ten years, he's like a ghost. No employment trail. No taxes recorded. No bank or credit card activity."

"Not liking the sound of that." He heaved a sigh, "And today?"

"He was flagged yesterday by the Carbon County Sheriff's Department for having a faulty brake light. He made a stupid error by trying to outrun them, probably because the trunk of his car was filled with drugs and drug paraphernalia, including meth and possible fentanyl. So, they gave chase. His car skidded into a tree, and he was injured. Paramedics did a quick fix, and he was taken to jail. As the night wore on, it became apparent that he needed medical attention that the jail was not equipped to offer."

"Tate, you're on speaker with the rest of us," Mace said. "What's the situation?"

"Someone I know is the nurse attending him. They brought him into the hospital but didn't go through the ER. Brought him up through the service elevator, and he happens to be in a room at the end of the hall where my dad is. I told Nora... the nurse that I'd keep an eye on things."

"Nora?"

He recognized Blake's voice and sighed. "Yeah."

"Do you need anything from us?" Mace cut in.

"As long as he gets stitched up and gets the fuck out of here, then no. I just didn't like her dealing with a situation that I wasn't apprised of. I'll let you know if I need anything more." Thanking them, he disconnected and walked toward his dad's room. *Time to get Dad discharged.*

Thirty minutes later, he stood by Caroline's SUV, supervising as his dad climbed into the backseat. *They're going to wonder why I'm not coming along.*

"Dad, I'm going to hang around the hospital for a bit."

His dad cocked his head to the side. "Something I should know about, Son?"

He hesitated for a few seconds, then said, "A prisoner was brought in for medical care, and Nora's been assigned. It just doesn't feel right leaving—"

"Stay. Knowing that possible threat, I'd rest a lot easier being assured that she's safe. Take your time. Lord knows your mom and sister will have me at the ranch with my feet up. At least I'll get them to prop me in front of the TV for a while."

Grinning, he gently clapped his father on the shoulder, then stepped back and shut the door. Looking at his mother's worried face, he said, "I'll be home as soon as I can." Watching as Caroline pulled away, he turned and stalked back into the hospital.

With David Carlson handcuffed to the bed, Nora noticed the guards seemed to relax. A portable x-ray machine had been brought up from radiology to do the initial evaluation on David's arm and ribs. Drug toxicology came back, and while David was clean, due to a history of drug use the doctor only prescribed a mild pain reliever. He seemed comfortable lying in bed, the medication allowing him to rest.

Billy had gone downstairs to the cafeteria to get lunch, leaving the other deputy in the room. Originally there had been two deputies in the room, one older, heavier, with a sharp eye and a no-nonsense attitude. He had left just before lunch, and Nora overheard him giving instructions to the younger deputy who looked as though he was barely in his early twenties and irritated that he was being lectured.

He walked around the room, stopping by the window and stretching, flexing his arms. She sucked in her lips to stifle the grin, thinking the deputy looked more comical than muscular. He turned and patted the weapon at his side, puffing out his thin chest. When she did not comment, he continued to walk around the room, finally moving to the other side of the hospital bed.

"I was surprised when you got assigned to be the nurse." The deputy's smile was wide as he stared at her.

Glancing at his name tag, she said, "Deputy Oliver, I assure you, I'm a perfectly capable nurse."

Eyes popping open, his head jerked quickly back and forth. "No, no, that's not what I meant. I just meant that I figured they'd give us some big, older male nurse. Not someone so pretty." His eager attempts at flirting passed over her, but it appeared he was not finished. "And you can call me Bart."

"I think, Deputy Oliver, that it's best if I stick with a professional title."

He chuckled, but the sound was too squeaky to be sexy. "Then maybe I'll have to take you to dinner, and we can get rid of the titles."

A snort came from the bed, and her gaze landed on David. He moved his head slowly, his narrow eyes focused on the deputy. "Boy, if you can't see that she's not interested, you need to get glasses."

Bart, now scowling, jumped to his feet, his fingers fisting at his side. Sneering, he looked down at David. "Don't forget who works at the jail... I can make your life hell."

"Okay, that's enough," she cut in, her eyes flashing. "I would think maintaining your cool would be part of being in law enforcement."

Shooting her a glare, he walked toward the window and looked out, his hands on his hips, his back to the room. She turned toward the door, hearing footsteps approach, and her gaze landed on a man in green scrubs. She didn't recognize him, which was unusual, considering the hospital was small. She glanced toward the identification badge attached to his chest, but it was flipped backward, keeping her from seeing his name. "Yes?"

Nora watched with wide-eyed shock as he lifted his hand and pointed a gun straight toward her. She gasped, and with eyes pinned on the weapon, was barely aware of the sound of Bart turning from the window, now facing the room.

"What the hell—"

"Shut up and stay quiet."

The man in scrubs now pointed the weapon toward Bart. "You, Deputy Dog, keep your fuckin' hands where I can fuckin' see them. Missy, you stay right where you are and don't move a muscle." Looking down at the bed, he grinned. "David, how you doin'?"

"Better, now that you're here."

Sure that her pounding heart could be heard throughout the room, she fought the desire to look down at David, refusing to take her eyes off the weapon that was now pointing in the direction of Bart.

"Nora?"

Her name came from the bed and, keeping her head still pointed toward the door, she shifted her gaze toward David.

"Keep real still and do exactly what we say, and no one will get hurt. You got that?"

Her nod of agreement was more random jerking of her head, but it seemed to placate him.

"Deputy, get these cuffs off me and don't do anything to piss off my friend. His gun is going to stay on you, and he's got no problem putting a bullet through your brain if you do anything other than unlock these cuffs."

The sound of movement from across the bed could be heard along with the clink of metal. With the gun still pointing toward Bart, she dared to turn her head slightly. Bart's teeth were clenched and his hands were shaking, but whether from anger or fear she couldn't tell. *Just get him unlocked and let them go. Please, Bart, don't try to be a hero.*

The cuff fell away from David's wrist, and he shifted toward Nora, pain creasing his face. Looking over his shoulder, he ordered, "Snap that on your own wrist."

Bart croaked, "Fuck that!"

The man with the gun swung it back toward Nora and grinned. "Do as you're told, or I'll put the bullet through her head."

Gasping again, she jerked, then hardened like stone. Terrified to move, each breath dragged in and out.

David's hand landed on her arm, and she jumped as he moved her slightly to the side. Bending, he grabbed the plastic bag his accomplice tossed his way. He pulled out a pair of jeans and quickly slid them up his legs. Jerking the hospital gown off, he tossed it to the side before donning a thick shirt. Jamming his feet into the shoes by the side of the bed, he grinned.

Reaching into the bag again, he pulled out a roll of duct tape and ripped off a small section. As he moved around the bed toward Bart, the man in scrubs shifted so that the gun was once again directed toward the deputy's head.

Nora glanced toward the door. *If only I could... it's too far... I can't make it.* Her mouth felt dry and she tried to swallow as fear threatened to choke her. David pressed the piece of tape over Bart's mouth before turning toward her. Expecting him to do the same to her, she was not surprised when he hustled around the end of the bed and stopped directly in front of her.

"Let's go."

Eyes wide, she could not comprehend his order until she saw the barrel of a gun pointing directly at her once again.

Waiting on the first floor for the elevator, Tate spied Billy walking toward him holding a Styrofoam box. "Taking your lunch upstairs?"

Grimacing, Billy nodded. "The deputy they have in the room is young. I thought I'd at least be on the floor while I eat my lunch."

"Is he from the jail?"

Shrugging, Billy said, "Yeah. They have their own deputies assigned just to the jail. Technically, I'm here as a courtesy backup." He looked around, then asked, "Did your dad get discharged?"

"Yeah. I thought I'd stick around since Nora's in charge of the prisoner."

Billy grinned, shaking his head slightly. "I remember the two of you in high school. Figured you'd be married by the time I graduated."

Heaving a sigh, Tate admitted, "Thought so too at one time, but life took us in different directions."

"'Bout broke everyone's heart when Nathan got killed over in Afghanistan. Sorry, man, you and he were best buds if I remember right."

Not having anything to add, he simply nodded.

"Well, maybe life's brought you and Nora back together again. Who knows? Stranger things have happened."

A scream from the end of the hall pierced the muted sounds of the hospital floor just as they stepped off the elevator. A nurse ran toward the nursing station, her hands waving as she continued to scream.

Tate, dodging others in the hall, raced to the last room and darted inside. Standing next to the bed was the young deputy, duct tape over his mouth. The bedsheets were shoved to the side and the hospital gown was puddled on the floor. The deputy jerked and rattled the handcuff linking him to the now-empty bed.

The room filled with hospital personnel and Billy rushed in, ordering everyone out. Pulling his keys from his pocket, he found the one needed to release the cuffs. The deputy's eyes filled with tears as he tried to gently pull the duct tape off his mouth.

Reaching him in two steps, Tate ripped the tape off, unheeding the cry of pain coming from the deputy. "Nora? Where's Nora?" He grabbed the young man by the shoulders and gave him a shake, looking at his name tag. "Deputy Oliver! Where the fuck is the nurse?"

"Gone," the deputy rasped. "They took her. They had a gun and they took her… the service elevator."

As others stood outside the room, he pushed into the hall and over to the elevator. Glancing out the window by his side, he looked down into the parking lot and spied a man in green scrubs dragging Nora toward an old green Jeep. An older man was with them, climbing into the back seat.

Tate's palm slammed against the glass as he watched Nora struggle, then curled into a fist when the younger man hit her in the face. She crumpled and was unceremoniously dumped into the back of the SUV before the driver stepped on the gas.

Darting through the stairway door, he pulled out his phone, hitting the direct link for LSI.

"Hey, man, you forget something—"

"Fucker's escaped... and taken Nora as a hostage."

11

Nora's face exploded with pain as she blinked her tearful eyes open. Her body moved gently with the sway of the vehicle. Uncertain if it was best to keep her eyes open to discern where they were taking her or closed so they would not know she was awake, she decided on open. The engine rumbled with power but sounded rough. An old blanket covered the area she was in, giving her little comfort, but at least the only smell emanating from it was a slight musty odor.

As they bounced on the road, she felt every pothole, every curve. Scanning the interior, she tried to keep her movements indiscernible. *I'm in the back of an SUV.* Bits of rust clung to the middle of the back door, and along with the crack in the back glass, she assumed the rattle-trap vehicle was old.

As her body rolled slightly at the next turn, she realized they were not hurtling down the road. *They don't want to get pulled over by the cops again.* When they came to a stop, she looked at the back door to see how the handle worked. She felt a nudge against her shoulder and jerked her gaze upward, seeing a man with a gun pointed over the back of his seat, down toward her.

"Don't get any ideas." He grinned and wiggled his eyebrows. "Or I might just have to take care of you myself."

"Shut the fuck up."

She recognized David's voice and twisted her head slightly to see him sitting in the back seat next to the man with the gun. Remaining quiet, she quickly learned he was in charge.

"She's a nurse, and I still fuckin' need her. So, keep your mouth shut, Bob, or I'll make damn sure you've got nothing else to say."

Bob's mouth scrunched to the side as his brow furrowed. He ducked his head slightly and turned back toward the front. She let out a long but silent breath, her eyes darting around.

Her jaw ached, and she slowly opened and closed her mouth several times to make sure it wasn't broken. She reached up and gingerly touched the tight skin, the swelling making her face feel lopsided. They had not bound her hands or feet, but she assumed they didn't want her to sit up and be seen by anyone through the untinted windows.

"You're bleeding," Bob said.

"You think I don't know that? Just get us the fuck outta here, and I'll get it taken care of."

Rawlins was not a large town, and soon they were no longer hindered by red lights or stop signs. As they rolled along, she peered out the windows from her reclined position and could see the cut hills rising from either side of the highway, the yellow stone covered in scrub brush.

Her gaze landed on a sign for the other side of the road heading into Rawlins. *We're heading east, toward Laramie.* Having lived her whole life in this area, she knew what lay ahead... craggy hills and mountains. Lakes and valleys. Sunsets that streamed color over the tree-covered mountains in the distance. Uninhabited land as far as the eye could see. And lots of places to disappear.

With at least two of the men in the vehicle sporting weapons, she battled with what to do. *Do I try to escape now or see where they take me and try to escape later?*

Closing her eyes, Nora's mind filled with the image of Tate. His clear, rough voice whispered in her ear. *Stay safe, Nora. No matter what, stay safe. I will find you.* She jerked her eyes open, but all she could see was that she was still very much alone. She had no idea what types of jobs Tate did working for a security company... *but surely, as soon as he finds out I'm missing, he'll look for me.*

Tate paced the hospital conference room, barely hanging on to his shit. Thirty minutes had passed since Nora was taken. By the time he had slammed through the door leading to the parking lot at the bottom of the stairs, the old SUV was gone, too late for him to get the license tag number. Still on the phone with LSI, he ordered Josh to look at the security cameras for information on the vehicle.

Having rushed back inside, he headed straight back into the hospital room, grabbing Bart by the front of his shirt, slamming his back against the wall. "How the fuck did you let him get the drop on you?"

"It was the other guy," Bart yelled in return, his voice whiny. "The other guy had a gun."

Billy pulled Tate away. "Not now. You gotta keep your head." Looking around, Billy said, "I've got detectives coming for forensics. We need to take this somewhere else."

Within a few minutes, the Carbon County Sheriff arrived, and along with the hospital administrator, they hustled into a hospital conference room one floor down.

Still pacing, Tate listened as Bart gave his accounting, aware that other law enforcement were arriving. His phone vibrated and he stepped to the side. "Yeah?"

Josh jumped in immediately with his information. "The vehicle is a seventeen-year-old, dark green Jeep Wagoneer, registered to a man named Robert Heller. I'm working on the cameras in town, and the last visual clocked it leaving Rawlins, heading east toward Laramie."

"What have you got on Robert Heller?" As he asked Josh the question, he noted the others in the room now quiet, centering their attention on him.

"Sending you a picture of him now."

As soon as the picture arrived on his phone, he held it up to Bart's face. "Recognize him?"

Bobbing his head up and down, Bart said, "That's him. He was wearing green scrubs and stepped into the room, pulling his gun on us."

Billy shook his head. "Never heard of him. Not local, that's for sure." Glancing toward the county's sheriff and police chief, he received the same head shakes.

Talking to Josh, he said, "No one here knows him other than he's the one who came into the hospital. Find out everything."

Mace joined in, "Tate, I've called our FBI liaison and he's already been in contact with an agent close to you. Levi Amory from the Wyoming office should be there in less than thirty minutes. He's been instructed to look for you."

"What do you need? Drew and Babs are gone but we can get anyone else to you."

Tate recognized Blake's voice, but his friend's concern barely registered. "I was hunting these hills from the time I could carry a gun. I just need to get to my parents' ranch, get my hands on some weapons, and I'll go hunting."

"You gotta play this smart," Mace said. "We'll do everything we can here, and I've got Blake here to assist Josh, and Clay is itching to get there to you on his way to another mission."

"Boss, I'll leave that up to you. I'll take whatever help I can get in any way I can get it."

"Consider this your new mission," Mace declared. "LSI is on it."

He turned and started out of the room, but just as he entered the hall, he felt a hand on his arm. Jerking his gaze to the side, it landed on Billy who leaned in close.

"Jurisdiction is the sheriff's. They're not going to be too keen on someone rolling in with weapons who plans on taking somebody out."

Rounding on Billy, a growl erupted from deep inside his chest. "And how do they feel about kidnapping and hiding out on their land?"

"All I'm saying is tread cautiously. You're not going to do Nora any good if you're arrested. It's shittin' me to say this 'cause I want to go in with you, but I can't without orders."

"You're not telling me anything I don't know, so are you really holding me here?"

"FBI will have that jurisdiction. If you're going to go in, go with the agent they're sending."

Tearing his hand through his hair, he bit back, "I haven't got time to fuckin' wait around on some FBI agent—" Billy's gaze shifted to the side and Tate heard someone step close.

"Then I guess it's good you don't have to."

His eyes cut to the side and he observed a tall, muscular man stalk toward them. Sunglasses pushed up on top of his head. Dark hair cut short but not military. Wearing cargo pants paired with a tight, black, long-sleeve shirt with FBI stitched over the left breast pocket, it wasn't hard to figure out who the man was. He headed straight toward Tate, his hand lifted in greeting. Grasping it firmly, he said, "Levi Amory. I'm the agent assigned to this area."

He held the agent's eyes as he gripped his hand. "Frank Tate. Go by Tate. How'd you get here so fast?"

Brow lifted, Levi nodded slightly. "You're in luck. I live in Laramie. Hell, when I got the call, I was only about fifteen minutes outside Rawlins."

Not wanting to waste any more time with bullshit introductions, Tate jerked his head toward the conference room he and Billy had just left. "There's little they can do in there. Not like we can."

"They can process what they have here, but as of now, I'm in charge and have been told to work with you. I've got no problem with that, but I can't let you go rogue."

"I've got my people working on everything they can find on Robert Heller and seeing what they can dig up on David Carlson. If you have your people talking to LSI, it'll save us a lot of time." He clenched his jaw, surprised his teeth were not cracking. "And time is not something we have to waste."

"Are you carrying?" Levi asked.

He shook his head. "I have a license, but I don't have my weapons with me. I was going to head out to my family's ranch and get what I can from them."

Levi grinned and jerked his head toward the elevators down the hall. "I always travel with what I think I might need. You'll be satisfied with the arsenal I've got."

Tate's phone rang again, and he jerked it from his pocket, putting it to his ear.

"Sending you the address for David Carlson's exwife. That happens to be the last known address of Robert Heller... he goes by Bob. Other than that,

Heller's like a ghost," Josh said. "But if anybody can find a ghost, it's me. I'll send you what I ferret out."

Lifting his gaze, he looked at Levi. "I'll take you up on your arsenal as it'll save me a fuck ton of time going by the ranch. I've got an address for David's ex-wife, which is the address Heller used when he registered the vehicle they're driving."

"Then that will be our first stop," Levi agreed.

"Fuckin' hell, I wish I could go with you," Billy bemoaned.

"You're better off here. You can be our liaison with anything they find and anything they come up with. Do your own digging with people you know here in town who might know anything about Bob or David." Tate quickly exchanged phone numbers with Billy.

"Bring your girl home," Billy called out as Tate stalked down the hall.

Without looking behind him, he offered a two-fingered salute as he and Levi stepped onto the elevator. *My girl. Fuck yeah... I'm bringing my girl home.*

Levi had been right—Tate was not disappointed with the arsenal available to him. A Glock, Custom .45, and a sniper rifle along with ballistic-resistant body armor vests were locked in a vault in the back of Levi's SUV.

"I cover a lot of distance, have to provide support to the Park Rangers and don't always have time to make it to one of our offices. This tends to keep me well-appointed at all times."

Tate agreed, still not breathing easy with Nora gone but feeling better about the quickness in which he would get her back. *And I will fuckin' get her back.*

Now they were in the SUV, Levi following the directions given so they could interview Betty.

As they turned onto her street, Tate noted small houses on either side of the road, some kept up more than others. Pulling next to the curb, he observed Betty's house to be neat and well-tended with a freshly-painted fence surrounding the small yard. Fighting the urge to rush, he walked side by side with Levi to the front door.

It was opened by a middle-aged woman, her immediate smile replaced by a look of wary suspicion. "Yes?"

"Betty Carlson?"

Her smile dropped completely. "I am no longer Mrs. *Carlson*. I'm Betty Frieder."

"Yes, ma'am. I'm FBI Agent Levi Amory and this is Frank Tate. We need to ask you some questions. May we come in?"

Her brow furrowed and she hesitated, glancing behind her. "Is this about my ex-husband? My children are here and—"

"Mom? What's going on?"

Tate's gaze jumped behind Betty to a teenage boy. She looked over her shoulder, her lips pinched tightly together.

"Dean, there's no need for you to—"

"Mom, I heard him say he was from the FBI. This is about Dad, isn't it?"

She opened her mouth, but Dean stepped up behind her and Tate could see that he was more young man than a teenager. And when he spoke again, that opinion was solidified.

"Let them in, Mom," Dean said, his voice soft and his hand on his mother's shoulder. "You can't shield us forever from what Dad's up to. And they wouldn't be here if it wasn't important."

Her expression fell, and she nodded. Looking back at Levi and Tate, she sighed. "Please, come in."

They stepped over the threshold into a small living

area furnished with a sofa and two chairs. A wood-burning stove was in the corner and a wide-screen TV was mounted on the wall opposite the sofa. Framed pictures sat on the end tables and hung on the walls and at a quick glance appeared to be of Betty and her two children.

"Can I get you something to drink?" she asked.

"No, thank you, ma'am," Levi replied. "We do need to ask you about David, and I'll tell you that time is of the essence."

At that, her eyes widened, and she plopped into the nearest seat, her son sitting on the arm of the chair, his hand once again on her shoulder. "Oh, Jesus," she breathed.

Levi glanced toward Tate and offered an imperceptible nod, permitting him to explain why they were there. Glad for the opportunity, he leaned forward and placed his forearms on his knees, his hands clasped in front of him. Holding her gaze, he said, "Ms. Frieder, David Carlson escaped custody this morning from Rawlins Hospital. He was being treated for an injury he sustained during his arrest the previous day. We've got questions for you and need any information you can give us because he didn't just escape alone. He kidnapped a nurse during his escape."

Her hand lifted to her heart as she sucked in a quick breath. "Oh, Jesus," she repeated, then shot a quick glance up toward her son before looking back at Tate. "I'll tell you anything you need to know, but you have to understand that I've had no contact with him in almost eleven years."

"We understand, but we need any information, even if you think it's minor, about where he might have taken her."

She shook her head and said, "I don't know. David and I met twenty years ago. He was a rambling man before we met, driving big rigs all over the west. He ended up working in construction and got a job in Wyoming. That's how we met. He had a few years on me and the tale as old as time was that I fell for him. We lived in a little apartment over my grandparents' garage and a year later I gave birth to Dean. Two years later I gave birth to Barbara."

Looking up at her son, she offered a little smile. "We were happy. He still worked construction and on weekends he and some of his buddies started building us a house. The problem was a year later, it still wasn't finished. He'd leave on Saturday morning and come back late Saturday evening after having a few beers, and it wasn't until later that I discovered he was drinking his Saturdays *and* our house money away."

"He was arrested, ma'am, for carrying drugs. Not just drugs he stole, but meth, which I'm wondering if he produced. Do you know if he was using drugs at that time?"

Sighing again, she nodded slowly. "Agent Amory, I don't know anything about drugs. I never used them, and I was never around them. I know he was arrested a few times when he was younger, but I put my foot down about that not being part of our lives. Eventually, he started coming home not acting like himself. He spent more and more time talking about needing to prepare for a government takeover. To be honest, I was so involved with my job and the children I ignored him when he'd start going on and on about needing to make sure we were prepared. At one time, he started storing food in the garden shed. I figured it was harmless."

"Was there anything in particular that made you worry drugs were back in his life?"

"I started getting suspicious because he sure wasn't acting like he'd just been drinking when he'd come home. One day, when Dean was about six, he came up to me with a bag in his hand and asked me what it was." She squeezed her eyes tightly and gave her head a little shake as though to dislodge the memory.

"I realized it was drugs, and I couldn't believe that David had brought that stuff into our home where we had small children. I got it out of Dean's hand, had him show me where he found it, but there was no more. I will tell you I searched the house, every nook and cranny, wanting to make sure there was no more lying about. And when David got home, I gave him an ultimatum. Clean up his act or lose his family. You can see what he chose. I haven't seen him in eleven years."

Dean slid his arm around his mom's shoulder, pulling her in close. "Nobody blames you, Mom. You did everything you could, and me and Barbara have a better life with Dad out of it."

"Ma'am, have you ever heard of Robert Heller or Bob Heller?"

Her face pinched again, and she nodded. "He was younger than David, probably close to my age. I never heard that he worked a job, but he always hung around.

To be honest, I thought he was a bit simple, but he seemed to worship the ground David walked on. David would start talking about wanting to stockpile supplies for the takeover, and Bob would be the first one to run out and start buying things."

"The vehicle David was in today was registered to Robert Heller but used this address."

Gasping, her eyes widened. "Oh, my God! Neither David nor Robert has ever been in this house! I moved here right after the divorce, and David paid a few years of piddly child support, so he'd know this address. But I assure you, Robert Heller has never set foot in here!"

"Ma'am, do you know who his friends were at that time? I know it was a long time ago, but anything you tell us could help. Do you know where he and his buddies would go?"

Shaking her head, Betty threw her hands up to the side, palms facing the ceiling. "No, I'm sorry. I know this doesn't sound too good but being around David was exhausting. I was working to pay our bills, took care of the children and the house, and found that the more he rambled, the more I ignored him."

"Mom, what about that old album in the basement?" Dean's voice was soft as he pulled her tighter against his side.

Tate was once again impressed with Betty's son. *He's handling her with kid gloves but wants to do the right thing.* Looking directly at Dean, he asked, "Photo album?"

Betty's brow furrowed as she twisted her head around to look up at Dean. "Honey, I don't know. I haven't looked at those pictures in years."

Pink hit Dean's cheeks as he admitted, "I've looked at them. Not a lot, but occasionally, I'll take a look." He lifted his gaze to Levi before shifting toward Tate. "I don't want to have a relationship with my dad, but I guess it's human nature to wonder about him. So, rarely, I'll take a look at the photo albums. Mostly, I was looking at pictures that had him and me in them, but I'm sure there are others."

Levi nodded. "Can you bring them up here or should we go down to look?"

"I can get them, sir. There's only one of 'em." Dean stood and hurried to a door in the hallway. The sound of his footsteps clomping down the stairs was soon followed by his return. In his hands was a faded photo album, which he immediately handed to Tate.

Opening it, he quickly scanned past the pictures of David and Betty when they were together, not seeing anything of significance in the backgrounds. At first, the photographs were all of them before they had their children. There were only a few pictures that showed David without family, but Tate immediately recognized one of the men on a fishing trip as Bob Heller. The background showed mountains, water off to the side. Sliding the picture from his plastic sleeve, he turned it around and showed Betty. "Do you have any idea where this was taken?"

She leaned forward, her fingers closing around the photograph, and brought it closer to her face. Shaking her head slowly, she sighed. "It's not familiar to me, but I remember David talking about the fish he would catch in the Medicine Bow River." Looking up from the photograph, she added, "I was never outdoorsy, so I didn't go on any of the trips. We didn't have enough money for hotels, so I guess he and Bob would just camp. And in case you're going to ask, I don't recognize these other men in the picture."

"Mrs. Frieder, would you allow me to keep this photograph if I promise to bring it back?" Tate asked. "I work with someone who can probably identify where this was taken."

"I don't mind, but that was years ago. I'm not sure it would have any bearing on where he is now."

"I understand, but it would serve as a starting place."

"We're digging into David's family," Levi said, "Is there anything of a more personal nature that you can tell us? Was he close to brothers, uncles, anyone?"

"He had an older brother who died years ago, but by the time we divorced, his sister-in-law was tired of him always asking for money and told him not to come around anymore. She once mentioned that she hated the influence David had over her son. His name was Kenneth. Kenneth Carlson. But Lordy, I haven't seen or heard from him in ages. Kenneth's mom died several years back, and she was the last of his family."

Levi stood and Tate followed his lead, both men thanking her and Dean. She walked them to the door, then reached out and placed her hand on Tate's arm. "I'm real sorry to hear about that nurse. I hope you find her safe and sound."

He thanked her, and with a chin lift jogged back out to Levi's SUV. Climbing into the passenger side, he held the photograph carefully, took a picture, and then sent it to Josh. Dialing LSI, he was not surprised when it was answered immediately. "I'm sending Josh a photograph. It's David and Bob Heller, taken many years ago, possibly near Medicine Bow River, near Elk Mountain. I know it's a longshot, but his wife said that was the only place he talked about going to. I was only in that area once as a teenager... some of my family went on a camping trip through there. It's remote as fuck and could be easy to hide there."

"Got it. I'll start scanning and searching immediately."

"Mace?" He knew he had all the Keepers listening. "I'm here with Agent Levi Amory. He's got me well suited and armed." Turning toward Levi, he said, "You're speaking to my boss, Mace Hanover, and some of the other people we work with."

"Agent Amory, thanks for letting us work with you."

Levi chuckled and said, "Call me Levi, and I don't know that I was given much choice. It seems you're on a first-name basis with the Director of the FBI. But that's okay with me. I'll appreciate all the cooperation we can get."

Mace replied, "Good to hear. What's your immediate plan, and how can we help?"

Levi looked over at Tate, then said, "Right now, we're going to head toward Laramie. While we don't know exactly where he is, indications are that he is somewhere nearby in an area that he knows and can hide in."

"What support will you have?"

"I've got the local FBI offices and sheriff's departments. They'll give complete ground support, but whatever backup you can give us would be appreciated," Levi said. "I've got someone from my office looking up the security cameras along Interstate 84 toward Laramie. From what Tate tells me, you've got a lot more power at your fingertips."

"I hear what you're saying. No problem. We're on it," Josh said.

Mace jumped into the call. "Tate, just letting you know that Clay is flying in. We've got a private plane that's flying him into Rawlins. He's rerouting from a mission in California, so it'll be middle of the night before he gets there. He'll be in contact."

Tate kept his eyes on the front windshield, watching the familiar landscape roll by. Hank Claiborne, known as Clay, was a former Ranger and a crack security specialist. And he'd be damn glad to have him as backup. Glancing upward, he sighed. "Gotta tell you, it looks like snow. Probably not what he was expecting when heading to California."

"He'll be prepared," Mace assured.

Closing his eyes for a second, a sense of relief snaked through Tate for the first time in hours. He trusted Levi, but another Keeper working on the ground with him would make their job much easier. "Thanks, Boss."

Disconnecting after Josh said he would send them what he could on the photograph, he leaned back in his seat. Neither man spoke, words not necessary. All Tate needed was for Levi to get him closer to where David might have taken Nora. *Then even God can't help him when I get my hands on him.*

13

It was as though they had forgotten she was in the vehicle with them. Nora inched upward to a seated position, and even though Bob occasionally glanced toward her, he made no comment for a while. Finally, when she was completely upright, he narrowed his eyes on her.

"She's sitting up."

His words hit her in the gut, only because she had no idea how volatile any of the men might be. Preparing to slump back down, she breathed easier when David shook his head and snorted.

"She can't go anywhere, and there's no one around. Leave her alone."

Bob appeared to accept David's directive, and she forced her breathing to slow so that her heart would not pound so heavily. Sitting up, even in the back of the SUV, it was now easier for her to see that they were off the main road onto a narrow but paved road. And they were climbing in altitude. The clouds that had been threatening snow were now sending a light snowfall, but she had no doubt it would soon get much worse.

Having grown up with the mountains practically in her backyard, she both loved and respected the land. She remembered both Nathan and Tate talking about the terrain when they came back from their many hiking or camping trips. Mountains could be beautiful to hike and yet dangerous if you did not stay on the trails. Wildlife was abundant and could be dangerous.

Some areas of the mountains and hiking trails were inundated with hundreds of visitors each year, but much of the land was uninhabited with plenty of places for someone to hide. She recognized they were heading in the direction of the Elk Mountains, not a place she had visited but knew that they could easily disappear in the thick forests.

She was familiar with how quickly snowstorms could turn into blinding blizzards, and she wondered how Tate would be able to find her. She did not doubt that he would try, but with each passing moment felt that his chances of success were lessened.

Looking down at the scrubs she wore, she was grateful she had included a long-sleeved shirt under her top. The Jeep had heat, but it did not reach to the back effectively. Her legs were cold, but thick socks encased her feet. She almost giggled at the outrageous idea of trying to hike through the snow in her footwear—her nursing clogs were hardly suitable for outdoor wear. *And in a snowstorm? Shit, I'd get frostbite before I got halfway down the mountain!*

The old Jeep slowed down and she watched as they

turned between tall scrub brush now dusted with snow onto a smaller, gravel road. This path was much less traveled, the potholes jarring her, bouncing worse with each mile. The snow now covered the scrub brush and trees, and if she had not been so scared, she would have appreciated the beauty. Looking out the back window, she spotted the tire trails through the snow on the road. As her heart leaped, she prayed that the snow would stay light enough that if someone was following, they would be able to track the movements.

Following? How would anyone know who to follow? She had been so terrified when Bob hit her and pushed her into the back of the SUV, she paid no attention to her surroundings in the hospital parking lot. *Had anyone witnessed what happened? Did anyone get a description of this vehicle?* She knew that David's escape would have been noticed, and surely her absence as well.

Hospital security cameras! Barely able to hide her audible gasp, she sucked in her lips. *Please, God, please, let someone have seen us on the security cameras.* She had no idea what Tate did for a living other than his family talking about his job working missions for a security company. *Would he have the skills to find me?* Thinking about their last conversation, she blinked back tears. *God, I wish I had a do-over. Or at least a chance to see him one more time.*

She looked at her watch. *I was recording David's information on the computer at 1 o'clock when I was taken.* Three hours had passed. Swallowing deeply, she kept praying.

The scrub brush gave way to trees that grew thickly along the sides of the gravel road. The snow had not reached the ground as the branches covered the area, allowing her to peer through the front windshield. Once more, the driver turned off the road, and this time it seemed as though he was driving on dirt tire ruts, not an actual lane.

Unable to see into the distance, she was surprised when suddenly, a small clearing opened, exposing a snow-dusted cabin and several outbuildings. Two pickup trucks were parked to the side, the darker one appearing to be more rust than metal. The other truck was white, and with the snow, there was little she could tell about it. Unless she could steal the keys and get away, the extra vehicles would do her no good, but she filed that snippet of a plan into the back of her mind.

Jerking to a stop next to the door of the cabin, she remained still, uncertain of what to do. Scanning the area, she ascertained she wouldn't be able to run fast enough to get away from the men and into the woods as long as they held weapons. *But if they ever put them down, maybe, just maybe...*

She couldn't remember the other men's names, so she blinked dumbly as David turned around and ordered, "Stay with Porter." A look of disappointment crossed the face of the man holding the gun, and she could only assume that was not him.

The driver had alighted from the vehicle and walked to the back. After he lifted the back door, he wiggled his fingers toward her. "I'm Porter. Come on."

Those were the first words he had said in her presence, and she stared dumbly for a few seconds. He wiggled his fingers again. With no other recourse, she scooted to the back of the old SUV and dropped her feet to the ground gently. Considering that her legs felt like jelly, she was glad her hand still grasped the tailgate. Porter maintained a blank expression, but he waited for a moment until her legs were steady underneath her. With a lifted eyebrow, he jerked his head toward the cabin. "Let's go."

He didn't have a weapon that she could see, but the other man with David still had a gun in his hand. Glancing to the side, she could see that blood was dripping from David's arm. *As long as they need me, they'll keep me alive. I think... Oh, Jesus, please.*

"Now."

Jumping at the sound of the order, she nodded, her head jerking up and down. A sharp wind whipped by the group as they trudged toward the cabin. Uncertain what she would face once inside, she hesitated before entering, the desire to run almost overwhelming. Then heat hit her and she welcomed the relief from the cold in spite of the shivers still wracking her body.

Shooting her gaze around the interior, the air in her lungs rushed out when she saw that there were no others in the cabin. Three men were bad enough... the idea of more was terrifying. The cabin appeared like most of the small hunting cabins throughout the area, although this one had minimal upkeep. A wood-burning stove stood in the corner of the small living area. A worn sofa and two threadbare chairs were the only furniture nearby. In the other corner stood a refrigerator, stove, and sink. A small table was nearby, the top covered with boxes and plastic bags. A short hall was directly in front of her, three doors visible. Not wanting to think about what rooms were in the back, she jerked her gaze away.

A whistling sound came from the left, and she spied chinks in the insulation around the window. With the wind seeping through, she was surprised the room felt as warm as it did. Unsure what to do and afraid to move, she stayed rooted to the floor. She wrapped her arms about her waist, pulling tight as though hugging herself for comfort as much as for warmth.

David settled on the sofa and looked up at her. Porter nudged her from behind and she took that to mean she needed to get to work. Lifting her hands slightly, she managed to speak. "Mr. Carlson, I... I don't have any medical supplies with me."

"I've got some."

She turned to the sound of a voice coming from the back hall, another man entering the room. *Shit, there's four of them.* Hating the odds that were increasingly not in her favor, she wondered if she would have a chance to escape. Blinking to keep the tears at bay, she glanced out the window and the deep snow forced the idea of escape further from her mind.

The new man looked over at David and smiled. "Good to see you, Uncle David. How are you?"

"Kenneth." Grimacing, he nodded toward the other man. "I'll be doing a lot better once Nurse Nora takes care of me."

"Nurse Nora," the man with the gun chuckled. "That's funny."

"Bob, shut up, asshole."

That comment came from Porter, and while she hated to find that she had anything in common with these men, she had to admit she agreed with his assessment of Bob. Turning her attention back to David, she found his gaze on her.

"Just need you to get me patched up and make sure I'm good. You've got nothing else to be afraid of."

She wished his words were reassuring but knew they could not possibly be true. Her tongue darted out, licking her dry bottom lip. *Once he's patched up and better, they won't need me. And they sure as hell won't let me go.*

Kenneth carried a box over and set it on the sofa next to David. Looking up, he said, "I got medical supplies here."

She tried to take a calming breath, but her lungs spasmed and it was more of a gasp. Jerking her head up and down, she looked toward the kitchen corner. "I need to wash my hands." Not receiving an answer, she took that to mean she could move about freely. Forcing her legs to continue holding her up, she walked over to the sink. A few dirty dishes were piled to the side, and the kitchen, as well as the whole cabin, looked as though it had not been cleaned in forever.

Uncertainty filled her, but she turned on the water. Waiting, it never became hot, and with no soap in sight, she rubbed her hands briskly under the stream of luke-warm water. *In this cabin, what will my dirty hands matter?* Out of habit, she leaned forward and turned off the water faucet with her elbow. A roll of paper towels sat near the sink and she grabbed several to dry her hands.

Turning around, she noticed they were all watching her, but no one spoke. "Okay, I guess I'm ready."

Kenneth jerked his head toward the sofa where he'd placed the box. After walking over, she peered inside and found it filled. Alcohol wipes, antiseptic cream, bottles of aspirin, and rolls of gauze and bandages. Reaching her hand into the box, she moved other items around and discovered bottles of prescription antibiotics, anti-inflammatories, pain medication, cold and flu medication, and, as she dug deeper, revealed more supplies.

A chuckle from David drew her eyes up to his, and he asked, "Surprised to see us so well-equipped?" He didn't wait for an answer but added, "Readiness. It all comes down to readiness."

Uncertain of his meaning, her brow furrowed as she tried to decide if a response was expected.

"Readiness!" Bob piped up from the corner, his grin wide. "When they come—and we all know they're coming—everyone will be wiped out except us. We'll be ready! Food, guns, drugs, money. We've got it all."

Just as Kenneth was telling Bob to 'shut up' once again, her gaze jumped back to David's. "I don't understand. Who's coming?"

David shifted on the sofa, grimacing in pain, but kept his gaze pinned on her. "Mark my words, Nurse Nora. The government's been plotting for years. They'll snatch up everyone's land, take away jobs and livelihoods, separate families. And only those smart enough to prepare will be able to fight this battle."

She fought the desire to bark out a laugh at the

absurdity of his words, but a glance at the faces of the other men in the room caused her to swallow back any sounds. Knowing it was best to play along, she simply nodded. "Yeah... um... I can see... that's smart." Unable to think of anything else to say, she turned her attention back to the contents of the box. Pulling out several of the prescription bottles with shaking fingers, she noted the expiration date had passed, some much further than others.

"Um... I'll need some scissors, and it would be good if you had a thermometer." She leaned forward and placed the back of her hand against David's forehead. "I know you have antibiotics here, but they're not going to be very effective because they're way past their expiration date. Without antibiotics, your infection will only get worse."

"Shit," David bit out. "Why the hell didn't we keep this up?"

"Because none of us have been sick or got hurt," Bob said. "I can't remember the last time anybody had to get in that box."

Now uncertain that the preppers she was being held by were very good preppers, fear kept her holding still as she waited to see what they would do.

Porter walked to a kitchen drawer and jerked it open, pulling out a pair of scissors. Handing them to her, he looked down at David. "I should call her. She could get antibiotics up here."

Bob snort-chuckled from the other side of the room. "Kind of funny, isn't it? All the shit we've got here, and we don't have the drugs he needs to get better."

"Shut the fuck up," Porter ordered, drawing a scowl from Bob. Turning his attention back to David, he asked, "If you want, I'll give her a call."

David shifted on the couch and grimaced again. Through gritted teeth, he said, "The hospital will be hot. Tell her she needs to watch her back and make sure no one sees her take the stuff."

Porter nodded and pulled out his phone, moving to the back room. Not knowing what they were talking about, unease snaked through Nora as she considered their possible meaning. *Is there someone at the hospital that brings them drugs?*

"Nora? You just focus on the task you were brought here for. Got it?".

She sucked in her lips and nodded as she stared at David. Taking the scissors, she cut away the bandages that were on his arm. "You know, some of these lacerations are deep. I'm sure the doctor was going to put in stitches once you'd had your arm x-rayed."

"Is that something you can do here and now?"

Shaking her head slowly, she said, "I'm sorry. We don't have anything here for me to use."

"So, what can you do?"

"Well, I'll clean the wounds again, place the antiseptic cream on it, use bandages to hold the edges together, and wrap it tightly with the gauze. That's the best we can do right now. The pain medication is not expired—"

"No! I want to keep my wits about me."

"Oh, okay. Um... there's aspirin in here that hasn't expired, so that will take the edge off the pain."

He nodded but said, "Don't worry about the pain. I can take care of that."

She glanced toward the others, not understanding his cryptic statement, but no one was paying them any attention. Looking back down at David, he nodded again and she took that to indicate he was ready for her to begin. She walked to the corner kitchen again to see if there was a clean receptacle large enough to hold warm water. Looking around, it did not appear there was anything remotely clean.

"Whatcha looking for?" Kenneth asked.

"Do you have a bucket, or a large bowl, or even a pot that I can put clean water in?"

Bob, now sitting in one of the chairs, laughed again. "Got lots of buckets and bowls in the back room."

"Okay..."

No one moved. *Do they want me to go get it?* She turned and started for the door when Bob laughed again.

"Forget about it, lady," Kenneth said. Turning toward Bob, he said, "If you'd stay away from the ice, you might have a brain cell left in your head."

Rooted to the floor, she turned her wide-eyed gaze from Kenneth to Bob, then back again.

Kenneth shook his head and said, "Ignore him. The only thing you can use is here."

Swallowing past the lump in her throat, she nodded. Spying a pot, she walked back over to the sink. Running water in it, she used a paper towel as best she could to scrub out the inside. Her efforts were almost fruitless, but after several long minutes she gave up trying to make it any cleaner. Filling the pot with lukewarm water, she grabbed more paper towels and moved back to the sofa. Not sure where to set it, she opted for the floor. Using the cotton pads found in the medicine kit, she wet them with the warm water and cleaned the lacerations on his arm and forehead as best she could. The pads were small, and the process took a while to clean the whole area needing to be washed.

Beads of sweat broke out on David's forehead.

"I know this hurts. I'm sorry."

"Just do what you've gotta do, Nora."

That worked for her considering she wanted to have as little contact as possible with them. Offering a slight nod, she continued. Using bandages, she pulled the edges of his lacerations together and secured them. Checking the expiration on the antiseptic cream, she squeezed some onto her fingers and applied it over most of his arm and forehead. Then, taking a roll of gauze, she began to wrap his arm from bicep to wrist. Once that was completed, she used the available tape to secure the ends.

Her lower back ached as much from stress as stooping. *And the uncomfortable three-hour ride in the Jeep didn't help.* Straightening, she winced and longed to dig her fingers into her sore muscles but not until she had a chance to wash them again.

"That's all I can do for now. Your wounds are clean, but without antibiotics, there's not much I can do about an infection."

Porter walked back into the room just as she

finished. "Don't worry about it. Got someone who'll bring what we need."

His implication kept her from wasting her time asking what he meant. Hospitals tried their best to keep track of all the medication, but there would always be a few people who stole what they wanted to either use or sell. She sucked in a quick breath through her nose, then let it out slowly. Bending, she picked up the pot of now-bloody water and took it to the door. Looking over her shoulder toward Porter, she said, "I just need to toss this outside. There's no way I want this to go into the sink."

Not surprised when the quiet man said nothing, she was glad when he came up behind her and pulled open the door. She stepped through, the blast of cold air hitting her causing her to shiver. Looking around, she hurried to a bush about ten feet from the door and dumped the soiled liquid from the pan, turning the snow-covered ground light pink.

Standing, she glanced around, observing the sun had already descended beyond the tree line and the mountains to the west. The snow had continued to fall while they were inside, a couple of inches already blanketing the ground. Deepening shadows crept forward as the wind swirled the snow all about her. She shivered but closed her eyes tightly, sending a prayer upward that Tate would be able to find her in the wilderness.

14

"Webcam at the last light in Rawlins clocks Heller's Jeep passing two hours ago."

Tate was informing Levi what he had just learned from Josh. "Obviously, you know this, but there aren't any other cameras around where we can see where he went after that. He's got access to some satellite images, but it's gonna take a bit to see what we can find out."

Eyebrows lifted, Levi shook his head. "Damn, you boys have access to the good stuff."

Tate didn't reply but simply continued to look out the windshield, his gaze scanning the area. The snow had blanketed the ground, and he was on the lookout for any tire tracks leading off the road. They had just passed Laramie heading back toward Rawlins, hoping Josh would be able to tell them something from the picture they had gotten from Betty.

"Lighthouse Security Investigations."

That came from Levi, and Tate looked over at him. "You asking about it or just saying it?"

Chuckling, Levi said, "I guess I'm asking about it."

"We do private investigating, security installations, and security missions. Some private, some contracted by the government. We're based out of Maine but work everywhere."

"Were you military?"

"Yeah. SEALs. So was the owner of LSI. He was a SEAL who was recruited by CIA Special Ops."

Levi whistled, nodding. "So, does he only hire ex-SEALs?"

"No. He prefers people with military backgrounds, but also those with some special ops experience. SEALs, Rangers, Deltas, CIA Ops, and more." He looked back over toward Levi and asked, "Why? You thinkin' of applying?" Much to his surprise, Levi did not reply. "I hope that didn't seem offensive."

Levi shook his head. "Nope. Not at all. I was curious and asked. There are times I get tired of the red tape and bureaucratic bullshit I have to put up with working for the FBI. I did my time in the military before this, so I know how to follow orders and complete missions. Jesus, just once, I'd like to be able to do what needs to be done without worrying about every fuckin' rule."

"Yeah, I hear you." After driving in silence another moment, he asked, "Which branch?"

"Army. Ranger."

"No shit?" It was on the tip of his tongue to let Levi know that he would fit in with the other Keepers, but decided it was too soon to make that evaluation. *Hell, just because someone's been in operations doesn't mean they could fit in with us.* Glancing to the side again, he just prayed that Levi had it in him to do what needed to be done to find Nora.

He looked out the window on his side of the SUV, hiding the anxiety that was slashing across his face. He could only imagine how scared she was. *Jesus, keep her safe... keep her strong.*

"They need her to take care of David," Levi said.

Tate remained silent, not trusting his voice.

"They could've taken anyone as a hostage to assure that they got out of town, but they sprung David before he had his medical treatment. They need Nora."

"I hear what you're saying, but that doesn't make me feel any better."

Silence settled between them again. Finally, Levi asked, "Who is she to you?"

"Not much to tell. Nora and I are friends from way back. At one time, we planned on getting engaged. Her brother was my best friend until he was killed in the service."

"Damn, that's tough, man."

"Let's just say that I didn't handle that time of my life well. It's been ten years, and in that time we've barely spoken. This trip was about my dad being in the hospital, but it's forced me to face some things. It's now become my chance to rectify my situation with Nora."

"Of all the shitty luck," Levi said.

"I'll get her back. Failure is not an option. I'll get her back from the assholes that took her and then work to get her back to me."

Tate's phone rang and he quickly answered. "I've got you on speaker, Josh."

"The mountain range in the background of the photograph is the Elk Mountains. That's about—"

"I know where they are. I'm familiar with the area. I used to camp and hike there when I was a teen. But they're a big fuckin' range. Can you get any more detail from the picture?"

"I'm working on it. I'm scanning it through right now, and hopefully, we'll have something for you soon," Josh said.

Mace got on the phone. "Clay is on his way. He'll be in touch with you as soon as he can."

"Thanks, Boss. I didn't come here expecting a mission but thank fuck I've got you in my corner." Disconnecting, he turned to Levi. "I was a teenager when my friends and I used to hike and camp near the Elk Mountains. At the time, I thought it was God's country. Still do, but now I'm thinking of all the places David Carlson could hide. You got any ideas?"

Scrubbing his hand over his face, Levi sighed. "Right now, let's pull off at this visitor center rest stop. We can grab some coffee, take a piss, and check the security cameras to see if the Jeep stopped here while Josh is looking at the cameras."

Agreeing, Tate looked over at the log and stone visitor center. The snow had already coated the ground, and the mountains in the distance would have seemed majestic in their beauty if he was not staring at them, wondering if Nora was uninjured and warm enough. Inside, he quickly took care of his business and then headed to the vending machines.

"Save your money."

He turned and spied Levi leaning out of a doorway near the back. Joining him, he walked into the Rangers' office where Levi was checking the security camera.

"So far, it doesn't look like they stopped here." Levi jerked his head toward the side and added, "You don't have to waste your money on crappy vending machine coffee. Pour a cup over there and we can take it with us."

Walking to the back counter, he poured fresh coffee into a travel mug. "Anything useful?" he asked, nodding toward the screen.

"Nothing. They didn't stop here."

He blew out his breath in frustration, then felt his phone vibrate in his pocket. Checking the caller ID, he answered. "Mom. You're supposed to be taking care of Dad."

"Honey, none of us can get settled until we hear from you. Please tell us what's going on."

"Dad doesn't need this now—"

"And if you think he's going to stop worrying, then you don't know your father!"

He squeezed his eyes shut for a few seconds, uncertain of what to say.

His mother sighed. "I know you're doing everything you can to bring Nora back to us. Can you just give me anything that I can tell your father to ease his worry?"

"We've got a line on where she was taken. My team is working on getting more intel, and I'm nearby with the FBI agent. I've even got a team member who's on his way out to help. Mom, all I can tell you is that I will bring her back. Your job is to convince Dad to rest and trust in me."

The airwaves were silent for a few seconds before he heard, "I can do that, Frankie. I'll take care of your dad and we trust in you." He was about to disconnect when she jumped in again. "And when you find her, tell her we all love her."

"Will do, Mom." Disconnecting, he leaned his head back against the glass window, his gaze out over the snowy vista beyond the visitor center. Even with a storm predicted, there were vehicles still on the road. Just like in Maine, the people here were used to driving in inclement weather. Several pulled in to the visitor center, probably for the crappy coffee as much as a chance to run to the restroom.

Taking a sip of his, he had to admit Levi was right—it was definitely better than what he would have paid for at the vending machine.

After a moment, he noticed a woman walking from the parking lot, and as she entered the center, she headed directly to the ladies' room. A niggling of recognition moved through him, but he couldn't remember why she seemed familiar. She was wearing a heavy coat, but her legs were clearly covered in nursing scrubs.

Walking toward the main doors, he moved into a position that allowed him to keep an eye on the ladies' room door. Surreptitiously holding his phone, he aimed the camera toward her as she moved back through the reception lobby. Snapping several pictures, he watched her carefully as she walked to the vending machines.

Levi walked near and whispered, "What have you got?"

"That woman. I've seen her before but couldn't

figure out where. She's a nurse at the hospital. I've seen her for the past two days in the cafeteria."

"There's probably a lot of people that work at the medical center in Rawlins that live in Laramie. She may travel this road every day going back and forth to work," Levi said.

"Maybe." He glanced to the side and held Levi's gaze. "Right now, we've got shit. Unless you've got something better to do, I say let's follow her for a little bit, just to see where she goes." The woman was leaving the building, and he watched to see which car she was heading to before looking back toward Levi.

"Works for me. I've followed a lot of leads in my career. Some went nowhere and others turned into gold. I'm not about to ignore anything right now."

They headed out to the parking lot and climbed into the SUV. Calling LSI again, Tate said, "Sending you a photograph of a woman. I know she works at the medical center in Rawlins, but I need to know anything else you can tell me about her." Sending the picture of her as well as her car tag, he heaved a sigh. "Jesus, this is a long shot."

After leaving the visitor center parking lot, they followed her at a safe distance and immediately noticed she was not driving toward Laramie. She soon turned off the highway onto a smaller road, heading to the west in the direction of Elk Mountain.

"There are less than two hundred people that live in Elk Mountain town," Levi commented.

Tate was impressed with Levi's surveillance driving in the sparsely populated area. Far enough away so that she would not realize she was being followed, and yet they could easily see where she was going. Turning onto a smaller road before she got to the little town, she slowed her speed as the snow fell heavier. Levi fell back so that she could not see him in her rearview mirror, but the snow made it easy to discern her tire tracks.

Radioing his location, Levi asked, "Billy? What's your location?"

"South of Walcott on Highway 130, on my way to Saratoga."

"How close are you to Pass Creek Road?"

"I just passed it. Why?"

"We're following a nurse that Tate recognized from the hospital. She's turned onto Pass Creek Road just before you get to the town of Elk Mountain."

"Nobody lives out there except a few ranchers," Billy said. "I'm on the western side of Elk Mountain. Do you want me to go back north and get on that road coming from the West?"

"Yeah. It's just a hunch we're following, but it's all we've got right now. Tate's people have told us that the Jeep passed highway marker 252 according to the cameras, but we don't see them on any of the cameras closer to Laramie."

"So, they got off around Elk Mountain, too," Billy surmised. "Gotta tell you, though, with the snow coming down, I don't know how long our vehicles will be able to make it. I'll call for snowmobiles and can get the sheriff's snow coach."

"Put that call in to have them ready but not

dispatched right now. I want to continue to follow her to see if she's meeting someone."

"I'll come from the other direction and squeeze her in between both of us."

Just as Levi disconnected with Billy, Tate's phone rang again. Levi chuckled and shook his head. "Hell, it's like Grand Central Station here."

Silently agreeing, Tate answered, knowing it was Josh. "Got something on the woman?"

"Her name is Mary Bingle. You're right about her employment. She's a pharmaceutical tech at Rawlins Medical Center. Twenty-four years old. Single. Lives in an apartment complex in Rawlins. Here's the interesting part. Her record is clean, but I did a quick check on her immediate and extended family. She's got an uncle named Porter Watkins, who did time in the Wyoming State Penitentiary for meth production about fifteen years ago. Before that, he'd been in a local jail at the same time David Carlson was incarcerated. Coincidence? Maybe. I'll dig and see if I can find more."

Tate turned his head and met Levi's gaze. "Still may be a hunch, but she may be our best lead."

Continuing to follow the tire tracks in the snow, they discerned her turn onto a smaller road climbing in altitude.

"Slow down!" Tate called out. "She stopped up ahead."

Calling Billy, Levi gave their location. "She turned onto Mill Creek Road but stopped about half a mile up. If you can make it to the intersection we just passed, I'll let you know what happens."

"You think she's going to meet someone?" Billy asked.

"I think she's gone as far as she can in the snow, and she's just sitting in her car. My guess is she's calling for rendezvous."

Tate's fingers itched for action. It was part of almost every mission to have to sit and wait. He often thought his teen years spent hunting in the hills and mountains around the ranch gave him the perfect mental attitude for that endeavor. Waiting for the prey. Patiently watching. And then striking when the moment was right.

But now, with Nora's life in someone else's hands, the terror that clawed at his heart made it hard to just sit. *If there's any way You can send this message to her, God, let her know I'm coming.*

15

Nerves stretched tautly, Nora perched on the edge of the sofa. As strange as it seemed, sitting closer to David felt safer than in one of the chairs by herself. The sound of a phone ringing cut through her thoughts, causing her to jump.

Porter put the phone to his ear. "Yeah? How far did you get? So, where are you?"

She listened to Porter's barrage of questions and, having glanced at the continuing snowfall outside, wondered if he was talking to the person bringing the medication.

"We'll send somebody down." Disconnecting, Porter looked at David and said, "She got almost here, but her shit car can't get up the mountain. She's right at the bottom on Mill Creek Road."

David nodded and sighed, lifting his hand to gently touch his forehead. "Go. Your old truck should make it down and back just fine."

She knew that Kenneth had left through the back

door of the cabin earlier but had no idea where he was. Porter grabbed a heavy coat and tromped out the front door. Five minutes later, he returned, shaking and kicking the snow off his clothes and boots. "I told him that I was getting ready to head out."

A flash of light moved across the front window, and Nora watched as the truck's headlights backed away and then turned. David leaned his head back against the sofa cushions and closed his eyes. Glancing to the corner of the room, she observed Bob in a similar position, snores indicating his sleep. Kenneth came into the room and looked down at her. She wanted to hold his gaze to show bravery, but her entire being quivered in fear, so she stared at her clenched hands instead.

"I gotta go to the back."

His announcement caused her to look up, uncertain of his meaning. "Oh... okay."

"I can't just leave you free here. I'm going to have to secure you." Before giving her a chance to respond, he added, "Do you need to go to the bathroom first?"

Secure? Pushing that new fear to the side, she nodded. *If he was going to lock her into a room, she didn't want to be stuck without a bathroom.* She forced her legs to hold her as she stood and nodded. "Yes, please." She followed him to the door right behind the kitchen. The door across from her stood open and she glanced inside. Two bunk beds sat against the far wall but most of the room appeared to be filled with boxes.

Answering her unasked question, Kenneth said, "Uncle David likes to be prepared."

She assumed he was referring to David stockpiling

for the *inevitable* government takeover or foreign invasion. A few of the boxes looked old and she wondered if his supplies were as outdated as some of his medicine. Having never met a prepper, she was uncertain what to expect. She sucked in her lips, kept her thoughts to herself, and turned toward the bathroom.

"There's no window in there. No way to get out. Don't waste my time trying, so just do what you gotta do."

Jerking her head up and down in a nod, she moved by him. Closing the door, she looked for a lock. A small slide bolt was the only thing available, and she quickly latched the door before she noticed there was barely any room to move around. Besides the toilet, there was a tiny shower and a minuscule sink. Taking care of business, she washed her hands then shook them dry, not trusting the old towel draped over the shower curtain. Looking into the mirror, she stared at her reflection. Pale, bruised, and shaky, she barely recognized herself. *And this nightmare is less than a day old!*

As soon as the latch was slid back, the door opened to Kenneth standing right outside. Her gaze dropped to his hand, and her breath caught in her throat as she saw the length of thin chain in his hand. "No, please, no!"

"I got work to do and can't trust you. Got no choice."

"There's a snowstorm outside, and I don't have a coat or boots. There's nowhere for me to go," she argued.

"Come on." He grabbed her by the arm and escorted her back to the living room. He wrapped an end of the chain around her wrist and snapped it with a small padlock. The other end of the ten-foot length was locked around the handle of the refrigerator. He looked at his handiwork and chuckled. "Not the most secure, but it'll work." Pulling on his boots and heavy coat, he opened the back door and once again disappeared outside, letting in another blast of cold air.

Stepping through, he slammed it shut, leaving her shivering as she sat perched on the sofa. Bob was still snoring, and David appeared to have fallen asleep. Not wanting to wake them with the noise of the chain rattling, she wiggled her wrist to see if there was a way for her to escape. He had secured it tightly, keeping her from sliding it off her hand. Her gaze followed the length of chain to the refrigerator and she wondered if that end would be easier. *I've got to do something.* Swallowing the fear, she stood and walked into the kitchen, praying that there would be something she could use to pry open one of the chain links.

Tate nodded toward Levi, and they slipped along the shadows next to the road, separating as they neared Mary's vehicle. The small SUV would have performed well on most of the snowy roads, but it was not suited for snow-covered mountain terrain.

As he crept along, he could see that she was sitting in the driver's seat, wrapped in a thick coat. Levi knocked on her window, and she jumped. With the snow swirling, visibility was low and they hoped that worked to their advantage.

Rolling down her window, she said, "Took you long enough to get here! I'm freezing—"

"FBI. Keep your hands where we can see them," Levi announced.

Mary squeaked but immediately lifted her hands in front of her. "What is this? I got stuck on my way home and need help!"

Tate opened the passenger door, spying the bag sitting next to her purse on the passenger seat. She jumped and her hand darted out toward the bag, causing Levi to order her to keep her hands up, once again.

Hearing someone approach, Tate looked over his shoulder and nodded as Billy pulled to the front of Mary's SUV. Alighting from his vehicle, Billy and his partner jogged over to the passenger side next to Tate.

"What have you got?" Billy asked.

"Good timing. This is your jurisdiction, so I'll let you take a look inside the bag."

Tate slid to the side, allowing Billy to lean into the SUV. He opened the bag and said, "Well, well. What have we got in here?"

Tate leaned close, but the swirling snow made visibility difficult. Billy turned and held the bag open for him. After looking at the contents, he stood up and called out to Levi. "Prescription antibiotics from Rawlins Medical Center, and it looks like enough pseudoephedrine to keep a meth lab going for a bit."

"Those are for me! I've been sick!" Mary called out.

Tate snagged her phone from the passenger seat and checked her call log. "She received a call almost two hours ago from a number in her contact list as Porter. She called back to that same number twenty minutes ago."

"You don't understand—they'll kill me if I don't meet them," she cried as Levi reached in to place his hand on her arm. He handed her to Billy's partner who escorted her toward the sheriff's SUV while Billy placed the sack of prescription drugs in an evidence bag. Once it was secured and labeled, he did the same with the phone.

Billy handcuffed Mary, then assisted her into the backseat. Slamming the door, he turned to the others. "Do you want me to take her in now or wait for someone else?"

"She called someone to meet her here. She must be expecting them soon or else she knew her car would get buried in the snow and she might not get out. Why don't you back up to stay out of sight and wait to see if we can get whoever was sent to meet her?" Levi suggested.

Nodding in agreement, Billy climbed into the front of his SUV and backed down the road. Levi looked toward Tate and grinned. "Want to pretend you're Mary?"

"Fuckin' hell. Just what I always wanted to do." Moving back to Mary's vehicle, he leaned in to push her driver seat back to allow for his long legs and climbed inside. The snow had already coated the windshield, and he left it alone, allowing the white blanket to obscure who was sitting inside. Knowing Levi would have moved out of sight, he leaned his head back and waited.

Almost ten minutes later, right on cue, a black shape was moving toward him. Finding a spot out the driver's window that he could peer out of, he watched as a pickup truck rumbled to a stop. He remained still as someone alighted from the truck, wrapped in a thick coat and boots, and began walking toward Mary's SUV.

Pulling up the hood of his coat, he turned his face away from the window. A sharp rap of a knuckle on the glass was followed by, "Wake up! Give me what you brought. I gotta get the shit up to David before he gets sicker, and you've got to get outta here before you get stuck here all night. If you freeze to death, it's not going to do us any good."

As Levi came up behind the man, Tate threw open the door.

"FBI. Keep your hands where we can see them," Levi ordered once more.

"Shit!" The man turned as though to flee, and Tate jumped from Mary's vehicle, his weapon drawn.

Billy approached, making another arrest. "Looks like I got my quota today, boys."

Pulling out the man's wallet, Levi perused his ID. "Porter Watkins. I believe we have your niece sitting in the back of Deputy Perkins' vehicle, ready to be taken to the county jail. Looks like you'll be joining her for a family affair."

Porter remained silent, his face cut in stone as Billy handcuffed him and marched him over, placing him with Mary in the backseat.

"How do you want to play this?" Levi asked Tate.

"Leave Mary's vehicle here. It's worthless to us in

this weather, but we'll keep the keys so no one else can use it. I'm going to keep Porter's phone. I can always send or receive a text if I need to without giving myself away. Billy might as well go ahead and take Porter and Mary to the jail. I'm going to take Porter's truck and follow his tracks back up the mountain—"

"By yourself?"

The snow was swirling and there was little time to waste before the tracks around them were obliterated. "I've got to go now to get as close to where they are as possible. My team member, Clay, will be landing in Laramie in a couple of hours. Get your hands on a snow coach or snowmobiles that are going to be needed soon."

"So, I go to Laramie, pick up your team member, and arrange for the snow transportation to get back to here," Levi reiterated.

"That makes the most sense. If I can get to them tonight, I can deal with them." He observed Levi's eyebrow lift and growled, "If I can subdue them alive, I will. But make no mistake. My mission is not to shut down their meth lab and arrest them. My mission is to rescue Nora. If you've got a problem with that, you need to say it right now."

Levi held his gaze for several long seconds, then shook his head. "I'll have your team member on the mountain by the first light of day."

Reaching out, the two men clasped hands and then separated. Tate jogged over to Porter's truck, fired the engine, and carefully turned on the snow-covered road, heading back up the mountain. The darkness of the night was lessened by the white snow blanketing everything in sight. The headlights glistened off the drifts, allowing him to see the ruts that Porter's truck had made. *Thank fuck we didn't spend any more time bullshitting around or these tracks would be completely covered.*

His progress was slow but steady. The silence was only broken by his breathing as he continually scanned the area while making sure to follow the tracks. Soon, he came to thick trees lining the road whose branches created a canopy keeping the snowfall at bay. Needing Intel, he dialed LSI. "Have you got me on location?"

Each of the LSI Keepers sported the tattoo of a lighthouse on their shoulder. Embedded under the skin of the beacon was a tracer. LSI was able to track their Keepers anywhere at any time.

"You've got Josh, and yes, I can see where you are."

"Is there anything you can see on a satellite further up the mountain than where I am? I'm following the trail of Porter, the man we just arrested who came down from the mountain."

"There are no recorded homes or residences in that area, but there are probably hunting cabins, which are either too small or hidden to show up on my satellite views. There are a few clearings around. The closest one to you is about four more miles. I'll see if I can get a close enough scan to locate any cabins."

If David had taken Nora to a cabin buried in the woods, it would be almost impossible to find it in the middle of the night. Focusing on the road ahead, he continued to follow the tire tracks from Porter's trip. Not wanting to get stuck in snowdrifts or go off the edge, he crawled along, gaze pinned straight ahead as the wipers kept the snow from sticking to the windshield but did little to assist his vision. His phone rang and he hit connect, glad to hear Josh's voice again so quickly.

"Okay, looking at the satellite view in daylight, I can see that you're about three and a half miles from the clearing. There is a small building on the north side of the clearing with two smaller sheds nearby. I'm trying to bring the view into more focus, but right now, that's the best I can tell you. This is from yesterday's satellite pass, and there were no vehicles evident at that time."

"I'm going to get as close as I can still following the tire tracks and then cut the lights. From there, I'll go on foot and report in."

Excitement began to move through his body, nerves tingling in anticipation of taking down the men who dared to put their hands on Nora.

16

Nora tiptoed into the kitchen, carefully gathering the chain in her hand as she moved. Once there, all her movements resulted in the chain rattling. David's pale skin and sweat-covered brow indicated that he was not well, and she didn't think he would be a problem. Bob, on the other hand, made her nervous. He didn't seem as smart as the other men, and in the few hours that she had been with them wondered why they tolerated him. But, considering he kept a gun with him, she could not dismiss his presence.

And Kenneth? Where did he go, and what is he doing? He said he was going to the back, but with a snowstorm pounding outside, she could not imagine him wanting to be anywhere but close to the fire.

"If you'd stay away from the ice, you might have a brain cell left in your head." Porter's words to Bob slammed back to the forefront of her mind. *Ice... meth! Of course, that's what this is about!* Billy had told her that the car

David was driving contained drugs, including meth. *Holy shit! They're making meth up here!*

She glanced around the short counter and her stomach turned at the nasty mess. Her gaze searched each pot and dish carefully, trying to discern if meth had been produced in the cabin. Uncertain exactly what she was looking for, she could only ascertain that the residue on the plates and pots were just dried food. *So, maybe one of the sheds is used for their drugs... that would explain where Kenneth went.* Her gaze shot down the hall to the last door that Kenneth left through and she hoped it led to the outside and not to another room where cooking drugs occurred.

She jerked at the thought, and the chain rattled again. Whipping her head around to see if David or Bob heard it, she held her breath until ascertaining neither stirred. She opened the refrigerator and was shocked to find that it was packed with food. Cheese, eggs, bread, and lunchmeat. Reaching up, she opened the cabinet and found it contained canned vegetables, rice, a jar of spaghetti sauce, and peanut butter. Upon careful inspection, it appeared the expiration dates had not passed. *They must have known the storm was coming and prepared.*

Turning the situation over in her mind, it hit her that David's accident and subsequent arrest had thrown whatever plans they had out the window. *If he's the leader of this group of meth producers, they needed to get him away from the police quickly.*

Hoping to find a utensil that she could use on her chain, she pulled open the top drawer in the counter. A large spoon, a spatula, and a knife were all she found. The second drawer was stuck and made a loud screeching as it opened. Glancing down, she spied a screwdriver, but just as her hand moved forward, Bob stood from his chair.

"What are you doing?" His words were slurred with sleep, and he scrubbed his hand over his face.

Holding up her hand, showing the chain dangling from her wrist, she prayed her words were less shaky than she felt on the inside. "I was looking for something to eat. I thought about cooking something but there's nothing clean."

He yawned and scratched his stomach, the gun dangling in his fingertips. As he walked toward her, she reached down and grabbed another large spoon from the drawer. Holding it up, she said, "Well, I found *something* clean. If I had a pot, I could heat some of the soup you have here."

"You had a pot earlier."

Unable to keep the wide-eyed, dropped-jaw expression of incredulity from her face, she stared at him. When he didn't say anything else, she realized he was being serious. "That pot was dirty to begin with, and I cleaned it as best I could but then used it to help wash away the blood from David's injury."

Bob blinked, still sleepy-eyed. "Yeah? So what?"

"The pot had *bloody* water in it," she repeated, emphasizing each word, thinking he would surely understand the error of his suggestion. When it became obvious that he was waiting for her to say something, she simply shook her head. "I can't cook food in a pot that had blood in it."

His gaze dropped to the sink where there were other dirty dishes. "Well, find something. Go ahead and fix some soup now." He looked around, his brow furrowed, and asked, "Where's Kenneth?"

"He said he had business to take care of. That's why he chained me here."

She observed Bob grin before turning and walking into the bathroom. Blowing out a breath, she looked to the other side of the room and saw David's eyes on her. With the chain continuing to rattle, she walked the short distance to the sofa, and asked, "How are you feeling?"

"And why do you ask, I wonder? I can't imagine that you're concerned about me."

"I might have been forced to come here, but you're still my patient." Her words to him were true, but the sentiment was not. She just knew that it was best to stay on their good side, at least until she could find a way to escape. Leaning forward, she touched the back of her hand to his forehead and felt the warmth. "You'll feel better as soon as we can get the antibiotics."

"I thought Porter would be back by now. What time is it?"

Looking at her watch, she said, "It's a little after six o'clock."

She glanced outside, and even though it was after dark, the white snow reflected light and made the world seem brighter. "It probably took him a while to get to wherever he was going. The snow is still coming down really hard."

Deciding to fix the soup, she walked back to the kitchen. *I don't have to eat whatever I fix for them, thank God.* She found another pot in the sink and washed off the dried food as best she could. Setting it on the hot plate, she opened three cans of chicken noodle soup and poured them into the pot.

While it was heating, she thought about the screwdriver she had seen in the drawer. *If I take it now, where can I hide it? Will they miss it? If I leave it in the drawer, will I be able to get to it later?* No answers came to her, but with Bob and David both awake, she decided now was not the time to sneak it out of the drawer.

Rinsing out a cruddy bowl and spoon, she finally gave up trying to make them clean. Pouring some of the now-heated soup into the bowl, she carried it over to the sofa, dragging her chain beside her. Handing it to David, she said, "You need to eat something to help your body fight the infection."

He peered up at her with suspicion in his eyes, and she snapped. "I've been in full view of both of you the whole time. There's nothing in the soup that didn't come out of that can. You can eat it or not." She walked back to the corner of the kitchen counter and called over her shoulder to Bob. "Should I just leave some here for Kenneth?"

"Yeah. I don't want to let you out to take some soup to him, and I sure as fuck don't want to go out into the cold."

She ladled more soup into a bowl, walked over to

Bob, and handed it to him. Having nowhere else to sit, she perched on the edge of the sofa where she had been earlier. Feeling David's eyes on her, she turned and held his gaze.

"Aren't you hungry?"

"I saw some crackers in the cabinet and thought I might have some in a little bit."

Snorting, Bob said, "She's going on a hunger strike."

David's lip curled in a snarl. "Maybe we'd all be better off if *you* went on a hunger strike."

"Huh?" A little soup dribbled off Bob's chin as he cocked his head toward David, his brow furrowed.

"Never mind. Just don't talk about shit you don't know anything about."

Sitting silently, Nora wondered about the four men. Kenneth had called David his uncle, so she assumed there was a familial relationship between those two. Porter was quiet, his task uncertain, but seemed to be efficient in whatever he was doing.

But Bob?

"Wondering why we keep him around, aren't you?"

She jerked her head around, unable to hide her surprise at David's words. Lifting her shoulders in a little shrug, she admitted, "I am curious."

"We go way back. Times like those make relationships hard to change."

She still had no idea what he was referring to but simply nodded.

"Bob, like me, firmly believes that the government is gonna come to take our land, our possessions, our weapons, our livelihood. And when you know you might be in a war, it's always good to have someone who'll follow instructions implicitly."

She glanced toward Bob who was slurping his soup, smiling as though he did not understand he was being talked about. *Or he doesn't care. It sounds like he's the one they keep around because he's reliable enough to follow orders without questions!* She tucked that bit of information away, wondering if he was easily led by anyone other than David.

David finished his soup and handed the bowl back to her. Bob held his out as well, and she stood to take it. Assuming they expected her to deal with the dishes, her chain rattled as she walked back to the kitchen corner. Turning on the water, she rinsed the dishes. Opening the cabinet, she grabbed the box of saltine crackers and opened a pack. Popping one into her mouth, she munched, thankful they were fresh. Turning around, she leaned her hip against the counter and found David's eyes on her again. "You're very well-stocked here."

"One day, more people will wish they had gathered their resources around them. I want to stay ready so that if Armageddon comes, I know I'll be prepared."

She blinked, having no response to that comment. Turning back to the sink so that she was facing the wall, she closed her eyes as she gripped the counter.

"Go to the back to see what Kenneth is doing. Tell him we've got soup in here."

She looked over her shoulder to see if David was talking to her, but his attention was focused on Bob.

"It's cold out there!"

"Do it."

Bob grumbled, remaining seated, but David continued to keep his steady gaze on the other man. Finally, Bob's shoulders slumped and he stood. "I'll go tell him, but I'm not staying in the cold." He made a big production of putting on his boots and heavy coat. After jerking the hood up, he opened the back door, and once again the blast of cold, night snow, and wind swept inside causing Nora to shiver.

Glancing toward David, she watched his eyes close once again. *He's weak, and I'm now alone with him.* She felt certain she could overtake him but had no idea where she would go. *Could I make it to the forest and stay warm until the morning? Would I be able to find my way down the mountain?*

Thinking of the cold outside, she dismissed that plan. *If the cold doesn't kill me, they would.* David's eyes were still closed, and she turned to open the second drawer, slipping out the screwdriver. With her back to the living room, she turned on the water and pretended to wash a few more of the dishes. Jamming the end of the screwdriver into the chain links closest to her wrist, she worked the metal, attempting to loosen her bindings. Occasionally glancing over her shoulder, she then moved closer to the refrigerator and did the same on the links that were near the door handle. She didn't want to break the chain at this time but weaken them just enough so that when she had the opportunity she could get away. Not wanting anyone to become suspicious, she placed the screwdriver back into the drawer.

A few minutes later, Bob came back in, once more

stomping and shaking the snow off his coat and boots. David roused up long enough to glare at Bob.

"Just as I thought, Kenneth's in the back cooking up ice. He says he'll eat when he gets in."

"Call Porter. Find out where the fuck he is," David ordered.

Bob pulled out his phone, pressing buttons before putting it to his ear. Shaking his head, he said, "Not answering. This storm is probably keeping the signal from getting through. I'll check Mary." Going through the same process, he shoved his phone back into his pocket. "Nothing with her either." He grinned before it turned into a chuckle. "Maybe the two of them have found a way to keep warm."

"She's his niece," David growled.

"So what?" Bob asked, his brow lowered. He looked over his shoulder and winked at Nora. "This storm keeps up, maybe you and I can do the same."

"Shut up and sit down," David ordered. "She's here to help me, not entertain you."

Bob scowled as he shuffled over to the chair and plopped down near the fire again, the gun still in his hands.

Nora had watched the entire exchange, barely breathing for fear of bringing any attention to herself. For now, it appeared David was keeping her safe, but she wondered how long that would last. If Porter didn't get back with the antibiotic, David's wound could become septic and possibly kill him. Sucking in a ragged breath, she let it out slowly. A few minutes later Bob began to snore and she breathed easier.

Walking over to the small table piled with papers and boxes, she slumped onto the one rickety chair available. With little sleep the night before and the trauma of today, her body was heavy with fatigue. Placing her arms on the table, she dropped her head forward. Her thoughts turned darker as the storm continued to rage in the night. *No one knows where I am. Once again, I'm all alone. Just me. No one else.* Doubts now plagued all thoughts of Tate saving her that had lifted her spirits during the day. *Even he can't find me now.* She tried to hold it back, but a tear slid across the bridge of her nose and dropped onto the table by her arm. Soon, it was followed by more.

1 7

After driving at a creeping speed for two more miles, Tate halted. With Josh on the phone, again he asked, "How close am I?"

"Looks like you're just a mile away from the clearing."

"I'm going the rest of the way on foot. I don't want to take a chance of someone seeing the headlights. I'm sure they would assume I'm the man they expect to come back with the drugs, but I don't want to alert them to my existence at all."

Mace got on the line and said, "Just letting you know that Clay has met up with Levi in Laramie. They're getting ready to head out in a few minutes. Levi has arranged for snowmobiles and a police snow coach. He said at first light tomorrow, they'll head up Elk Mountain."

"My goal is to have taken this point and have Nora with me. But in case I can't get down in my vehicle, the snowmobiles will be perfect." Disconnecting, he suited up. He was still wearing the body armor but pulled on a thick white camo coat over the top. Pulling a knit hat over his head and gloves on his hands, he climbed from the vehicle.

As a former SEAL, he relished the feel of the FBI rifle as well as the other weapons. A backpack full of ammunition, protein bars, water, equipment, and a radio earpiece securely placed, he headed out. The moonlight reflected off the snow, making the night appear much brighter than normal. With Josh's assistance and the use of night-vision goggles, he headed toward the clearing.

Starting out, he stayed on the road, although the tire tracks were almost obliterated. The wind whipped the snow into a blinding storm and the drifts made the walking slow.

Even with his focus on the mission, he was reminded of winter hikes that he and Nathan used to take. It had seemed so easy back then to think of the future. *Go off to war... serve our country... come back to home and family. I would marry Nora and move her to the ranch. Nathan would find someone to love and live nearby.* Blinking at the onslaught of ice crystals slamming into his face, it brought his thoughts back to the here and now.

Wiping his goggles, he noted a faint light in the distance. By now he was no longer able to tell where the road was but moved toward the trees and stalked through the forest. As he got closer to the light ahead, he could distinguish more than one light. The light reflecting off the snow had made the climb up the mountain easier to see, but now it cut down on the protection of dark cover.

With the mini camera and radio attached to his headset, he knew LSI could see what he was seeing but had no doubt the view was blurry due to the storm. "There's a cabin, lights on the inside, and smoke curling from the chimney. Two vehicles are parked outside. One buried under snow, and the other appears to be the Jeep Wagoneer. There are two smaller outbuildings that I can see. No lights. Another slightly larger outbuilding that may be connected to the cabin in the back, lights on inside."

After reporting to LSI, he continued around the clearing, staying in the protection of the woods. Deciding to check on the lighted outbuilding first, he slipped around the back of the cabin and could see it wasn't connected but was built so close to the back of the cabin a person could go between the structures in just a couple of steps.

Creeping toward the window, he stayed out of sight as he maneuvered to a position where he could peer inside. He could only see one man on the inside, but the tables were strewn with empty bottles, two hot plates, glass tubes, pots and pans, bags of cat litter, Mason jars, and more shit that he could not identify through the dirty window. With stealth, he crouched and made his way around to the front and scanned the area. The door was propped open about an inch, and the chemical smell of rotten eggs and cat urine hit him. *Fuckin' hell... a fucking meth lab going in the middle of a blizzard. Jesus, how can he work in that?*

He moved his head slightly from side to side to allow the camera to take in the whole view, knowing LSI would let Levi know a meth lab was present and DEA would descend to get rid of the lab. The man turned slightly to the side and he recognized the picture of Kenneth Carlson.

When active duty, he would have easily taken the man out... quietly and permanently. But as a civilian, he needed to subdue Kenneth, keeping him alive if possible. *Easy if he wasn't in a volatile fuckin' meth lab.*

Desperate to find Nora and assure her safety first, he noticed an open hasp for a padlock attached to the door. With a grin, he slipped a zip tie through the clasp. It would hold Kenneth until he could get back. With the noise the man was making on the inside and the wind whipping outside, Kenneth would not be able to hear any noise that might come from the cabin. Satisfied that Kenneth was secure for the time being, he slipped off his jacket and laid it by the back of the cabin so that movement was easier. Pulling the neck scarf over his nose to help keep the cold at bay, he tramped back through the snow.

Checking the other unlit outbuilding, he saw that it was unoccupied but filled with boxes. Levi had mentioned that David Carlson was a prepper and it looked as though he had stockpiled for years. Dismissing those thoughts, he knew Levi would deal with everything David had been involved with. *My mission is Nora.*

The cabin appeared to be sturdier than the outbuildings, and as he approached the side, he observed one small window near the front coated in a layer of ice, obscuring his view. Creeping soundlessly around the back, he clocked a window facing the woods and a narrow door. There was no light emitted from the window, but the glass was somewhat protected by the woods, therefore keeping it clear of heavy frost.

With his goggles in place, he ascertained empty bunk beds and more boxes. Continuing around the next corner, he discovered that side also did not have a window but did have a pipe coming out of the wall, smoke billowing from the hole. *Woodburning stove.* The only joy that thought gave him was if Nora was in that room, she had some heat.

At the far corner, he was able to peer around to the front of the cabin. There was no porch, and besides the front door, it only contained one window that faced the meadow. While it was evident light was shining from inside, heavy ice adhered to the glass, creating a blurred image.

Pressing his thumb to the lower-left corner of the glass, his body heat soon melted a tiny hole in the ice. He positioned his head so the mini camera on his head-piece was aimed directly toward the small area of cleared glass and stared down at the screen of his phone showing the images from inside the cabin.

Near the wood-burning stove was a chair, and he recognized the man identified as Bob Heller slumped over in sleep. There was a sofa just below the window, and it appeared that someone was sitting in the corner. From that view, he was unable to discern if it was male or female. Angling the camera, he could see that the back corner was set up as a kitchen with a small counter, cabinet, and refrigerator. Identifying the edge of a table near the front corner, he was unable to see more. He hated that there were no more windows in the cabin but assumed it was built by hunters who were simply seeking shelter against the elements.

He grimaced, the desire to kick down the door and take out David and Bob almost overwhelming. Knowing he needed to take them alive if possible while keeping Nora safe made the mission problematic. He was not willing to place her in more danger than she already was. *I lost you once. I'm not going to lose you again. Promise.*

Crouching, he silently moved to the other side of the window and repeated his earlier process. With a postage-stamp-sized area in the lower right corner free of frost, he looked through his camera again. Bob was definitely asleep in the chair near the fire. And while still unable to see the head of the person on the sofa, he was now certain that the body and legs were not Nora's. He could see the person's arm was bandaged, giving further evidence that he was looking at David. *Both men in the front room. So, where the fuck is Nora?*

He had not seen anyone in the bunk beds in the back room, so she must be in the front room near the table. That was the only area he was unable to clearly observe.

Shifting back to the left side of the window, he created a slightly larger ice-free section to peer through this time, and something caught his eye near the refrigerator. Using the zoom application on the camera, he detected a chain was looped around the refrigerator door handle. He scanned the length of the chain as it dropped to the floor and snaked toward the front of the room, disappearing at the edge of his viewing screen.

Chain? They've fucking chained her? Rage colored his vision red.

"Steady. Focus." The voice came through his earpiece and he recognized Mace had seen the view from his phone and knew what was going through his mind. He hated that his boss had to send him a reminder to stay cool but wondered if Mace spoke from experience, once having to rescue Sylvie and her son, David.

Tate slowed his breathing which in turn slowed his heartbeat. Calm. Methodical. Work the problem. Stepping back from the window, he decided to enter through the back door. With its close proximity to the woods, the wind and snow blew with less ferocity against the back.

He made his way noiselessly around the cabin again. He did not hear any sounds from the man inside the meth lab and assumed he was still unaware that his outside door was effectively locked. Reaching the back door of the cabin, he twisted the knob to the narrow door. It was locked, but he ascertained it was nothing more than a simple locking doorknob, not a deadbolt. Sliding his knife between the door and jamb, he jiggled the knob and it turned easily. He was surprised that preppers didn't have their stores more secure. *They weren't expecting anyone. They sure as fuck weren't expecting someone like me.*

Even with his large size, he slipped through the door with ease. In a narrow hall, he glanced to the left to see the tiny bathroom was empty. To the right was the bedroom, and another glance inside proved his earlier assessment that it was unoccupied.

Soundlessly stepping forward, he spied David sitting in the corner of the sofa, his head slumped to the side. His face was pale and forehead sweaty. *He needed the drugs Mary was bringing.* He could now see a small table pushed into the corner of the front of the room, piled with boxes and papers. He forced his heartbeat to remain steady as his gaze landed on Nora, sitting at the table, bent forward with her head resting on top of her arms. Her eyes were closed, and he had no doubt she was exhausted. *But alive!*

The thin chain that he had seen snaking across the floor was now visible as it wrapped around her wrist. Not willing to waste another second, he stepped into the room, his weapon pointed straight at David with Bob also in his sights. "Get your fuckin' hands up!"

18

Nora was jolted from her restless sleep at the shout of a deep-voiced, authoritative order. Gasping, she jerked upward, her fatigue-slowed mind unable to perceive the presence now filling the room. A large figure with his back to her was holding a gun toward the other side of the room. Until the vision in front of her twisted ever-so-slightly giving her a chance to see its profile, she was sure she was going to die.

As recognition slammed into her, she screamed, "Tate!" at the same time Bob shouted, "Fuck!" and David bolted upward, his eyes blinking as he looked around.

Stumbling to her feet, the chain rattled about her. She wobbled on unsteady legs but remained rooted to the spot, not wanting to distract Tate from whatever he planned on doing.

"Keep your fuckin' hands where I can see them," Tate ordered the men.

His familiar voice now resonated with a timbre she didn't recognize. He barely glanced her way, but in that second, she saw his eyes move, doing a full-body scan. He appeared calm on the outside, but as he focused his attention on the two men in the room, his rage was evident, its fire sucking the oxygen from the room.

"Go ahead and twitch... fuckin' move a fuckin' muscle and your fuckin' brains will hit the wall."

"Shit, man," Bob said again on a heavy exhale, this time with wide eyes.

Her gaze landed on Bob, and she jolted out of her stupor. "Tate, he has a gun with him."

"Keep your hands up where I can see them," Tate repeated.

David remained still, and she looked at him carefully. His eyes were slightly red and sweat still beaded his forehead. She had no doubt he was feverish, but he remained unflappable. In a defiant voice, David said, "I know the law. I know you need to take me in, not execute me with no provocation."

Moving one step closer, Tate growled, "I'm not the law."

David lifted a brow, tilting his head slightly.

"You took something of mine, and I'm just itching for a reason to put a hole through you and end your worthless life."

David's gaze shot between Tate and Nora, his jaw tightening. Still standing where she had leaped to her feet, she was uncertain what to do. Battling the desire to rush to him, burrowing into his arms for protection, she didn't want to distract him from whatever he needed to do.

"Nora?"

Barely hearing over the pounding of her heart, she realized he had spoken. "What?" she blurted.

"We gotta get you out of those chains, babe."

"I can do it. I know where there's a screwdriver." She rushed to the drawer and jerked it open. With shaky hands, she jabbed the sharp end of the screwdriver into a link and pried it open. Slipping her wrist free, she let the chain fall to the floor with a clink. She looked up, relief beaming, holding her wrist upward. "It's done! I had it mostly open earlier, and it didn't need much now to pop it loose." She clamped her mouth shut to stop the babbling, her chest heaving with the slight exertion.

"Good job, babe. Now, I need you to move over here… get behind me." Tate kept his gaze pinned on David and Bob.

She hurried forward, reaching her hand out to touch his back, letting him know she was there. Leaning slightly forward, she whispered, "Just tell me what to do."

"We need to secure these two."

"You won't get away with this! We've got friends," Bob blabbered, his eyes darting around the room.

David jerked his head around and shouted, "Shut up! Just keep your fuckin' mouth closed, Bob!"

"If you're referring to your friend Porter, I'm afraid he's enjoying the comforts of the local jail. So is his accomplice, Mary."

Her hand had gently touched Tate's back, but hearing that Porter was no longer a threat, she gripped his shirt for a few seconds, afraid her legs would give out from under her. "Thank God," she breathed. *Shit! Kenneth!* "Honey, there's a man out in the—"

"I'm afraid he won't be any help to these two either. He's locked in. And as soon as the authorities get here, your toxic lab and prepper compound will be shut down and disposed of."

"I always knew the government would send someone in to try to take over." David's face contorted. "Persecution, brute force, taking over our land and our lives."

Tate shook his head. "Shut the fuck up. You're on common ground, not your own land. I don't give a fuck what your personal beliefs are, but I'm not the government." Grinning as he captured David's attention, he said, "That's right, asshole. I'm private. And right now, I'm not answering to anyone but me. So, like I said earlier, you took Nora, and I'm here to get her back. Killing the two of you in the process makes no difference to me."

She had no idea if Tate meant those words or not, but it had the effect of keeping David and Bob quiet. She reached out and touched his back again, wanting to feel the solidity of his body against her fingertips.

"Babe, I need to get them secure."

"What do you need me to do?" She had no idea if she could help but was determined to do anything Tate needed.

Keeping his weapon directed on them, he reached behind her and drew her to his side. "Bob. Stand up and turn around with your back toward me. Put your wrists together behind your back."

She watched as Bob swallowed heavily several times, his eyes working as though to decide if he wanted to follow Tate's directions. He must have come to the conclusion he had no choice if he wanted to stay alive, so he stood. The gun Bob no longer held in his hand lay on the chair cushion. He did as Tate asked and turned so that he was facing the wall with his hands held behind him.

"Nora, get his gun."

She scooted around to the right, hating that the room was so small she was close to Bob. Tate quickly had Bob's wrists held tight while his weapon was still securely in his hand. She picked up Bob's gun and turned to move toward Tate when David jumped to his feet, a hidden knife flashing in his hand before being thrown.

She screamed. Tate shoved Bob to the floor and lunged in front of her. The knife embedded in Tate's shoulder.

Bob cried out and her gaze jumped to take in the whole scene. When Tate pushed him, Bob landed on his knees, his face perilously close to the woodburning stove. Bob jerked back, falling to the floor. David, the weapon no longer in his hand, attempted to run toward the door. She stood with Bob's gun still in her hand, frozen to the spot as Tate jerked the knife out of his shoulder and rushed forward, tackling David against the wall.

Sure that he was going to snap David's neck, she blinked as Tate kept his injured arm pressed against the much smaller man, smashing his face against the wood.

Reaching into his pocket, Tate pulled out restraining ties and quickly subdued David's wrists. Kicking David's feet out from under him and causing him to crumple to the floor, Tate bent and secured his ankles as well. Looking back at Bob, she saw him squirming on the floor, unable to escape.

If she had not witnessed it, she was not sure she would have believed it possible. *How did Tate handle both men so quickly after getting knifed in the shoulder?*

He looked back at her, his eyes once again going from head to toe in a body scan as though to assure himself she was all right. "Babe, are you okay?"

She jerked her head up and down, still trying to suck in air. "Yes. Yes." Seeing uncertainty in his eyes, she said, "Honey, I'm fine. Shocked and feeling rather foolish at not helping, but I'm fine."

As he stood and turned toward her, she noticed blood running down his arm. "Oh, shit, Tate, we need to take care of that."

He shook his head and reached his arm out to her. "I've got to take care of them first."

Stepping closer, she peered into his eyes. "Tate, if something happens to you, I don't know what I'll do—"

"Babe, it's a knife wound. Burns like shit, but it's in my shoulder. We're not talking major organs here. I need to get rid of them—"

"Get rid of them?" she squeaked.

He bent slightly to hold her gaze. "I want to get them tied up and put into one of the outbuildings. I've got Kenneth locked in the lab, but I'll put these two in the other little shacks." He turned and looked down toward

David still on the floor, and his lips curled into a grin. "You, asshole, I'll secure in the lab. We'll see how long you last when you're breathing in those fumes."

Standing so close she could feel his warmth radiating onto her, she held onto his bicep. "What do you need me to do?" Tate hesitated, and she jumped in to explain. "I know I didn't react fast, and I'm sorry. I'm so sorry you got hurt."

He wrapped his good arm around her and lifted his other hand to touch her face. "Babe, there was nothing you needed to do. It's all good. But I can only carry one of them out at a time, so I need you to stand guard over the other one. Can you do that?"

"Yes. Absolutely."

He nodded toward the gun still in her right hand. "Can you use that if you have to?"

Sucking in a deep breath, she let it out slowly and held his gaze. "You and Nathan taught me how to shoot when I was little. It's been a while, but I haven't forgotten. I was caught off guard earlier, but I'm together now. You go do what you've got to do, and I'll take care of what's in here."

He grinned and bent forward, and for a second, she thought he was going to kiss her. Instead, he rested his lips on her forehead, and the touch warmed her deep inside. "Go, Tate. I promise, I'm good, and the sooner you go the sooner you can get back to me. I need to take care of your arm."

Still grinning, he said, "That's good, Nora. You sound like yourself again."

She stared in amazement as he hefted Bob onto his

good shoulder and stepped through the door, letting in a blast of cold, snowy air. She held the gun on David as he lay on the floor, moaning.

"He ripped open my arm again and you know I'm sick. You're a goddamn nurse. Help me!"

"You're right, I am a nurse. But you gave up the right to my medical concern when you kidnapped me, threatened me with a gun, and lastly, put a knife in my man's arm." David didn't reply, but her own words hit her. *My man.* She had no idea if the sentiment was correct, but it sounded right.

A few minutes later, the front door flung open again and Tate hustled back into the cabin. He scanned the room and grinned as she confidently held the weapon on David who was still on the floor. "That's my girl." Once more, she didn't know if the sentiment was correct, but being called his girl lightened her heart.

19

Tate bent, hefted David onto his good shoulder, and trudged through the heavy snow, glad that neither Bob nor David were overly heavy. With Kenneth still locked inside the larger outbuilding, he had placed Bob in the smaller one. Zip-tied and chained to the wall, he knew Bob was going nowhere.

Now, with David in his arms, he looked around. *What I'd really like is to leave him in here to choke on his own meth fumes.* The last thing he wanted was for David to find something in the room that could be used as a weapon or a method to get free. It was obvious he could not leave David in the lab, so he turned, spied another building, and grinned. Standing near the edge of the woods was an old-fashioned outhouse.

He jerked open the door and plopped David unceremoniously onto the wooden bench. "You're out of the weather, but I can't help if it smells like shit in here. Personally, I think it's fitting." Securing him to the wall as well, he knew David was going nowhere. "It won't kill you to spend the night here and your escort to prison will arrive tomorrow."

Leaving David sitting on his *throne*, he walked out, securing the door behind him. David's curses drifted off with howling winds.

Now, to deal with Kenneth. Looking through the window again, he carefully observed Kenneth inside still working. It had only taken him about fifteen minutes to deal with David and Bob, and it did not appear that Kenneth was aware that anything untoward had happened.

Sliding his knife out of its sheath, he silently cut through the tie, inching the door open. He could see Kenneth had his back to him, still sitting on a stool and hunched over the table. Tate rushed in, knowing his presence would be announced by the cold rush of air when the door was thrown open.

Grabbing Kenneth from behind, he clamped his hand on his mouth and put the knife blade to his throat. Kenneth kicked out, knocking over a small table with jars on top. The noise was muffled by the sounds of the storm outside, but fumes rose in the air. "Give me a fucking reason not to slit your throat right now for taking her." With his head to the side, he could see the man's eyes bug out.

"I find out you hurt her in any way or put your hands on her, I will slit your throat. Or maybe I'll just leave you in this cesspool to choke on the toxic fumes." Chuckling, he threw out, "Or drag you into the woods and let the animals have you."

With a quick movement, Tate put him in a chokehold. Kenneth slumped to the ground, the bottle of liquid in his hand dropping to the side. Tate kicked it out of his way, then quickly pulled out zip ties and secured the man's arms behind his back before doing the same with his ankles. Pulling out duct tape, he slapped it over Kenneth's mouth to keep him quiet when he regained consciousness.

Scanning the mess in the room, he grimaced. Leaving Kenneth here with the toxic fumes would certainly kill him, something he was tempted to do. Grabbing him by the arm, he hauled him into the back of the cabin and into the room full of boxes. A quick slice of the tops of several revealed cans of food and household products. Shoving a few boxes to the side and stacking others, he made space on the floor to hold his unconscious prisoner. Unceremoniously dumping the man inside, he closed the door. He fought the urge to set the lab on fire, knowing it would send toxic fumes into the air. *I'll leave this for Levi to deal with.*

Stepping back into the hall, he looked toward the kitchen and found Nora standing with Bob's gun in her hand, her eyes wide. "It's okay, babe. It's me." He kicked the back door shut and hurried to the front of the cabin.

Now, standing in the small room, he watched as Nora rushed toward him. Barely stopping, she threw herself against his chest and burrowed in. Wrapping her in his embrace, he finally let his heartbeat ease.

"Oh, Tate, I kept telling myself you'd come. I just knew you'd try, but then the storm got worse—"

"Babe, you've got to know that even a blizzard wouldn't keep me from getting to you."

It felt so good to have her cheek pressed against his chest, her body safely tucked in his arms. Everything clicked into place… the past, the present, and what he hoped would be the future.

She leaned back and her gaze landed on his shoulder, concern marring her brow. "Come on. You've got to sit down. I need to take a look at this."

She tried to pull him toward the warmth of the fire, but he stilled her movements. When she looked over her shoulder at him in surprise, he said, "Nora, we've got to get out of here."

Her head jerked slightly as her gaze shot between his face and the dark, snowstorm-filled night outside the window, then back to his face. "We can't go anywhere now!"

"Honey, there's a meth lab that's right behind this cabin. The fumes are dangerous. The materials in there are volatile. And I don't want you around it any more than you've already been exposed."

Her eyes still wide, she argued, "I can't make it down the mountain dressed like this! I know you can do anything, but Tate, I can't!" Her gaze shot to his shoulder again. "And you're still injured!"

Hit with unprecedented hesitation on a mission, he wrapped his hand around her arm and pulled her gently back to him. "Okay, you can treat my shoulder, but then we have to make a plan and follow it through. I won't allow you to stay in this meth-infested cabin all night long. I'll talk to my people and find another cabin close by. It might not be as big, but as long as it's shelter, I can keep you safe. All you have to do is trust me, Nora."

He watched as emotions moved across her expressive face before she slowly nodded. "I trust you, Tate."

Those words shot through him, piercing his heart as he wrapped his arms around her and pulled her tight against his chest. "I promise—*promise*—to take care of you, babe." They stood embracing for a long moment before she finally stepped back and nodded toward his shoulder.

He allowed her to pull him over to the sofa where she pushed him gently to sit. She quickly divested his outer shirt and helped him to pull the thermal undershirt over his shoulder so that she could see the extent of the injury. Just as he knew, it was a clean stab wound. He could have dealt with the injury himself but understood she needed to tend to him, giving her something to do while the adrenaline was still coursing through her body. "I've got a stocked medical kit in my pack, Nora. Everything you need should be in there."

"Good," she said as she jumped up and hurried to his pack. "They had some medical supplies here, but I hated to use it on you unless I had to." She bent over to dig through his pack and his gaze dropped to her ass. Whirling around, she held it in her hand. "Got it!" Rushing back over, she assessed his wound.

"Tate, you know you're going to need stitches. I can disinfect the wound and bandage the edges together, but it goes down into the muscle. What I can do is patch it tonight and then, when we get back to town, you'll need to be seen in the hospital."

He knew she was right but didn't want her to worry.

"Just do what you need to do tonight, sweetheart. We'll figure everything else out tomorrow."

Using a clean, sterile gauze that he had in his pack, she gently pressed on the wound until she was sure the bleeding had stopped. Her finger traced over the tattoo of a lighthouse on his shoulder. It was not marred by the higher injury. He wondered if she would ask about it, but she remained quiet, simply allowing her delicate touch to trace along the lines.

Her gaze jumped to his and she turned quickly. Not wanting to lose the connection, he said, "All the Keepers have this tattoo."

Her head tilted slightly as her gaze dropped back to his shoulder.

"There's a small tracer chip in the light. They can locate us… anywhere in the world."

Her eyes widened. "Seriously?"

He nodded and her lips curved slightly. "So, if we leave the cabin, someone will still know where we are?"

He lifted his hand and cupped her face again. "Yeah, baby. I promised I'd take care of you."

She sucked in a deep breath and let it out slowly. "Well, then I'd better get your shoulder taken care of." Turning, she moved back to his bag. "I don't trust the water coming out of the tap," she said, pouring hydrogen peroxide over the area, making sure the wound was clean. Using the over-the-counter antibiotic cream before closing it with butterfly bandages, she then wrapped his shoulder with long strips of gauze. Finally, she tied off the ends and carefully looked over her work.

By the time she finished, she was kneeling on the floor between his knees, her hands resting on his thick thighs. Every movement she made captured his attention.

"I heard the scream, Nora."

Her brow scrunched as she tilted her head slightly.

"The scream from the nurse down the hall. By the time I got there, you were gone. I ran toward the service elevator and there was a window overlooking the parking lot." He lifted a forefinger and ran it gently over her bruised jaw. "I saw them hit you and throw you into the back of the Jeep."

She leaned her face into his palm, her gaze never leaving his.

"I've never felt so fuckin' helpless in my entire life. Not even when Nathan died. All I could think about was getting to you."

"I had no idea what we were doing. I didn't know where we were going. I had no way of contacting anyone. But I kept telling myself that if anyone could get to me, it would be you."

He held the back of her head in his hand and leaned forward. With his thumb on her chin, he tilted her face toward his. Hesitating, he wanted to give control over to her. She did not hesitate when she lifted on her knees and settled her lips over his. *Thank fuck!*

It had been many years since he had tasted her lips but found them just as sweet as he remembered. Kissing Nora had been a favorite pastime of his when they were teenagers, but back then he had little control, and they often ended lying on the hay in the loft of the barn, their hands grasping for each other. By the time they were adults, the kisses were little different but usually led immediately to clothing tossed to the side.

After so many years without her, Tate simply wanted to savor the feel and taste of her. Soft lips, little moans, small hitches in her breaths. His cock swelled, but no longer led by his dick, he had no problem simply losing himself in her lips.

His shoulder stung as he moved his arm, cupping her face with his large hands. Pulling back, he swept her cheeks with his thumbs, reveling in the petal-soft feel of her skin. Her eyes were large and luminous, staring directly into his. Past and present collided, opening up the possibilities of a future.

Moving in for another kiss, he tilted her head slightly so that their noses would not bump as he took her lips again, this time sliding his tongue into her welcoming mouth. Her warmth enveloped him as he both explored the new taste of her while remembering the effects of her mouth on his.

Her tongue tangled with his, hesitantly at first. Sliding his hands from her face to her waist, he leaned back on the sofa, pulling her up with him so that she was soon straddling his lap. Her arms slid around his neck, her breasts pressed against his chest, their lips never separating.

He had no idea how much time passed as they lost themselves in their kiss. After a while, her hips began to move, and she pressed her core against his crotch. One hand moved to the bottom of her shirt, slipping underneath the material and gliding along the skin of her back. The pads of his fingers were calloused, but he could swear there was nothing as soft in the whole world as Nora's skin.

Her hands slid down his chest, finally landing at his waist, where she traced his muscles through the material of his shirt. With one hand still on her back, the other slid around to the front, resting at the bottom edge of her bra. His thumb swept upward, over her satin-covered, tight nipple, and her groan nearly caused him to come in his pants.

Maintaining control over his actions was usually easy with his SEAL training, but with Nora, it was all he could do to keep from stripping her naked, worshiping her body, and taking her right there in the cabin.

The cabin. As though he'd jumped into cold, icy water, reality slammed back into him. No way was he going to make love to her on a nasty piece of furniture in a cabin that had been inhabited by a meth head. Pulling back, he loved the little mewl of discontent she made as she pressed forward to continue the kiss. He brought his hands back up to cup her face and hold her in place.

"Nora, there's nothing I want to do more than keep kissing you, holding you, and doing whatever comes natural, but baby, I respect you too much to subject you to that in this place." He watched as reality seeped over her, her kiss swollen lips forming a pout as her brow crinkled. Sighing, she offered a slight nod but didn't move off his lap. That was fine with him because the feel of her so close made the world seem right.

"We've got to get ready to leave."

"Are you hungry?"

Her question caught him off guard and his fingers flexed against her soft hips. "Hungry?"

"If we're going to go out into the storm, I wondered if we should eat first." She glanced toward the corner kitchen and crinkled her nose. "They have a lot of food here, but nothing clean to prepare it with."

"Hop up, babe. I've got protein bars in my pack, so we can at least eat something that we won't be afraid will poison us."

With a little nod, she slid from his lap and moved over to his pack. While she bent over to rummage inside, the sight of her perfect, heart-shaped ass snagged his attention, and he took the opportunity to adjust his cock in his pants to ease the pain, if not the arousal.

She stood with bars in each hand and turned toward him. "I can offer you peanut butter chocolate or peanut butter chocolate."

Chuckling, he rolled his eyes toward the ceiling, pretending to think. "Hmm, I guess I'll take the peanut butter chocolate." As she bent to gather a water bottle, he glanced down at the sofa he was sitting on, really seeing it for the first time. *Jesus, this thing is ancient... and I don't even want to know what's been on it.* Jumping to his feet, he accepted the proffered protein bar and they munched in silence for a few minutes, washing it down with their bottled water.

He reached into his pack and pulled out a thermal shirt. Handing it to her, he said, "Put this on over your other tops. It will be large but will help to hold in your body heat." He pulled out a pair of thick sweatpants and handed them to her as well. "I'm going to call my team, and you work on getting wrapped up."

She looked at the clothes, a dubious expression on her face, but she acquiesced. Satisfied, he turned and pulled out his phone. "David and his men have been subdued, but this place is a meth lab nightmare. I'm not letting Nora stay here, so you need to find another shelter that I can get to. It doesn't matter how crude but get the closest one you can. All she's wearing is nursing scrubs and whatever else I can get on her. Take a look and send me the coordinates. I want to give Clay a call."

"Will do," Josh replied.

Disconnecting, he hit another button on his phone, his gaze naturally drawn to Nora. She had pulled on the thick pants over her nursing scrubs, rolled down the waist, and tied them tightly to keep them secure.

"Clay? What's your location?"

"Met up with Levi. He's coordinated to have snow-mobiles and a snow coach at daybreak tomorrow to go up the mountain. Right now, the FBI and sheriff have set up a base at the rest stop a few miles from the road to get to you."

"Put me on speaker so Levi can hear as well."

"Got it."

"David, Robert Heller, and Kenneth Carlson have been captured. They're separated and locked in a couple of outbuildings. You saw my feed, so you know the meth lab is right behind the cabin. It's a fuckin' mess, completely unstable, and volatile as shit. Josh is getting me the location of another shelter that I can get Nora to for tonight. Something close. As soon as I get there, he'll get the location to you."

"You need me to get there tonight?" Clay asked.

"No, first light will be good. You can get to us, and Levi's group will need hazmat suits."

Levi piped up. "Don't worry about it, DEA is here, itching to shut down that lab."

Glancing to the side, he observed Nora staring up at him, looking both ridiculous in her oversize clothes and adorable at the same time. Grinning, he disconnected. "Come here, babe."

She stepped to him, her palm placed gently on his chest. Bending, he kissed her lightly. Glancing down at her feet, he said, "I'm gonna look in the back room and see if I can find a pair of boots."

"I can look—"

"No!" She jumped and he winced. "Sorry, but I've got Kenneth restrained in the back room. I don't want you near him. I'm also going to check on the others before we leave. Stay here and I'll be right back."

He slogged through the snow toward the smallest outbuilding. Throwing open the door, he scanned the interior, satisfied that Bob was still securely bound. Popping off the top a water bottle, he tilted it up and allowed Bob several sips.

"You gotta let me out here," Bob cried.

Skewering him with a glare, he said nothing but secured the door before he made his way over to the old outhouse.

Opening the door, he saw that David was still sitting on the wooden platform. Offering him a few sips, he said nothing, checked the bindings and then closed and locked the door after him.

Not wanting to be away from her for another moment, he tramped through the high snowdrifts and made it back to the cabin. His next check was on Kenneth in the back room. Repeating his actions, he assured that Kenneth was still bound before giving him a few sips of water as well. No begging for mercy came, and Tate figured Kenneth was smart enough to know it wouldn't happen anyway.

Looking around, he opened several boxes, finding nothing but canned goods. He glanced down at the boots on Kenneth's feet but immediately dismissed taking them for Nora, considering they been all over the meth lab.

Leaving the room, he closed the door behind him. He jerked his head around at a noise from the hall and spied Nora walking out of the bathroom.

A light pink blush hit her cheeks. "After drinking a whole bottle of water, I was about to pop."

He chuckled and said, "I think I'll take care of the same thing." He slid off his jacket and handed it to her.

He headed back to the tiny bathroom and quickly took care of his business. Once back in the living room, he said, "Pull on my socks over your nursing clogs. We'll get a couple of plastic bags and tie them over your feet and lower legs. It won't be perfect, but it'll work to keep your feet warm and dry until we can get to another cabin."

With only a lifted eyebrow giving evidence of her surprise at his request, she immediately grabbed the socks. Pulling out his phone when it vibrated, he said, "Talk to me."

"Sending GPS coordinates," Josh said. "Not much around, but it looks like a small wooden structure about a mile to the southeast."

"That's away from the truck I used, but it'll be covered by now anyway. Clay will get us down by snowmobile tomorrow." Disconnecting, he turned back to Nora and watched as she pulled plastic bags over her feet and tied a string around the tops to secure them to her ankles. "Looks like we're moving."

20

Once Tate knew where they could go when they left the cabin, everything seemed to go at full speed. *Perhaps to keep me from worrying about what we're doing.* She looked as though she was wearing a padded suit considering she had on several shirts, pants, and socks. Glancing down at her plastic bag-covered feet, she wondered if facing the snowstorm was truly better than staying in the cabin regardless of the possibility of meth contamination. But, having given her trust over to Tate, she remained quiet.

He pulled a face mask hood over her head so that only her eyes showed. He started to wrap his huge coat around her, but that's when she finally objected. "Tate, I can barely move as it is! If you try to get that coat on me, I'm not going to be able to walk." He started to retort, but she placed her hands on his lips to still his words. "Look, the faster we get there, the better it will be. At least start out with a coat and you can hurry and I'll be able to keep up."

"There's no way I'm going to let you walk for a mile without some kind of outerwear."

She turned and hurried to the table and picked up a smaller coat from one of the chairs. Wrinkling her nose, she said, "This was what Bob was wearing. It looks clean enough." She slipped it on and zipped up the front. "It'll work."

Now, both somewhat appropriately attired, Tate threw open the front door. The blast of icy wind whipped through and she shivered. She had not taken a step outside and already regretted their decision to leave. With his hand clasping hers, he stepped out into the snowdrifts and she followed, shocked when the snow came almost up to her knees.

The moonlight reflected on the white ice crystals, making the dark night much brighter than normal. She tried to look around, but the snow hitting her face stung and she ducked her head.

"Follow my footsteps," he called out. "It'll make it easier."

Concentrating on the path he was creating, she appreciated his attempts to shorten his gait to match hers. She reached out and held on to his backpack, focusing on one step at a time. It only took a few minutes and she was already winded, the cold seeping through her feet. They crossed the open area in front of the cabin and reached the tree line away from the lane. As soon as they neared the trees, she was grateful for the forest rising in front of them. The snow was less deep under the thick branches and the wind was not able to batter them with such ferocity.

She wanted to ask how much further they had to go, but a glance over her shoulder proved that the cabin was still visible in the distance. *We haven't even gone the length of a football field!* She stumbled, and he turned to grab her arms. Steadying her feet, she nodded, not wanting him to stop and worry about her.

They pushed through the thick forest, keeping a quick pace. With the snow under the canopy of trees being less, they were still able to see where they were going. Another time and for another reason, she would have loved the scenery—nighttime walking through snowy woods with Tate—but now, she just wanted to get to their destination. Deciding to focus on counting her footsteps to keep her mind off their situation, she made it to fifty but discovered it wasn't working.

Tate stopped suddenly, and she ran into his back. Jerking her head up, she started to ask him what was wrong when she noticed he had something in his hand and was looking around. Assuming he was checking their directions, she remained quiet.

He turned around and wrapped his arm around her, bending low so that his face was directly in front of hers. "How are you?"

"Okay."

He held her gaze, his eyes searching deep.

She reached out and grabbed his arms, giving a little shake. "Really, I'm okay." Glancing down at the instrument in his hand, she said, "I know we haven't come far."

"We're about a fourth of the way there."

Her eyes jerked wider before she had a chance to

hide her reaction. He pulled her in tighter and she reveled in his strength. *He's worried about me.* Leaning back, she assured, "I'm okay. Let's keep going."

His smile warmed her heart and he turned, and they continued through the woods. With a multitude of clothes and socks on, she was no longer feeling as cold as when they first started out. The terrain grew rockier, and they came to the edge of the woods, where the snow had piled higher.

He yelled over the wind, "We've got to get to the other side of this and then down the mountain just a bit."

She offered a nod, not having any other choice. No longer shielded from the wind or the deep drifts, she trudged forward, stumbling often. Once again, trying to stay on the path Tate's feet and legs were creating, exhaustion set in, causing her to stumble. Whatever adrenaline she had been running on, her tank was officially empty.

Tate turned, and before she had a chance to object, he scooped her up into his arms. He carried her as though she weighed nothing. Grabbing around his neck, she held on, her objections dying in her throat. Even with her weight, they seemed to make better time. She was grateful when they reached another line of trees, although not nearly as thick as what they had been in.

He set her feet down and lowered his head again so that she could hear his words. "According to my GPS, we don't have too much further to go. It's downhill, but we can stay in the edge of these woods for most of it."

Nodding, she was grateful for the reprieve and glad they were going downhill instead of up. Once again holding onto his backpack, she followed along. The plastic bags provided no traction, and she found that while her feet were not wet, she slipped continually as though skating on solid ice.

Tate stopped again and said, "New plan. I should've thought of this earlier." He slid off his backpack and jerked it around to the front, putting his arms through the loops and securing it next to his chest. With one hand braced against a tree, he squatted and shouted, "Climb on."

Protesting would've been fruitless, so she simply obeyed. Wrapping her arms around his neck and with her thighs perched on his waist, she was jostled as he stood and shifted to balance all the weight. Continuing to move through the snow at the edge of the woods, his feet were sure and steady. She closed her eyes and tried to remain as still as possible to make the progress easier for him.

After a few minutes more, he shouted, "There it is!"

She could have wept with gratitude, holding on tight as he finished the last of the trek to their new shelter.

With his hand braced against another tree, he twisted his head and said, "You can climb off now, babe."

Finding it harder to move her limbs than she thought was possible, she managed to clamber off his back, her hands grabbing his coat to keep her legs from buckling underneath her. He dropped his pack to the snow-covered ground and turned toward her.

"Let me go in and see what we're facing."

Not waiting on her to answer, he moved away and she obtained her first clear view. More of a tiny lean-to than a cabin, it appeared ramshackle and she could not imagine what critters found their shelter inside. The door was hanging askew on its hinges, and Tate jerked it open, shining a light inside. Another blast of icy wind sliced through her and she suddenly no longer cared if she shared the protection with all the animals of the forest. Forcing her legs to move, she stepped closer to the entrance.

He turned around and nodded. "It'll be fine."

She nodded and followed him in.

When he said 'It'll be fine', he should have added the caveat 'fine for just a few hours of being out of the storm'. As he ducked his head to enter and stepped inside, it was easy to see how crude the shack really was. The wind whistled through a few cracks in the wood, and where a previous visitor had placed stones in the corner to bank a fire, they'd also cut a hole in the roof to allow the smoke to ascend but now allowed snow to fall in.

The floor was hardpacked dirt, a few leaves blown into another corner, and no windows to allow in any light. The shack was only about eight feet square, and he had to continue to duck considering the height was only about six feet tall. It was hard to imagine this crude structure was technically better than the much larger and furnished cabin, but not being next to a meth lab made it superior. Shining his light toward Nora as she entered, one look at her face and he knew she did not share his opinion.

Eyes wide, her head swiveled as she took in the rudimentary interior before her gaze landed on his face. Schooling her expression, she simply nodded. With his light still illuminating the area, he grinned. That had always been Nora, even as a child. No matter what he and Nathan got into, she always went along—usually having as much fun as they did.

But the light also illuminated the fatigue etched on her face. Dark circles under her eyes. The droop of her shoulders. And a shiver. That last jolted him into action. "I'm gonna run out and see if I can grab some wood."

He headed back out and within a few minutes came back with an armload of sticks and a few larger pieces of cut wood he found behind the shack. Stepping inside, he noticed that she had already swept the leaves to one side with her foot.

"Do you think you'll be able to get the fire started?"

He looked over his shoulder and grinned. "Babe, as a SEAL, I learned to start a fire in almost any situation or weather. This will be a piece of cake." Chuckling, he added, "Plus I've got a firestarter in my bag."

He worked efficiently and soon had a small fire in the corner, banked by the same stones placed there before. The smoke rose to the ceiling and escaped out the hole in the roof.

"Wow, you did it!"

Nora's soft voice, full of awe, humbled him. Still in a

squat, he twisted around and looked up at her standing close by, her fingers reached out toward the flames. "Come on babe, let's get you as warm and dry as possible."

He pulled off his coat and held the inner lining close to the fire for a few minutes. Once warm, he lay it on the ground, weather-proof side down, and said, "Sit down and we'll work on your feet."

There was little room to maneuver, but the advantage was that the interior of the shack soon warmed a little with the fire even though it was not weatherproof. Once she sat on part of his coat and stretched her legs out, he joined her. The plastic bags had kept her feet from getting wet, but they had become caked with packed snow and ice. With those now off, they peeled off the larger socks that had been put on over her nursing clogs. By the time he got down to just her socked feet, he had her twist around so that her feet were closer to the fire.

Reaching inside his pack, he pulled out two more protein bars and another bottle of water. She seemed a little lost, and he was sure she was about to succumb to exhaustion. Unwrapping one of the bars, he handed it to her. "Eat this and then we can rest."

She accepted it and began munching, alternating bites with sips of water. Several minutes later, she seemed revived, smiling as she passed the bottle back to him. The wind continued to howl outside, but the quiet in the shack was comfortable, something he always remembered about Nora. Even as a young girl she never felt the need to prattle endlessly, but instead, when she spoke it was usually something interesting or relevant. Nathan, like himself, had been an adventurer, but Nora was the calming member of their trio.

Finishing her protein bar, she crumpled the wrapper and set it to the side. After brushing her hands over her pants, her gaze glanced around the shack before landing on him once again. "How did you find me?" She smiled and continued to prod. "Was it some of your super-secret security systems, otherwise known as SSSS?"

He barked out a laugh. "SSSS? I'm going to have to remember that." As his mirth slowed, he reached over and took one of her hands in his own. "The answer to your question is yes and no. We were able to use the cameras at the hospital to get the license number and registration of the vehicle. I worked with the FBI and my own people, and I interviewed David's ex-wife."

"He was married?"

"Yes, many years earlier." Seeing Nora visibly shudder, he added, "She thought he was a normal guy, but when he started using and selling drugs, she didn't want that around their children. She kicked him to the curb and hasn't seen him in eleven years."

Her eyes widened. "So, she wasn't able to help, was she?"

"Her teenage son remembered that there were some pictures in the basement. He found one that showed his dad and some others outside a little cabin with mountains in the background. I scanned it and the Keepers were able to identify it as Elk Mountain. It was a long-shot but considering the highway cameras had him heading this way, we thought it was a good lead. We were at the rest stop when I saw one of the nurses from the hospital. It seemed strange that she was out in the middle of the snow, heading to the mountains. Turns out, she was stealing drugs from the hospital to bring here. So, you see, babe, investigations can be a lot of legwork and we can never discount luck."

Sighing, she held his gaze but shook her head slowly. "I felt sure you were going to find me, but when the storm got worse, I was no longer as certain. I was afraid I would be stuck here for a long time."

"I hate to ask this, but did they... hurt you?"

Her fingers jerked in his, clamping tight. "Oh, no, Tate. The only time they did anything was when Bob hit me right before we got into the Jeep. He threatened a few times, but David always shut him down. I got the feeling that Bob was not particularly smart and the others put up with him for the reason of having a stooge to do their bidding."

"You're probably right." They sat in silence again, continuing to drink their water. The inside of the cabin was warm from the fire. He opened his mouth to ask another question but snapped it shut, hating to bring up anything that would cut into the easiness that they had found.

"You want to know about the pregnancy, don't you?" Her voice was soft and her eyes warm.

"You always could read my mind."

"It's not that difficult to imagine that you're curious—"

"Babe, you've been through a harrowing experience

and the last thing I want to do is bring up anything bad for you. We can talk about this later."

She remained quiet for a moment, sipping more of her water. Looking back at him, she said, "No, it's fine to talk about it now. I'm tired and yet very awake. Once tomorrow comes and we get outta here, it's going to be a bit crazy. Right now, Tate, it's just you and me." She shifted slightly, keeping her legs crossed, but now was facing him directly. "What do you want to know?"

He lifted his heavy shoulders in a shrug, wincing at the sting of his injury. "Honestly, I don't know, Nora. I guess I want to know anything and everything you want to tell me. But I especially need you to know that I'm so sorry you went through everything alone. So, don't spare me… give it to me straight." Continuing to hold her hand, he also held her gaze. *I've got a lot to atone for, and it starts right now.*

2 1

Nora sat cross-legged on Tate's warm coat in front of the fire... in a ramshackle shack... in the middle of a blinding snowstorm. Looking around the tiny room with all the events of the past day running through her mind, it was hard to tell if she was stuck in a surreal dream or if this had become her reality.

He sat in front of her, his long legs stretched out, extending far beyond the edge of his jacket. His face was lit from the firelight that both illuminated and cast shadows. There was no pain etched in his expression, and she hoped the aspirin was working and that he was not stoically ignoring discomfort.

So much had happened in the past twenty-four hours, she was not sure it was in her to delve into deep emotions, but what she told him was true. As soon as they were rescued, there would be little time for a long, heartfelt conversation. He would go back to his life on the other side of the country and she'd return to her job at the hospital and her little apartment.

She cast her mind back to Nathan's funeral. She sucked in a deep, cleansing breath before letting it out slowly. "You and Nathan used to talk about living on the ranch when you were young, but then you two spent just as much time talking about sailing the seas. Selfishly, I'd hoped that you would both ignore the siren's call and stay on dry land. I thought you'd marry me and we'd have a bunch of kids to raise on the ranch." Looking down at her hands in her lap, she sighed. "I now know they were the silly daydreams of a young girl."

"Nora, they weren't silly. And you're right, at one time, those had been my dreams, too." He reached over and placed his large hand over her much smaller ones, the touch warm and comforting.

Lifting her head, she held his gaze, nodding ever so slightly. "But you were always destined for more adventure, Tate. I knew it and didn't fight it. I just always thought you'd come back to me." She chuckled, then added, "Or that you'd take me on your adventures with you. I suppose, to be honest, that was what I hoped for. That you'd take me and we'd discover new things and new places together."

"You've got to know, Nora, that when I left to join the Navy, that's what I thought would happen. And even when I decided to become a SEAL, I had no idea it was going to be so hard or push me beyond all my limits. I had no clue how much focus it would take. I had fellow team members or commanders who were married but knew their wives were back home raising children mostly as single moms while their husbands were out on missions. Those men missed birthdays, holidays, anniversaries. Some of the marriages didn't last, and I knew more than one who got a Dear John email in the middle of a mission."

At the mention of a breakup email, she remained quiet but lifted her eyebrow, holding his gaze without wavering.

He sighed heavily and squeezed her hand. "I know, I know. That's what I did to you. It wasn't until Nathan was killed and I saw your anguish and felt it mirrored in myself that I knew I'd do anything to protect you. Even from me."

"And the night of Nathan's funeral? When we made love in the barn loft? I've got to tell you, that it felt different that night. I know that's such a girl thing to say—"

"No, it wasn't just you. I felt it too. It was as though we couldn't get enough of each other, and I wanted to drown my sorrow and grief and guilt in your sweet body."

"And I felt the same, Tate. I wanted you to take away all the pain."

"But we didn't use a condom. Never even thought about it."

She shook her head slowly, sighing heavily. "It was dumb and irresponsible, but I think we were so caught up in what we needed from each other at the moment that the idea of birth control flew out the window."

They sat again in silence, before he asked, "When did you know?"

She shrugged and said, "Not for a while. I know that

there are early detection pregnancy tests, but I just didn't think about it. I'd lost my brother and was drowning in grief. My father's heart problems only got worse and losing his son made it scarier. To be honest, it was right about the time I got your email."

He sucked in a quick breath and winced. "I think that was the worst decision I've ever made in my life, Nora. I saw your grief at Nathan's funeral, and all I could think of was if something happened to me. I didn't want you to have to go through that again. It was stupid, but it didn't hit me that breaking up with you was still losing me. I swear... I think... somehow in my mind, I still thought I could come back to Wyoming someday and we would be together."

The wind outside and the crackling of the sticks in the fire was the only sound heard for a moment. She picked up the water bottle and took a long sip, allowing the fresh water to help her focus.

"The timing sucked, that's for sure. If I'd realized I was pregnant sooner, I could have told you, and then we could've planned together. It might have given you hope on your missions that when they were over, you had something to look forward to." Shrugging, she added, "Or maybe it would've just made you feel trapped."

Shaking his head vigorously, he said, "No! I would never feel trapped by you. Making a child with you would be the greatest honor."

His words pierced her heart and she winced before being able to hide her pain. Pinching her lips together for a few seconds, she then forged ahead. "It was at that time that I finally realized I hadn't had my period. For a week after I got your email, I didn't leave my bed. Caroline finally dragged my ass out, and when I told her my fear, she was the one who got a pregnancy test. I took it that day and it was positive. She wanted to tell you right away, but you were on a mission. And I didn't want you to be with me out of a misguided sense of duty." Another sigh left her lips, and fatigue pulled at her. "A couple of days later, I had a lot of cramping. Caroline took me to the ER, and I was miscarrying. I was about nine weeks along."

She dragged in a ragged breath, but no tears came. This time, the silence between them was heavy with deep, unspoken emotions.

"I can't imagine your pain, Nora, And I'm so sorry that I wasn't around to share it with you."

Setting the empty water bottle to the side, she reached out and took both of his hands with hers. "I used to think there were reasons why bad things happen, but I've come to realize that in our lives we have incredible highs and incredible lows. Often, there's no explanation or reason other than it's just part of life. I've already told you that I was pretty messed up for a while. I missed a semester of college, but finally got my degree and started working. If it hadn't been for your family, Tate, I don't know what I would've done when I lost Dad and then Grandma and Mom. I know it was hard on your family to be so close to me and yet have me hide away whenever you came home, but I just didn't think I was strong enough to see you. Even ten years later, I wasn't strong enough."

"Babe, you're the strongest woman I know. Hell, you're the strongest person I know."

She threw her head back and laughed. "Oh, I hardly think I could outlast your former SEAL buddies or your new coworkers."

He shook his head and said, "There's all kinds of strength, Nora. I've got friends who can do whatever it takes to get a mission done, but I'd put your emotional strength up against any of them."

Uncomfortable with his praise, she glanced down at their clasped hands. *He thinks I'm put together now, but he didn't see me at my worst.* She lifted her gaze and it settled on his shoulder, thinking of his injury and how he received it. "How does your shoulder feel?"

"There's a dull ache, but then I'm not doing much with my shoulder right now, so it feels a lot better than it did."

"You threw yourself in front of me." *It had happened so fast, but, as though in slow motion, he managed to push Bob down and get his own body in front of me, the knife hitting him instead.*

"I hope you know I'd do anything to protect you. I failed in that years ago, but I don't plan on failing again."

She shook her head slowly, fatigue pulling at her. "You didn't fail me, Tate. Failing me would've been to leave me *after* I told you I was pregnant. You didn't do that. You never knew. By the time I was listening to Caroline and ready to tell you, I miscarried."

The feel of his strong fingers wrapped around hers warmed her heart more than the fire. *How can fingers be strong? How can everything about him make me feel protected?* She lifted her gaze to his and, with a great deal of hesitation, asked, "Did you ever think of me?"

He nodded, his eyes searching hers but full of guilt. "Yes. I know I was the one who broke up, but you never left my mind. I carried a picture of you in my wallet... it's still there. It was one of you, me, and Nathan. It served as a memory of where I came from but also a reminder of what I wanted. When you avoided me so much over the last ten years, I figured that ship had sailed and I'd completely lost my chance with you."

"Was there ever anyone else special?" She asked the question but hated the idea of what his answer might be.

"No. Not special. I dated some but nothing ever satisfied me like being with you. I figured I would end up being an old bachelor."

She sucked in her lips tightly, trying to keep the smile from emerging.

"But what about you, Nora? I know you were dating someone seriously."

Her smile dropped from her face. "I did. I tried. It was a mistake."

"A mistake?"

She shrugged and sighed. "I thought what I needed was the absolute opposite of you. Caroline hated him, but I figured he was around, steady, and not adventurous. By then, my dad had died, and I really just wanted some stability. But as we got closer, I think I knew it was never going to be forever. I would've ended it at some time, but he beat me to it."

"He broke up with you? Was he stupid?"

Jerking back, she blinked. "Well, *you* broke up with me!"

"That's what I mean. I was stupid and admit it!"

A rueful chuckle slipped out and she shook her head as her heart pounded, wondering how he would take the words that were coming next. "The reality is when he found out some things about me, he was no longer interested in taking a chance on me."

Tate raised his eyebrows, his chin jerking back, but he remained quiet.

Continuing, she explained, "In the ER, because there was a lot of heavy bleeding when I miscarried, they did some uterine scraping. Later, my doctor said there was scar tissue and the result was that I might not be able to have children."

"Oh, fucking hell, Nora."

His voice was full of anguish, and she winced at the strong emotion lacing his words. Shoulders slumped, she dropped her gaze to her lap, starting to pull her hands away from his. He gripped tighter, and her eyes jerked back up to his in question.

"Babe, I don't know what to tell you except to say this. Any man would be lucky to have you by their side, children or no children. Just being with you would make every day better. And if that's not how he felt, then he was not worthy of your time."

A shiver ran through her at the intensity of his gaze. It blazed through her, and she couldn't understand how she felt so cold and so hot at the same time. He lifted his hand and cupped the back of her head, leaning forward to place his lips on her forehead. Her breath was so shallow she was afraid she might pass out, but she closed her eyes and memorized the feel of his lips on her skin. He pulled back slightly only to lift her chin upward and placed his lips on hers. The kiss was gentle. Yielding. Giving what she needed at that moment: comfort. She had no idea what his thoughts were about their future. Old wounds had been exposed and she felt raw. And yet, for the first time in many years, healing eased into her mind. *But where does that leave us?*

Too tired to figure out her tangled emotions and too afraid to ask him, she simply said, "We've gone over a lot of heavy tonight, Tate."

He reached up and brushed her hair from her face, his thumb gently moving over her bruised jaw. "Do you want to lay down and rest?"

She nodded.

"I'm going back out to grab a few more sticks for the fire, then we can catch a few hours of sleep. I know someone will come for us tomorrow on snowmobiles."

"What if they can't get through because of the storm?"

He kissed her forehead again and stood. "Baby, these guys know what they're doing. They'll get through."

She pushed up to stand, stepping off his coat. Once he was bundled against the weather, he headed back outside. She looked out the door, but he was out of her sight. The snow was deepening, and in a different time and place and situation, she would think it was beautiful. Now, it had created an oasis for her and Tate to reconnect. *But when the morning comes, where will we be?*

22

As soon as Tate stepped outside the cabin, the blast of snow and ice slapped him in the face. He sucked in a quick breath, but the frosty air pushed tangled thoughts to the side. *Maybe this will keep my mind on the mission.* Focus had never been a problem, but it was increasingly harder to be around Nora and not want to take her into his arms and make love to her. But just like it was obvious that sex after Nathan's funeral had been ill-timed, this was not the right situation either. *When I'm with her, I'm going to take care of her... in all ways.* With that vow first and foremost on his mind, he tramped through the thick snowdrifts.

Her words had burrowed deep inside him. When he told her that she was the strongest person he knew, he hadn't exaggerated. But he was done with leaving her alone to face whatever life threw at her.

Still full of recrimination, he quickly moved into the nearby woods and managed to find more sticks to go along with the few other chopped pieces that had been piled behind the shack. Ducking his head again as he went through the doorway, he dropped his armload and turned to secure the door as best he could. It did not fit well, but he tried to keep most of the wind from entering the interior.

She was huddled near the fire and a shiver moved across her. Stepping closer, he dropped to his knees next to hers. "You cold?"

She shook her head. "No, not cold. I just... this is all so..." She dropped her head and lifted her hand to her forehead at the same time. "I suppose I'm just tired."

He did not doubt that she was exhausted but was equally sure that everything they had talked about stirred up emotions that she had not had a chance to process. "Nora?"

She responded to his gentle voice and lifted her head, holding his gaze. Dark circles had formed under her eyes and the bruise on her cheek was still swollen. Her eyelids drooped, but she gave her attention to him.

"We're going to lay down and try to sleep for a couple of hours. We're done talking for now, babe, and things have been heavy. But I want you to try to sleep and everything else we'll deal with tomorrow."

She held his gaze for a long moment, her eyes searching his. He did not look away. She must have found what she was looking for because she gave a little nod before scooting down onto his coat. He lay next to her, and it did not escape his notice that she placed him on the side that allowed him to not put pressure on his injured shoulder. Lifting his arm, he wrapped it around her, offering his chest for her pillow.

He hoped she would be able to find sleep, and it did not take long before her body grew heavier and her breathing deepened. He smiled, knowing she might be exhausted but that she felt safe in his arms.

Sleep did not come easily for him, the multitude of thoughts still running through his mind. He had no idea what the future would bring, but knew with Nora back in his life, he was not going to let her go.

Her bed moved and Nora blinked slightly, aware that light was seeping into her room. The illumination seemed odd, but she closed her eyes, hoping for a few more minutes of sleep. When the mattress shifted again, she jerked her eyes open and realized she was not in bed but lying mostly on Tate.

With her hand on his chest, she pushed herself up, eliciting a grunt from him. "Sorry," she mumbled, still trying to clear her mind. "What time is it?"

He sat up and stretched, then, crouching as he stood, moved to the door. "It's still early, but the sun reflecting off the snow makes it seem extra bright."

"Is it still snowing?"

"The wind has died down, so it seems the storm has passed even though snow is still falling."

She pushed up and stood, mimicking his stretching. Walking over, she nudged under his good shoulder, encircling his waist with her arms. He pulled her in tight, and they stared out the door for a moment. "It looks really deep out there. Do you think anyone will come today?"

He dropped his chin and looked down at her, a smile on his face. It was the most beautiful sight she imagined waking to and prayed it would not be the last time.

"Absolutely. The FBI, DEA, and police will want to get up here and shut down the meth lab and get their hands on the producers. I've got a team member working with the local FBI agent who has snowmobiles. They won't have any problem getting up here."

"Will they be able to find us?"

"Babe, stop worrying. I promise, they'll get here."

"Oh, yeah, I forgot about your tattoo tracer." She felt assured and gifted him with a smile. Glancing at his shoulder, she said, "I need to take a look at that."

His arm squeezed her waist. "Other than being a little stiff, it's okay. I'll get it worked on when we get to the hospital."

She held his gaze, judged him to be truthful about his level of pain, and then turned to look around the room. "This feels strange." He squeezed her arm and she continued. "I just slept on the ground in a little shack and yet it seems better than the cabin. I didn't even want to eat anything there because it was so unclean." She crinkled her nose as she turned her gaze up to him. "I thought that someone that was stockpiling for some kind of takeover would be super organized and, well, maybe not clean, but just have everything in its place."

"I don't know how long David collected things out here," Tate said. "There's plenty of food, but some of those boxes that are in one of the outbuildings are pretty old. This may have been a place that he started years ago for the eventual government takeover that he thinks is going to happen right here on Elk Mountain, but as he used more drugs and got more involved in that business, I'm not sure his mind was very sound."

"What about the others?"

"Kenneth is his nephew, and it doesn't seem like there's a lot of family, so that may just be a relationship that Kenneth clung onto and David used. Bob, as you say, does not appear to be very swift, but he made an excellent gofer and possible fall guy. If he'd gotten caught trying to get David out of the hospital, I think David and Kenneth would've given him up easily to the police."

"What about the drug lab? I didn't see it, but you said it was close to the cabin. Wasn't that dangerous?"

"Absolutely. There's always a risk of fire or explosion because a lot of what they're using is volatile. They're also breathing in those toxic fumes even if they're not ingesting the drugs themselves."

"Who was Porter meeting to get the drugs from?"

"She was a pharmacy tech from the hospital that I saw at the rest stop. She's been stealing and getting extra prescriptions of pseudoephedrine. That's what they used for the meth."

"Oh, my gosh! What was her name? It's a small medical center and I would probably know her."

"Mary Bingle."

Eyes wide, she nodded. "I know her." She shrugged, then amended, "Well, I've never talked to her, but I've heard of her. I've seen her name on prescriptions when I had to send doctor's orders for meds."

"Well, I'm sure the police will investigate what's going on at the hospital to make sure she was the only one involved."

Shaking her head slowly, she thought about everything that had changed in the past twenty-four hours. Turning so that their bodies were flushed together, she lifted her arms to go around his neck. Standing on tiptoe, she pressed a kiss to his lips and loved the feel of his muscular arms banding tighter around her. The kiss flamed hot as their noses bumped and tongues tangled, and he pulled her tighter against him.

Her breasts felt heavy, and as his tongue thrust into her mouth, she felt the electricity shoot straight to her core. Squeezing her legs together, she longed to ease the desire for friction.

He finally pulled away, dropping his head forward so his chin rested on the top of her head. He winced as her fingertips grazed over his injury.

"Are you okay? Is it your shoulder?"

His lips curved into a grin as one hand slid down to her ass and pressed her closer. She felt his hard erection against her stomach and her eyes widened.

"No, I'm not okay. Right now, my cock wants to be buried deep inside you, and no way can that happen."

Before she had a chance to respond, the distant sounds of an engine met their ears. Squeezing her waist, he kissed her quickly. "Looks like we can roll out the welcome mat, babe."

23

———

Nora felt the loss of Tate's warm body as he patted her ass and then walked over to snag his coat off the floor. Pulling it on, he fastened it securely and then kissed her forehead before throwing open the door and moving through quickly.

She wanted to run after him, but the blast of icy air for the few seconds the door was open reminded her that the weather was still harsh even if the worst of the storm had passed. Standing at the door, she peered out at the sparkling winter wonderland. The mountains were magnificent in all seasons, but there was a special beauty when the entire world lay in a clean blanket of white snow. Casting her mind back to the cabin, she shivered, thinking of how such a picturesque scene could hide such evil.

Increasingly louder engine sounds drew her attention back to the edge of the woods where the lane led to the cabin. It did not take long for a snowmobile to burst through, heading directly through the clearing.

Tate stayed near the front door, his smile wide and his arm raised in greeting. Wanting to be at his side, she looked around to see if there was something she could put on for warmth, then sighed heavily, knowing he would want her to stay inside the safety of the shelter. Continuing to stare out the door, she observed the snowmobile driver cut off his engine, climb from the seat, and unsnap his helmet.

The man approaching Tate was as large as he, dark-haired and wide-shouldered. *Must be his teammate.* They greeted with tight, back-pounding hugs. He winced and she knew a slap landed on his injured shoulder. No longer willing to stay in the cabin, she threw open the door and rushed outside. She immediately halted, her nursing clogs inadequate in the deep snowdrifts and the snow hitting her face causing a squeak to leave her lips.

Tate turned and hustled to her, immediately unsnapping his jacket so that she could push her body next to his. The jacket was large enough that he could wrap it around the back of her, pressing her body close to his warmth.

"Nora, you shouldn't be out here. It's freezing."

Looking up, she said, "I'm sorry, but I couldn't stay. Plus, I know your shoulder hurts." She shifted around inside his jacket so that she could peer out at the man who approached. "He was stabbed in the shoulder."

The other man immediately dropped his grin, but Tate just shook his head. "Hate to admit it, but I let the fucker get a blade in."

"That's not true! He threw himself in front of me and took the knife instead."

Tate's chest rumbled against her back as he chuckled. "Clay, I should introduce my defender. This is Nora Stiles, nurse extraordinaire. Nora, I'd like you to meet my teammate, Clay."

Clay continued to smile as he greeted her until his gaze landed on her bruised cheek. Tate squeezed her middle and said, "We need to get inside. I want to keep her warm."

She moved back inside the tiny shelter, not surprised that Clay stayed in the doorway even when Tate followed her.

"I came on up early," Clay said. He reached into his pockets and pulled out power bars, handing them out. "I wanted to get to you two while the others were gathering the snow coaches and heading up toward the cabin at a slower pace."

"How will we get down?" She unwrapped the bar and gratefully began munching. Clay and Tate shared a glance, words not appearing necessary between them. "Oh, no you don't," she argued. "Don't do the *silent talk* where I don't know what is going on!"

Clay grinned and inclined his head toward her. "I think I like her, Tate." Turning toward her, he added, "You keep him on his toes."

"Years of practice," she muttered, still watching them warily.

Tate scrubbed his hand over his head and sighed. "Okay, Nora. We have one snowmobile right now and the best thing to do is to have it take all three of us back up the mile to the cabin. There we can meet with the others, and I'll be able to borrow a snowmobile to take us down."

"Okay."

Tate's brows lifted and he cocked his head to the side. "Okay?"

"Um… yeah… okay." Now it was her turn to lift her brow. "Why not?"

"Because I hate the idea of having you go back into that place." He reached out and cupped her face, his eyes worried.

Smiling, she shook her head. "Tate, I'm not afraid of the cabin. It wasn't great to be there, but that's over with. I can move on. You probably need to be up there while they get David, and I know once we get back to town I'm going to have to talk to the police." She reached up and wrapped her fingers around his wrist, giving a little squeeze. "I'm with you… it's all good."

"Damn, now I know I like her," Clay said, gaining an eye roll from Tate. "I'm ready whenever y'all are."

"I just need to wrap my feet in plastic bags again."

Clay glanced down and shook his head. "Damn, I wish I could've brought some boots for you."

"Well, if I had my fuckin' head on straight, I could've told you," Tate groaned.

"It's not for much longer and being on the snowmobile will be a lot better than walking through the snow!" She sat and quickly tied the bags over her feet and secured them around her ankles. With Bob's coat wrapped around her and Tate's hooded scarf pulled over her head, she looked up. "I'm as ready as I'm ever going to be."

The three tramped over to the snowmobile and Clay climbed on, scooting as close to the front as he could and still be able to control the vehicle.

"You next, babe. You'll be more protected between us."

She threw her leg over the seat and scooted close to Clay, allowing Tate to settle on the back. It was a tight fit, but she immediately felt protected between the two large men. Clay fired up the engine, and with a jolt, they started forward. He kept the pace slower, and they took a path that skirted around the woods they had gone through the previous night. But with the powerful engine hurling them forward, they made it to the cabin in less than ten minutes.

As they approached, she heard the roar of more snowmobiles and snow coaches coming up the main lane that Porter had taken the other day... *yesterday... was it just yesterday?* Still stunned at how crazy the past day had been, she barely registered they had stopped. Still pressed between Tate and Clay, her body had been carefully protected. Now, as Tate climbed off, the cold air hit her back.

"Come on, Nora. I want you out of the cold for the few minutes that it'll take to get things done here."

She looked toward the men climbing off snowmobiles and descending from the snow coaches, some with FBI or DEA embroidered in large letters on the back of their coats. Twisting her head upward, she said, "Honey, I know you've got a lot of work to do. I can stay in the cabin by myself."

"I'll get you in there first, babe, and then go back out

to talk to everyone. I don't want you around when we bring David and the others out. Plus, Levi is going to be interviewing you and so will Billy. He's in one of the snow coaches that the sheriff's department sent."

Not surprised by that information, she nodded. Walking awkwardly with her plastic bag-covered shoes, she squealed as he scooped her up and carried her inside the cabin. She slipped out of her jacket and turned toward the first man who entered and greeted Tate before addressing her.

"Ma'am, you can call me Levi," the FBI agent said. "I'm going to have Tate take us around to secure the prisoners and take a look at the meth lab. As soon as I do that, I can turn the lab over to the people who'll work on dismantling it safely, and the sheriff's department will escort the prisoners back to jail. As soon as we can, we'll let Tate go and he can get you back down the mountain. Once there, we'll need to meet with you for an interview. Does that sound okay?"

She smiled and nodded. "Please, call me Nora. I'm sure you don't need my permission, Levi, but yes, that's perfectly fine."

His gaze shifted around, landing on the kitchen, and he grimaced. "What a dump." Looking at Tate, he said, "Let's go get 'em."

Tate bent and kissed her lightly on the lips, mumbling, "Be back as soon as I can."

She stayed near the door even though the cold morning air hit her. It was surreal watching the activity of law enforcement as they swarmed the area. The snow had come to a stop, and visibility was now clear, allowing her to easily see what was happening.

Two men with FBI jackets came out with Bob in handcuffs and he was led to one of the snow coaches.

She watched as the same procedure happened with Kenneth. She was unable to see where David came from, but he was marched forward, placed in a snow coach, also.

Turning away from the door, she stood in the middle of the cabin and looked around. *Tate mentioned that some of the boxes in the back and outbuildings were old.* She wondered how long David had been living this kind of existence... stockpiling food, ammunition, and weapons for the eventual war that seemed to exist only in his mind. Hearing a noise from the front, she turned and spied Billy. He grinned and opened his arms. Glad for the familiar face, she rushed forward and accepted his hug.

"Good to see you, Nora. Gotta tell you that when I realized you'd been taken, I couldn't believe it. I kept blaming myself, wishing that I had been up there in the room."

Shaking her head, she said, "There was nothing you could do. He came in with a gun and caught us all by surprise."

"Well, I've got to get your statement, but I know Agent Amory does too. As soon as we get back to town, we can go over it together."

"What about the other deputy? Was he okay?"

Snorting, Billy said, "Bart? Nothing hurt about him but his pride."

A few minutes later, Levi, Tate, and Clay stepped into the cabin as well. With the group of large men in the small cabin, the space felt tiny, and yet, with the smiles abounding between them, she did not feel crowded. Despite the mass of bodies, Tate easily maneuvered his way to her, wrapping his arm around her.

"You okay, babe? I know you're tired and hungry, and I want to get you back down the mountain as soon as we can."

She smiled up at him and nodded.

"Nora?" Levi began, "I want you and Tate to get back to Rawlins. You both need to be checked out at the medical center, and I know this ordeal has been exhausting. I need to stay up here with some of the deputies, DEA, and my fellow agents to process everything that's here, including the meth lab. If you're okay going back down the mountain with Tate on my snowmobile, I'll get a ride back in the snow coach. There are vehicles on the main road for you to take back."

"Thank you!" she exuded, squeezing Tate's waist while nodding with enthusiasm. "I'm so ready to get off this mountain."

"This will make the trip down the mountain better for you," Billy said, handing her a large ski suit and sheriff's department coat.

Grateful, she took them and pulled them over her scrubs. A few minutes later, she smiled up at Tate. "I'm ready when you are. Take me home."

"Babe, I've been waiting forever for you to say those words to me." Bending, he kissed her lightly. "Let's go."

They walked out with Clay to the snowmobiles. Levi had handed his helmet to Tate who made sure it fit snugly on her head. Climbing aboard, she wrapped her arms around Tate's middle, scooted her crotch to his ass, and tightened her knees next to his thick thighs.

He twisted his head to the side and called out, "Hold on, baby!"

Excitement scored through her as she grasped him tightly. The engines fired and as they lurched forward, she squealed in delight. Clay took the lead, and she did not doubt that if she was not on the back, Tate would have raced down the mountain. Instead, he made the trip as gentle as he could as they flew past thick forests, down to where the vegetation was more snow-covered scrub brush. She enjoyed this trip much more than the previous day coming up the mountain.

Her smile split her face as the wind whistled by. Sucking in the cold, fresh air, she hoped she would have another chance to take a snowmobile ride with Tate, preferably on a date instead of heading to the hospital and police station.

It did not take long for them to make it to the highway where several SUVs and an ambulance waited. As the engine shut down, she climbed off the back, immediately hating to lose contact with Tate's body. Pulling off her helmet, she stepped to the side to give Tate room to do the same. Uncertain what was expected of her, she looked to him for direction.

"I want you to go back to town in the ambulance."

She continued to stare at him, hearing his words but

not understanding them. "Me? Why do you want me to go in the ambulance? You're the one he stabbed!"

"Babe, you've been through trauma. I want to make sure you're okay."

"I'll be okay as long as I'm with you. I don't want to go back to town in the ambulance unless you're in the ambulance with me and I know *you're* being checked out."

Staring down at her with his hands on his hips, he said, "Are we seriously standing out in the freezing cold, arguing about who's worse off and going in the ambulance?"

Mocking his posture, her hands landed on her hips. "I guess we are."

He finally sighed and shook his head slowly. "Okay, you win. We'll both go in the ambulance and meet everybody at the hospital."

A bark of laughter sounded out behind them, and she looked to see Clay grinning at them. "And another one bites the dust," he muttered through his smile.

Rolling her eyes, she tugged on Tate's hand, dragging him through the snow toward the ambulance.

"Are you both coming?" the paramedic asked, a smile on her face as well, having obviously heard their conversation.

"I'm a nurse at Rawlins Hospital and this man has a stab wound in the shoulder. I treated it last night with what I had, but it needs to be looked at. For me, there's just fatigue and a bruised jaw."

As though to prove his shoulder was not too bad,

Tate boosted her up into the back of the ambulance before hauling himself in. "Looks like you heard from the boss."

He sat down on the bed, and the paramedic and EMT shifted around to make room for both of them. With his coat off, he slid his arm out from his shirt, exposing the bandaged shoulder.

Nora was seated to the side, her blood pressure and temperature being taken, but when she spied the blood on the bandage, she lunged forward.

"Nurse, have a seat," the paramedic ordered. "You need to take care of you and let us deal with this now."

She knew he was right, but she hated seeing Tate's blood. Settling back, she let the EMT finish her blood pressure reading while the paramedic began cutting off the bandage from Tate's shoulder.

"The main highway isn't too bad," the driver called back. "ETA is about forty minutes."

The paramedic cleaned Tate's shoulder, checked his blood pressure and temperature, and called ahead to the ER, letting them know what to expect. Looking at Tate, he said, "There's not a plastic surgeon on staff now, but the ER doctor should be able to stitch you up without too much of a scar."

At the scowl Tate aimed toward the paramedic, Nora could not contain the giggle that slipped out.

"Do I look like I give a fuck about a scar?"

The paramedic's brow crinkled, and she shook her head, laughing. "No, I don't reckon you do."

As soon as she was finished with Tate, Nora maneuvered around so she could slide onto the gurney with him. Curled up on her side, she rested her head on his chest and wrapped her arm across his abdomen. Just like laying on the floor hours earlier, she realized anywhere felt comfortable as long as she was with Tate.

24

Tate looked out of the ambulance's back doors and rolled his eyes. Billy must have called Caroline because she and Thomas as well as his parents were at the hospital waiting when the ambulance arrived. Nora scrambled out first, and they rushed to her, enveloping her in their hugs. He refused to be wheeled in, and as he climbed down from the back of the ambulance, his family added him into their embrace.

Nora, looking both exhausted and elated, snapped into nurse mode and said, "We need to let him get in. He has an injury."

Growling her name, he shot a glare her way, but she shrugged it off. Finally, the hospital staff sent his family back into the waiting room while he and Nora were taken to ER bays. It didn't take long for Nora to be given a clean bill of health and to find her way into his room. The doctor had already numbed his arm and was working on stitching the wound. Nora walked to the other side of the bed, hitched her hip onto the mattress, and sat next to him.

"Everything okay?" he asked her.

She nodded and squeezed his hand. "Everything's good. They told me to eat and rest, two things I already knew needed to be done."

Her gaze dropped, but he felt like there was more. This time, he squeezed her hand and she brought her gaze back to him. "Anything more?"

"They made sure that I had the number for a crisis counselor. Everything happened so fast, but they said that memories, nightmares, all kinds of things can hit me later. They wanted to make sure I had the number, even if I think I don't need it now."

"I want you to use that number anytime you think you need it," he said. He ducked his head slightly so that he could move closer and continue to hold her gaze. "Promise me."

She glanced from his face to his shoulder and back to his face and grinned. "I'll promise to use the number if I need it if you promise to hold still. I don't think Dr. Jernigan appreciates his patient moving around so much."

Grinning, Tate said, "Okay, okay, I'll hold still."

It did not take long for the doctor to finish stitching Tate's shoulder. With the paperwork complete, they were both discharged and walked into the waiting room.

Susan hurried over to Nora and patted her cheek. "Oh, sweetheart, we've been so frantic. But I knew with Tate going to get you, he'd bring you back to us."

Tate had shifted over to his dad and said, "Hell, Dad, you just got discharged yesterday and here you are again."

Frank said, "Don't worry. Your mom's been fretting over me and looking after me. Now, let's get ready to go home. Caroline and Thomas went to get the kids and head back to the ranch. We'll have a good meal and you guys can rest."

"My car is still here in the parking lot," Nora said. "I think I'm going to head home, and I'll see you—"

"You're not going home by yourself," Tate declared.

"Honey, you should go home with your parents and—"

"Yes, and you're coming, too. I'm not letting you go back to your apartment alone right now."

Her eyes widened. "You're not *letting* me?"

"Nora, this is not the time to argue about semantics. I don't think it's a good idea for you to be alone right now. Please, I'll drive your car, and we'll go back to the ranch. Eat a good meal, rest up, and prove to Mom and Dad that we're doing okay. Plus, Dad probably needs a nurse to keep an eye on him right now anyway."

Pursing her lips, she shook her head. "That's emotional blackmail."

He could tell she was yielding, and he grinned. "Whatever it takes, sweetheart."

They all left the hospital, Susan driving Frank in their vehicle and Tate driving Nora's little SUV. As they pulled out of the parking lot, she looked at him and said, "You know, you're not always going to get your way."

He chuckled and said, "I've known you since we were little."

"What's that supposed to mean?"

He reached over with his free hand and wrapped his fingers around hers, giving a little squeeze. "It means I know you're a woman of your own mind, strong and independent by yourself. But babe, I want to do everything I can to take care of you."

He glanced to the side and could see thoughts working behind her eyes, but she remained silent. *She's wondering what the fuck I mean by that.* He had a lot more that he wanted to say to her, but the time wasn't right. Not when she was emotional and exhausted. He only had a couple of days before he needed to report back to LSI and planned on making the most of his time left with her. *And when I go back, she'll know exactly the place I want to have in her life.*

Each movement felt like her limbs were made of cement. They had made it to the ranch, where Caroline and Susan quickly served a hearty meal of beef stew and homemade biscuits, topped off with Susan's apple pie.

Before eating, Nora checked on Frank, assured by him that he felt fine, but not long after the meal, he and Susan settled in the den so that he could rest in his recliner and watch TV. Thomas headed outside to check on the stock, and Caroline headed into the den with her parents.

Now, with a full belly, she forced her body to stand

and moved toward Tate. He opened his arms as she approached, and she encircled his waist with her arms and placed her head on his chest. So tired she was uncertain she could make the drive to her apartment, she wanted to complain that this was the reason she should have gone directly home.

Determined to keep the *fatigue-bitch* hidden, she said, "I need to leave. This was nice, Tate, but I'm really tired."

"Then let's go."

It was shocking—and a little stinging—that he was no longer fighting her but seemed ready for her to leave after having strong-armed her into coming. Deciding he must be ready to crash as well, she nodded and stepped back.

He took her hand and led her toward the front of the house but detoured before they got to the door. Turning at the bottom of the staircase, he began the ascent, his fingers still linked with hers. Her feet stumbled to a halt, and he looked down when her hand jerked in his.

"Where are you going?"

"Bed."

"Then where are you leading me?"

"To my bed."

Eyes wide, she sucked in a quick breath, her gaze jerking around to see if anyone was listening. "Tate," she hissed, "I can't get in bed with you here!"

"Why not? We slept together last night."

She jumped up onto the stair-step right above him and placed her hand over his mouth. "Shhh, your parents might hear."

"Baph," he muttered through her hand. Sticking his tongue out to lick her palm, she dropped her hand quickly, her eyes bugging out at him.

"Jeez, are you twelve?"

Laughing, he pulled her close to him and kissed her lightly. She stared into his eyes, mesmerized by the hazel that held her captive. She watched as the humor faded, replaced with concern.

"I've been on missions all over the world, Nora, and when it comes to difficulty level, this one was easy. But from the moment they took you until the moment I got you back into my arms, my heart didn't stop pounding, my emotions didn't stop grinding, and my rage wasn't close to quelling. Right now, I don't want you to go back to your apartment alone. I'd worry about you making that drive as tired as you are. And if you're determined to go back, then I'll drive you there. But honest to fuck, sweetheart, right now, I want to tuck you in bed and lay down beside you. I want to know that you're here, safe with me. Nothing else, just sleep. The peaceful sleep that comes from knowing the other half of my heart is pressed close to me."

His words moved through her and tears filled her eyes as she brought her hands back up to cup his jaws. Drawing in a ragged breath, she nodded. "Okay," she whispered, loving the way her one-word agreement brought a smile to his face.

He took her hand in his again, linked fingers, and led her upstairs and into the bedroom. She saw his duffel bag tossed into the corner and the en suite bathroom through an open door. The queen-size bed looked inviting, but so did the bathroom.

"Bath first or nap?"

"You must've read my mind," she chuckled. Sighing, she said, "Honestly? If I get into the bathtub, I'll fall asleep and never get out. But I feel disgustingly dirty and want to get out of these clothes. I think I'll opt to take a shower."

"You got it, sweetheart." He walked over to his duffel and pulled out a clean T-shirt. Turning around, he handed it to her. Kissing the top of her head, he said, "Put this on when you get out."

She wrapped her fingers around the soft cotton and instinctively lifted it to her nose and sniffed. It smelled like him, despite the fabric softener. She glanced toward the bathroom again, then looked up. "What about you?"

"I'll take a shower in the hall bathroom." He must have caught her lifted brow because he chuckled and added, "If I get in that shower with you, I'm going to want to do a whole lot more than just get clean."

She felt the heat of blush cross her face and rolled her eyes. Hurrying into the bathroom, she closed the door and quickly took care of business. Turning on the water, she soon stepped under the spray and luxuriated in the feel of the warm water pounding her tense muscles. After washing her hair and scrubbing with shower gel, she stepped out onto the thick mat and dried quickly. When a knock on the door sounded, she pulled on Tate's T-shirt, glad it hung to her mid-thighs. He stood in the open door, his hair wet, dressed in a clean T-shirt and drawstring flannel pants.

"Caroline thought you could use these." In his hands were a clean pair of panties and flannel pajama bottoms. "She's a little bigger than you, but this will keep you warm."

Delighted, she turned and pulled on the panties and bottoms, glancing over her shoulder to see that he averted his eyes. They both brushed their teeth and she used lotion to moisturize. It was early afternoon, but when she walked back into the bedroom, he had pulled the curtains, blanketing the room in shadows.

Suddenly hesitant, she stopped by the side of the bed. "This feels weird."

"It's only weird if you make it that way, Nora." He climbed into bed and jerked down the covers on the other side. Patting the mattress, he said, "Come on, sweetheart. We both need to rest."

No longer wanting to think about anything other than closing her eyes, she crawled into bed and curled up next to Tate on the soft sheets. He did not hesitate to wrap his arms around her and pull her in tightly to his chest. With the thick covers and his body heat, she was soon enveloped in warmth. If she had been more awake, she might have pondered the realization that she was in his bed, in his parents' ranch house. She might have worried what that said about her or him or their relationship. She might have fretted over what the future would bring for them.

Instead, she closed her eyes and fell asleep, safe in the knowledge that Tate would chase away any of her nightmares.

And when she awoke, it took a moment to figure out

where she was until she felt Tate's arms still wrapped around her. Blinking, she glanced at the clock on the nightstand and was surprised to find they had slept soundly through the evening and all night.

Waking in his embrace felt so right, but that was scary. *How easy it would be to get used to this... and how devastating it would be to lose it again.*

25

Tate's morning started out perfectly. He woke with Nora in his arms and his morning wood pressed against her ass. He battled back the desire to ease his aching cock by burying it in her warm body. She was beginning to stir, so he slid his hips away from hers. She rolled over, her gaze moving about his face before landing on his shoulder.

"How did you sleep? Does your shoulder hurt?"

"It's a little stiff, that's all. But as far as sleeping? With you tucked up close to me, I don't think I moved all night." She smiled and it struck him straight to the heart. Her sleep-tousled hair had dried naturally with waves. He reached out and rubbed his finger over her soft cheek before gliding his hand through her hair. *Nora, waking up in my bed.* There had been a time he wanted this every day and walked away from it. His noble notions now crumbled to dust, knowing he had been a fool.

A knock on the door interrupted the moment, and

she jumped out of bed, a blush painting her cheeks. He stalked over to the door and opened it, his mother standing just outside.

"I'm so glad you two were able to rest! Clay is in the guesthouse and Levi called to say you can come to the station whenever you can get there. Breakfast is ready whenever you want to eat, but Caroline thought that Nora would need some clean clothes."

After thanking his mom, he turned and walked toward Nora, handing her the clothes.

"I can't help but be embarrassed that your mom knows I spent the night in your bed."

Chuckling, he said, "Then we just need to keep doing it to get you over your embarrassment."

She stuck her tongue out at him but snatched the clothes from his hands. "Oh, this is perfect. A warm tunic sweater and leggings!" She walked over to the dresser and pulled off his T-shirt before slipping on her bra. He could have been a gentleman and turned away, but the sight of her smooth, naked back kept his gaze riveted on her. She donned the sweater and it hung below her ass. Mesmerized, he continued to stare as she slid the leggings up her legs. Turning around, she looked at him, then lifted her brow. "Are you seriously just going to stand there and watch me dress?"

"Abso-fucking-lutely."

She laughed and threw his T-shirt toward his face. He snagged it with one hand, watching her smile light her face. Stalking toward her, he threaded his fingers through her hair at the back of her head and brought her closer to him. "You're beautiful, babe." Bending, he took her mouth in a gentle kiss, wishing he could take it wilder and hotter, but knew their day needed to begin.

He assumed she was afraid that breakfast would be awkward, but Tate's family acted as though it was the most natural thing in the world for her to have spent the night in his bed and be sitting at the table first thing in the morning. Her nerves visibly eased, and he watched with pleasure as she devoured her meal.

Leaning back, she patted her stomach. "Wow, I was hungry."

"You didn't eat a lot last night," Susan commented, her gaze peering at both of them. "I'm glad to see you fill up this morning."

Hating to leave the cocoon of the ranch, Tate said. "We've got to go into town, babe."

Her gaze jerked up to his and he hated the specter of uncertainty that crossed her face. It was quickly replaced with a nod and they left the kitchen to grab their coats.

The nice part of the morning was over as he drove one of the ranch trucks to the police station, following her car. Her feet stumbled slightly as they entered the small reception area filled with men and he was glad his arm was around her waist. Billy was there with the local sheriff. Levi was in their huddle, along with Clay. The conversations halted as they approached, and he breathed easier at the comforting smiles that were directed her way.

Sitting next to her, he listened as she gave her statement, detailing what happened in the hospital room, the gun Bob held on her, forcing her along with them, hitting her, and the ride to the cabin in the back of the Jeep. His hands curled into fists, and at one point she reached over and placed her hand on his, giving a squeeze. *Fuck, she's trying to comfort me.* The detectives, along with Levi, sat in on her interview, and once her statement was over, they expressed how well she had handled the ordeal. Billy assured her that the three men were in jail and would not be a threat to her anymore.

Levi explained that the DEA and FBI had taken charge of the meth lab site and after evidence had been collected, it was being destroyed according to regulations. "I know you're a nurse and were only at the cabin a short time, but keep in mind that the effects of being exposed to meth can linger. Be sure to seek treatment if you experience persistent cough, excess energy, dizziness, or blurry vision." Looking up at Tate, he added, "You were actually in the lab for a few minutes, so the same goes for you."

As they stood to leave, Levi turned to Tate and asked for a moment of his time. Nora smiled and nodded, walking out into the hall with Billy.

Tate gave Levi his attention, silently waiting to see what he needed to talk to him about. Levi looked down for a moment, rubbing his chin before lifting his head and steadily holding Tate's gaze.

"Can't think of any reason to beat around the bush, so I'll just come out and say it. I'd like to get more information about your employer. I'm not saying that I'm ready to leave the Bureau, but I'm more than a little interested."

Tate sighed in relief and grinned. "Shit, man. I was

afraid something was going down with those assholes we brought in and afraid it would affect Nora."

Eyes wide, Levi shook his head quickly. "No, no. Everything with the investigation is fine. I will tell you that we're looking into Mary and the hospital more to make sure there's no one else who's been leaking drugs. But this conversation is all about me."

Tate reached into his back pocket, snagging his wallet. Pulling out a card, he handed it to Levi. "The information is on there. I've got to head back to Maine in a couple of days. I'll talk to my boss, Mace, and let him know that he might be hearing from you."

Levi studied the card, nodding slowly before smiling. "Thanks. This means a lot." Sticking out his hand, Tate clasped his firmly.

"It was a pleasure working with you, Levi. I appreciate everything you did." Turning, he walked down the hall, finding Nora waiting for him. She smiled up at him, and he immediately wrapped his arms around her. With his lips pressed to the top of her head, he said, "I'm so proud of you, babe. You handled yourself perfectly through your ordeal. It doesn't mean I don't want to go to that jail and beat the shit out of those men, but right now, I don't want to give them any more of my time."

"That's probably a good thing. I don't want to have to visit *you* in jail!" She leaned her head back and her top teeth landed on her bottom lip as she fought a grin. "So, what would you like to do now?"

"Let's get you home and then I'll show you." He was glad it only took five minutes to pull up to her little apartment. *The mission is complete... rescue is over... family*

*time has occurred... police statement is given. Now, it's our
time... new mission.*

The entire drive, Nora was a nervous wreck. *What did
Tate mean? He'll show me? Have all of the hugs and kisses in
the past day just resulted from a crazy, messed up, intense
situation? Does he want more? Do I want more?*

Before the answers to any of these questions were
revealed, she drove into her parking spot and a few
seconds later he pulled in next to her. Climbing from
their vehicles at the same time, she cast a glance his way,
wondering if he was as nervous as she. As usual, he
appeared relaxed and in charge. Now that she thought
about it, she could never remember seeing him
unsteady except for Nathan's funeral. Giving her head a
little shake, she pushed that thought from her mind and
they walked up to her apartment together.

Turning the key, she stepped into the living room,
tossing her purse to the side. Her feet came to a stut-
tering halt as she looked around, her breath catching in
her throat. Everything was the same, nothing out of
place. And yet, shivers began moving through her body
until violent shaking overtook her and she slumped to
the floor.

Tate dropped to the floor, his arms wrapping around
her. "What's wrong, sweetheart?"

Swallowing deeply, she slowly shook her head.
"Nothing. I just suddenly felt... oh, it's silly."

He gently turned her around and bent to hold her

gaze. "There's nothing silly about thoughts or feelings or emotions. What's going on?"

"I don't understand it, but things feel so different. I was just here two days ago, in this space that I've made my home. And yet, with all the craziness in the past two days, I walked in and everything felt strange. Like I don't recognize anything. All I can see is that cabin and those men..." Unable to bear the intensity of his gaze, she dragged in a ragged breath and dropped her eyes. "See, I said it was silly."

"Nora, listen to me." He shook her shoulders gently and she lifted her gaze again. "What you're experiencing is a type of PTSD. When you've suffered a trauma and then you step back into what was your life before, nothing quite seems right. You've been on a whirlwind for two days, and just because it's over, your mind and emotions are having to catch up with everything that happened."

"Okay," she whispered, her head bobbing jerkily. "I know you're right." She blew out a long breath and swallowed deeply again. As a nurse, she knew what he explained made sense. But never having experienced it, she was uncertain how to deal with the emotions. "What... what should we do?"

He looked around the room before bringing his warm gaze back to her. "Well, let's walk around your apartment and you can tell me about it."

Her face scrunched and she repeated, "Tell you about it?"

"Yeah, let's walk around and you can tell me about the things you have in your apartment. What you like...

what you wish was different. Let's just get reacquainted and take things one little step at a time."

With his arms around her, she looked around, nodding slowly. "Um… well, I got this place after I sold my parents' house." She turned in his arms and cast her gaze about the room again, thinking back to when she saw it the first time. "I know it's small, but it was only me, and since I was working full-time shifts at the hospital, I didn't need much. I didn't want a yard to have to take care of, but I wanted a view. It was late afternoon the first time I was able to see it, and the sun was setting." She lifted her hand to point to the large picture window at the end of the living room, the mountain range in the distance clearly visible. "As soon as we walked inside, the sunset was breathtaking that day. Clear skies, no clouds. Streaks of golden yellow and peach across the blue. It reminded me of—"

Her voice caught in the back of her throat, and she hesitated. Her back was pressed to Tate's front, and his arm still banded around her, holding her close, keeping her safe. "It reminded me of all the times you and I used to watch the sunset from somewhere on the ranch."

"I remember those times too, Nora. Good times."

She twisted around to look up at him with a tremulous smile curving her lips. "I told the building manager that I would take the apartment and I hadn't even looked at the rest of it."

Tate's arms squeezed her, and he smiled. "I hope the rest of it was okay."

Chuckling, she nodded. "It was fine. Small, but fine."

"Show me the rest," he encouraged.

"There's not much more to show. Obviously, the living space is connected to the kitchen and dining area. It's really more like just one room, with only the kitchen counter dividing the space at all. But, as I said, it's just me and I didn't want much to take care of. I usually work day shifts, and I'm out of here by six-thirty in the morning and don't get back until four in the afternoon at the earliest. If I have errands to run then I don't get back until dinner time. Occasionally, I have to work a night shift, and then I just need a place to sleep."

His arms let her go and he walked into the living room, looking at the photographs she had hanging on the wall. She watched as his attention snagged on the one in the center. It was a picture of her, Tate, and Nathan on their first visit back home after they joined the military. She was standing in the middle of both of them, all laughing at something amusing one of them had said. The expressions on their faces told of good times had and expectations of good times to come. She loved that picture, and no matter how much her heart had broken, she kept that picture on her wall.

Tate cleared his voice and twisted his head to look at her. "I remember the day that photograph was taken. We were out near the barn and Caroline came down and snapped it. I remember it like it was fuckin' yesterday."

"I was just thinking that no matter what happened, I never considered taking that picture down. It was in my room at my house and I made sure it was on this wall." She saw his intense stare, and she continued, "Even when the thought of you pierced my heart, I couldn't stand the idea of taking that photograph down."

He turned and it only took two steps for him to be right in front of her again. He lifted his hand and slid his fingers to the back of her head, his thumb sweeping over her cheek. His eyes were warm and his voice was gentle. "Show me more, babe."

She smiled and glanced toward the kitchen. "Are you hungry?"

With a chuckle, he shook his head. "Not with one of Mom's breakfasts in me."

She linked fingers with him and guided him toward the short hall. "It's only a one-bedroom apartment because I never have guests who spend the night. The bedroom isn't very big, but I admit that I like the bathroom. It's surprisingly large for such a small apartment."

The bathroom was on one side of the hall, behind the kitchen. He leaned his head in and then quickly jerked around to look at her. "Wow, you're right."

"The sunset through the picture window was the first thing that sold me on the apartment, but I have to admit when I saw the large soaking tub, I knew it was the place for me."

"Then I know exactly what you need to do next."

With her head cocked to the side, she looked up at him, waiting to find out what he thought she should do to make herself feel more at home.

Instead of speaking, he bent and plugged the bottom of the tub before turning on the water. Checking the temperature as it ran over his fingers, he said, "You need to soak."

"Now?"

Standing, he pulled her into his embrace again, tucking her head under his chin. "Right now, I want you to feel warm, safe, and secure."

She wanted to tell him that was what she felt when she was in his arms, but just circled his waist with her hands and gave a little squeeze.

"So, you're going to take a long, hot bath and relax."

"Are you leaving?" She asked the question even though she was terrified of the answer. She was so used to being alone, but right now that was not what she wanted.

"Hell, no, Nora. I'm not leaving."

Smiling, she felt the tension leave her shoulders. He bent and kissed her lips lightly, then stepped out of the bathroom. "Take your time, but I'll be close by." With that, he walked out of the bathroom and closed the door.

Stinging hit her eyes, and when she squeezed them shut, tears rolled down her cheeks. She had no idea how long she stood, but she suddenly jolted and looked down at the water that was rapidly filling. Turning off the faucet, she stripped, stepped over into the heated water, and settled back with her head on her tub pillow. Closing her eyes, the tears stopped, and she was filled with ease.

Fifteen minutes later, the water was cooling as she climbed from the tub. Her body was warm and her muscles relaxed, but the thought of Tate in her apartment caused tingles to run along her spine. Grabbing one of her huge, thick, soft bath towels she dried her body and moisturized. Glancing around, it dawned on her that she came into the bathroom with no change of clothes. With the towel wrapped around her, she opened the door and stepped across the hall into her bedroom.

Her mouth dropped open at the sight of Tate reclining on her bed, his back resting on the pile of pillows and his heated gaze on her. His shirt was off, exposing his T-shirt that stretched across taut muscles. His jeans fit tight in the right places, loose in others, ending in his bare feet which she found incredibly sexy. Uncertain of his expectations, she hesitated.

He swung his legs over the side of the bed and stood. It only took a few steps before he was right in front of her. Her head tilted back as she kept her gaze on his face, his large presence filling the room. He lifted both hands and cupped her cheeks, his fingertips gliding through her hair. Slowly, he lowered his head until his mouth hovered a whisper away from hers. She reached her hands up and clung to his biceps, careful of his injured shoulder, pressing her towel-covered body closer to his, and their lips met.

The past was over... mistakes that had been made could only be forgiven and previous good times were left to be celebrated in memories. The future was unknown... the great uncertainty that faces everyone. But in the here and now is where we decide who we are and what we want to do.

With his lips claiming hers, his arms holding her body tightly to his, she decided.

I'm his.

2 6

Tate could not believe the gift she was handing him and had no intention to squander it or take it for granted. When Nora had walked out of the bathroom with her hair piled on top of her head in damp tendrils hanging about her shoulders, her skin dewy from the warmth of her bath, and her body encased in a thick towel, he fought the urge to rush to her and claim her for his own.

Instead, his gaze scanned her from head to toes and back again, settling on her eyes where he could see hesitation. Wanting to erase the doubt, he moved swiftly to her and pulled her into his arms.

Offering control, he could have howled with male pride when she clutched his arms, pulled him close, and kissed him. Just as he knew it would be, her skin was warm and petal-soft, and her lips were pliable underneath his.

He drank her in, his tongue thrusting into her mouth, caressing and tasting. As the kiss moved from gentle to wild, he lifted her in his arms and carried her to the bed. Bending slightly, he jerked the covers down before lying her on the mattress. She rolled to one side and jerked the damp towel out from under her, tossing it to the floor.

He perused her naked body which was just as beautiful as he remembered from years earlier, acknowledging that maturity had only made her more desirable. Her breasts were full and the chilly air had her nipples pulled tight. She did not try to cover her nudity but smiled slowly as she reclined in comfort.

"Are you just going to stand there and stare, or are you going to join me?"

"As beautiful as you are, part of me could be satisfied just staring at you," he confessed, loving that her gaze no longer held doubt. "But considering I'm about to come in my pants, maybe I should join you." He reached behind and pulled off his T-shirt, carefully maneuvering it around his bandage. With a quick flip, his belt was undone, and he shed both his pants and boxers at the same time.

Her smile held appreciation, and she leaned up on her elbows, her gaze locked on his cock. He thought he was hard before, but with her perusal, he swelled even more. Crawling onto the bed, he knelt between her legs, kissing his way from her belly button to her breasts where he moved between them, circling her nipples with his tongue before taking the taut buds deeply into his mouth.

She fell back against the pillow, her hands encircling his neck, and her fingers lightly caressing the tops of his shoulders. Not wanting to rush the moment, he worshiped each breast before kissing his way to her collarbone, nibbling where her pulse was fluttering at the base of her neck. Her breath hitched and he sucked gently, leaving a small claiming mark. She lifted her chin as he continued to kiss along her jaw, his lips finally claiming hers once more.

Keeping his full weight off her chest with his forearms pressed into the mattress on either side of her, his body covered hers from head to toe. His hands cupped either side of her head as they clung together, their tongues tangling and his cock pressing near her heat.

It had been so many years since he'd held this woman in his arms, but it was as though he could remember each time. First when they were fumbling teenagers, then later as young adults, eager for sex any time they could find the time and the place. The last time had been after Nathan's funeral, with the storm raging outside and their desperate attempts to find comfort in each other's arms, yearning to feel alive as they buried their sorrow.

And while the past moved through his mind, he was determined to make this time different. Older and wiser. More about pleasure and less about desperation. More about her and less about his own needs.

With his tongue emulating the sex act, he felt her hips pressing upward and his aching cock seeking relief. Wanting her to be ready for him, he kissed his way back down her body before settling his mouth on her sex. She gasped, and her hands flattened on the mattress, her fingertips digging into the sheets.

Holding her legs steady, he licked and sucked, the taste of her as intoxicating as he remembered so many years ago. His dad had once sat him and Nathan down, telling them that sex with the woman they loved was unlike sex with any other woman they would ever be with. At the time he'd rolled his eyes, but now the evidence was before him. He had loved Nora all those years ago, and now, with her again, it was unlike anyone else.

Before his thoughts could travel anywhere else, he sucked on her clit and she cried out, her short fingernails now lightly scraping over his scalp. He felt her come on his tongue and he continued to lap his fill as her legs slowly stopped quivering.

Lifting his head, he grinned as he kissed his way back up her body again, landing on her lips. Kissing her hard, he let her taste her own unique essence and loved the moan that came from deep within her chest.

Their kiss slowed, and he lifted his head. "Babe, if we do nothing else today, believe me when I say I'm good."

With her hands clutching onto his arms, she gasped, "Please, Tate, don't stop now."

Grinning, he reached his hand to the side where he had tossed his wallet earlier. Pulling out a condom, he ripped the foil with his teeth and leaned upward to roll it onto his cock. Settling back between the cradle of her thighs, he entered her slowly.

He closed his eyes and grit his teeth at the sensation of her tight warmth gripping his cock. Inch by inch, he slid further until he was finally seated to the hilt.

"Tate."

Her voice was barely above a whisper, but he opened his eyes and stared at the sheer beauty lying under him. No longer full of doubt or hesitation, her smile and gaze radiated an emotion he was afraid to define but wanted to own. Sliding his nose along hers, he whispered, "What do you need, babe?"

"Take whatever you need, and in doing so, you give me what I desire. Just you."

Her words scored through him, and his breath left him in a rush. Holding her gaze, he trusted her words and began moving, thrusting deeply. They quickly caught their rhythm, the ebb and flow of a mating dance that was as old as time, but right now, for them, fresh and new.

Her hips lifted to meet his, and he shifted his angle for maximum penetration. Her smile had left, replaced by a heated look of intense need, an expression he was sure was mirrored on his own face. Her legs widened as she wrapped her feet around his back, her heels digging into his ass.

He could tell he was not going to last and wanted her to come again. He leaned down and pulled her nipple into his mouth, nipping the bud before easing the sting with his tongue. While still thrusting, he shifted his weight slightly to the side and skimmed his hand from her breast over her tummy to her clit. She cried out, tightening around his cock and digging her fingernails into his back.

His name on her lips as she came jolted through the past and pierced his heart. That was all it took for him to feel his balls tighten as he continued to thrust, finally roaring through his release. Keeping his weight on his arms, he continued to glide in and out of her warm, tight sex. He tried to drag in a breath but was uncertain he could take in enough oxygen to keep from passing out. Rolling to the side, he brought her body with him, falling to his back and holding her tightly onto his chest. There, bodies still connected, they panted through their smiles, their heartbeats mingling together.

After a few minutes, he reached down and snagged the covers, jerking them up to her neck, hating to hide her luscious body but wanting to keep her warm. Shifting her to the side, he kissed her lightly, mumbling against her lips. "Be right back."

He headed to the bathroom and took care of the condom before slipping back under the covers. Drawn together like magnets, they moved easily, her head on his chest and his arms pulling her in close. He felt so comfortable with her tucked into his embrace, it was as though the years had fallen away leaving them more worldly but bound just as tightly together.

Her fingers trailed along his jaw, and he stared into her eyes. "I'd give anything to know what you're thinking, babe."

Her fingers slid to the back of his head, gliding along his scalp. "This all seems so familiar, and yet everything about you is also different. Your body is bigger, your jaw more square. Your hair is shorter than when you were in high school but longer than when you were in the military. We both have more years and experience behind us, but it was as though there had been no one else. I know that sounds weird…"

"It doesn't sound weird at all, Nora. When I first saw you laying on the bed, all I could think of was that your body was so beautiful and familiar, and yet the years had only made you more desirable. You admitted that you never loved anyone the way you loved me, and I've told you it was the same for me."

"So where does that leave us, Tate?"

He knew the moment was coming when they were going to have to face the hard discussion of where to go from here. He knew what he wanted… *and that's her with me.*

"First things first. We get dressed, we get something to eat, and then we'll come back here and talk."

Lifting her eyebrow, she asked, "Just talk?"

Barking out a laugh, he responded. "We'll talk to begin with, but I have no doubt we'll end up right back here all night long."

2 7

Nora was changed and standing in her kitchen by the time Tate walked out of the bathroom, fresh from his shower. Wearing a slouchy sweatshirt and yoga pants with thick socks warming her feet, she grinned as he moved his gaze over her. Dropping a menu on the counter, she said, "Before you say anything, I thought I'd suggest we eat here. I know we could go out, but... well, I kind of like just having some *us* time."

Tilting his head to the side, his brow lowered. "Sweetheart, *us time* is my favorite time, but I don't mind taking you out. Are you sure?"

"It's cold outside and warm in here. There are lots of people out there, and in here it's just you and me. The idea of just the two of us *staying* just the two of us right now works for me."

Grinning, he nodded. "I couldn't have said it better."

After perusing the menu, she made the call. As she reached into her purse to pull out her credit card, his hand slapped down onto the counter, his credit card in front of her. Knowing it would be useless to argue, she read off the number and then disconnected. "I could've paid for dinner, you know."

He leaned in and kissed her. "It was my suggestion we go out to dinner, so it's my treat." He opened her refrigerator and pulled out two beers. Holding the long necks in one hand, he linked fingers with her, and they walked to her sofa.

It did not take long for their dinner to arrive and, setting the various containers on her counter, they piled their plates high. Eschewing her small table, they walked back over to the sofa. Making themselves comfortable, they sat in silence while their chopsticks moved effortlessly and their moans of appreciation filled the air.

Licking her lips, she asked, "What is it about Chinese food? It's always amazing and always hits the spot!"

Laughing, he shook his head. "I don't know, but you're right. I've had Chinese food all over the world, and it's all been good."

As they finished the food and placed the empty plates onto the coffee table, shadows slowly began creeping into the room as the sun was setting. The sky was cast in streaks of gold and rose, pink and blue.

"Do you remember lying on the hay in the loft of the barn, staring out toward the sun setting over the mountains?"

He turned and looked toward her, the smile playing about his lips indicating that he had the same memory. "Nora, I think I remember everything that we used to do. Playing, riding horses, me letting you ride on the tractor, and yes, you snuggled in my arms in the hayloft."

She smiled, reaching across the cushion to hold his hand. As memories continued to assault her, she sighed. "You know, Daddy and Mama thought the world of you. So did Nathan. I know he was your best friend, but he once told me that you were the only guy that he could imagine ever allowing me to be with."

Tate shifted so that he was facing her, his eyes warm. "I loved Nathan, but I had no idea he said that to you. That's good… I'm glad to know that." He looked down and linked his fingers with hers, giving a little squeeze. "I loved your parents, also, Nora, so it's good to know they felt that way about me. But I don't doubt that after I broke up with you, they didn't feel the same way."

Shaking her head, she squeezed her eyes tightly shut for a few seconds before settling her gaze back on him. "They still loved you, Tate. They knew how upset I was, and they were upset for me. Daddy told me that war changed men, but that you'd come back to me. I used to think he just said that because he missed Nathan so much."

Tate winced and his fingers twitched against hers.

"I'm not saying that to make you feel bad, honey. He missed both of you. Funny, though, Mama used to say the same thing. She'd pat my cheek and tell me that one day my prince would come. I'd roll my eyes and tell her that life wasn't like a fairytale, but she'd just smile like she knew something I didn't know."

He turned completely so that he faced her, and his back was to the sunset. Seeing the brilliant colors of the sky in the background behind him caused her breath to catch in her throat. "I always thought you were the most beautiful man."

"I was just thinking that I've never seen anything more beautiful than you, Nora."

Their hands were linked between them, their gazes never wavering. She wanted to ask him what they were doing and where they were going, but fear choked the words, holding them in her heart.

"Don't be afraid, sweetheart," he said.

How does he do that? How does he see so deeply inside of me? "I'm terrified," she whispered.

He lifted his hand and cupped her face, and she leaned her cheek into his palm. "So am I," he confessed.

Her eyes popped open in surprise. "You? Why?"

"Because now that I have you back in my life, I don't want this to end. You're the only woman I've ever loved. The only woman I've ever seen a future with. But we're not kids anymore. And I know that you've lived in Wyoming your whole life. You have a job here, friends here, and a life here. What I want you to think about is moving to Maine. I know that's asking a lot, but that's where my job is. My family is here, and I'll always come back to see them, so it's not like you'd leave them forever. But I also know it's asking a lot, and I know it might be asking too much. That's why I'm terrified."

Her chest depressed as the air rushed from her lungs. *Move? Move to Maine?* She had no idea why the suggestion of moving caught her off guard. *After all, if we were going to be together, one of us has to be willing to move.* She had been unsure that he wanted them to be together. The most she had allowed herself to hope for was that he would want to try a long-distance relationship to begin with. A slight snort erupted as she realized that, with Tate, his decisions were usually big.

As these thoughts crashed into her, she became aware of the expression of uncertainty on his face. She sighed heavily. "I suppose I wondered if you'd ever want to move back to the ranch, but I know that's not going to happen. I mean, even your parents have moved out of the main ranch house."

Squeezing his hand, she said, "I'm sorry, Tate, all kinds of thoughts came flying at me. I didn't expect you to want me to move. At least not now. I wasn't sure you wanted to be with me or thought that maybe you'd want to date long-distance for a while."

"I'm through fuckin' around, Nora. I'm older and wiser and know what I want. And what I want is you. You were the girl of my heart and now the woman of my dreams, and I'd be a fuckin' fool to let you go now that I found you again."

Her heart raced as tears threatened to spill. Leaning forward, she kissed him gently, finding it hard to catch her breath. Settling back, she sucked in a deep breath before letting it out slowly. "This feels really weird. I know you're on pins and needles waiting to see what I'm going to say, but it's not a simple yes."

"It could be. It could be just as easy as that."

Shaking her head, she said, "Tate, it's like you said. I'm also older and wiser. I get that your job is in Maine, and as a nurse, I can get a job somewhere else. I certainly don't think that Rawlins Medical Center is the only place to work. But before I make a move, I'd need to find a place near you and that would take time. I'd need to check openings at hospitals and doctor offices and that doesn't happen overnight. There's also the matter of your job."

He jerked slightly, his brow lowering. "My job? What are your concerns about my job, babe?"

"Seriously, Tate? You once broke up with me because you felt like your job was too dangerous. I'm assuming with the missions you go on now that you sometimes face danger. How is that different? I lost you once and almost lost myself in the process. If we move forward, I need to know that you're not going to get scared and leave me again."

"I can assure you that my job now is nothing like when I was a SEAL. That doesn't mean that sometimes I'm not in a risky situation, but I'm trained so that those risks are minimal. Most of what LSI does is security in one form or another as well as investigations. My job is a hell of a lot safer than the average policeman, and while I do have to travel, I'm home a lot."

He scooted around on the cushions and gently pulled her over his lap, settling her in his embrace. She closed her eyes as she allowed the feel of his arms around her sink into her very core. *God, this feels good. So, so right.* Opening her eyes, she saw that he was staring as though he could see deep inside her.

"Nora, you and I both know there are no guarantees in life. But I can promise you here and now that I will love you faithfully. The dreams we had when we were young about getting married, having a family, growing old together... those are still my dreams. I know they won't take place here in Wyoming on the ranch, but they can still take place."

"I used to dream of leaving Wyoming and following you around the world." Chuckling, she added, "After my parents passed, I guess I really hadn't thought about settling anywhere but here. I don't care where we are as long as we're together."

His breath halted as he cupped her face, holding her steady in front of him. "Please, be clear with me, babe. What exactly are you saying?"

Her top teeth hit her bottom lip for a few seconds, then she smiled. "I'm saying that I want to be with you, Tate. And if that's in Maine, then that's where we'll be." She saw his smile widen and she hurried to add, "But... it's not going to happen instantly. I need time to make sure what we're doing is right. Let's be honest... you kind of swooped back into town and we've had an intense couple of days. It would be so easy to assume that our love is just going to explode so big that nothing else matters. I know you want me to say a big 'yes', but I need to make sure we're doing this right and smart."

His lips curved and he kissed her soundly. "Sweetheart, everything you just said makes perfect sense. I want you, but I want you to be sure."

Sucking in her lips for a second, her brow crinkled. "So, how should we do this?"

"Well, I'm leaving tomorrow to meet Clay in California. We have an easy job there for a couple of days. I'd already told LSI to route me back through here on my way to Maine because I wanted to check on Dad one last time. That'll give you time to think about things. I want you with me, but I know it's asking a lot. So, we can arrange for you to come to Maine, check out employment opportunities and all that."

Smiling, she pulled him back in for a kiss. "Thank you, Tate. Thank you for wanting me and thank you for not rushing me."

Their kisses started out gently but soon flamed hot. With one arm on her back and the other under her knees, he stood and carried her back into the bedroom. Making the most of their time, they made love long into the night before they fell asleep in each other's arms.

Tate turned away from Clay to hide his grin. They had been in California for two days, reviewing the security system for an up-and-coming starlet who had just purchased and moved into a massive mansion. The original security system was older, not up to today's standards. She had been plagued by a fan-turned-stalker, and while the police now had him in custody, her agent wanted her system to be the best. LSI did not install systems but could go in, analyze a customer's potential weak spots, and design a security system. Then they could make recommendations as to the best company to install.

The reason Tate was hiding his grin had just walked into the room where he and Clay were finishing their work. Young, tan, white veneer teeth, blonde hair with extensions to her waist, and thin, honed body with enhanced breasts. He had no doubt on the silver screen she was beautiful, but in person, her appearance was so plastic that she looked like a human Barbie. And she had the hots for Clay.

After the initial few hours on the first day when her interest intensified the more Clay tried to separate, Tate promised that he would not leave the two of them alone. Not that Clay couldn't handle himself, but for his protection and the protection of LSI, it was best to make sure that neither of them was alone with her.

Having completed the analysis and security workup proposal, they were almost at the end of this mission. The starlet's ever-present giggle was beginning to sound more like a snarl as she realized the two men were getting ready to leave and she had not obtained the prize she was so sure was hers.

Clay offered an audible sigh of relief as her manager walked into the room. As they presented the paperwork to the manager for his review, she began a litany of complaints about the system and about them. With a practiced hand, the manager ignored her as he continued to deal with Tate and Clay.

They were gratefully finished just as her voice reached a level of screeching, but her manager jerked his hand up with his palm in her face and her mouth snapped closed. Turning back to the Keepers, he thanked them and said that LSI's office would have the signed papers for the system by the end of the day.

With a nod, they walked out of her huge mansion in the suburbs of LA into the bright sunshine. Climbing into their rental, they drove back toward the hotel.

Before Tate had a chance to say anything, Clay sighed heavily and said, "No drama."

Glancing to the side, Tate lifted his brow in question.

Clay shook his head and continued, "That's what I want. No drama. Sure as fuck not like her, but not even like the women you all end up with."

Considering wives and fiancées of the Keepers were all strong, intelligent, kindhearted women, Tate was uncertain what Clay was referencing. "What the fuck are you looking for?"

"Simple. A good woman who has no drama. And is pretty. And smart. Oh yeah, and can cook—"

Barking out a laugh that interrupted Clay's litany of female virtues, Tate shook his head. "So, you're looking for a smart, pretty, good in the kitchen woman, and presumably good in the bedroom, who has no drama? Where the hell are you going to find this paragon of womanhood?"

"Not on a mission, that's for sure! Hell, every one of you had to rescue somebody. I want to find someone simple that I don't have to worry myself sick about rescuing."

"Okay, that makes sense... most guys would want that. But you still haven't answered where you're going to find her," Tate continued, trying to contain his laughter.

"I don't know. Somewhere everyday... like in the frozen food section of the grocery store or in a line at a bank. The kind of place where you just go in, you're not expecting anything, and then you see her, and she immediately grabs your attention. You strike up a conversation, you trade phone numbers, and boom...

you start dating."

"Just like that?"

Clay huffed, scrubbing his hand over his face. "Yeah, just like that."

Pulling up to the hotel, Tate handed the rental off to the valet. "We got finished a little earlier today than we thought. Want me to see if Babs can get us an earlier flight?"

"Yeah, see what she can do. I'm ready to hit the hotel's gym and pool for some laps. Let me know if we're going to leave early."

Tate entered his hotel room, appreciating the accommodations that LSI always acquired. Glancing at the king-sized bed he had all to himself, he thought of Nora. *What would I give to have her with me right now?* Glancing at his watch, he knew she was at the hospital. Flopping backward onto the bed, he closed his eyes, counting down the hours until she got off her shift and they could talk. *Tomorrow... I'll see her tomorrow.*

It had only been two days and Nora missed Tate, thinking of him constantly. Somehow, the time they'd spent together, while short in duration, had managed to heal the breach of so many years. Now, able to look into the past through his eyes, thinking of where he was and what he was doing at the time of their separation allowed forgiveness to settle in. Understanding the past made thinking of the future so much easier.

Back at work, walking through the halls of the

hospital, it became clear that it would be so easy to work somewhere else. *I love being a nurse, but it doesn't have to be here.* When she was younger, she longed to see more of the world, but with one loss after another, it seemed as though Rawlins would be the only place she would ever live. Now, the idea of moving somewhere new and different with Tate slid through her, causing her step to be a little lighter.

"Nora!"

Her name had been called out from the office she just passed by, and she backtracked to peek inside, observing Dr. Hawkins sitting at his desk.

"It's good to see you again. I haven't had a chance to let you know how sorry I am about what happened. We were all so shocked and upset."

She smiled in appreciation of his concern. "Thank you. I was very shocked as well, but I'm fine and all the prisoners are in jail."

He glanced down at his desk, his fingers rifling through papers in front of him. "I don't suppose they gave away much information about their operation, did they?"

"Are you talking about the drugs they were producing?" Gaining his nod, she shook her head. "I know they had an outbuilding that they were using as a meth lab that was not connected to the cabin where I was held. I was never in that area and even though I was close, I wasn't there long enough to have been exposed to anything directly. I'm aware of the risks considering there were probably traces of meth in the cabin. So far, I'm fine."

"Good, good. I'm glad your ordeal was no worse than it was."

Glancing into the hall behind her and seeing it occupied, she looked back at him and leaned against the doorframe, lowering her voice. "Of course, besides me being back at work today, everyone is talking about Mary's involvement with them."

He jerked his head up and down in short nods, shifting in his seat. He slid his glasses off and pinched the bridge of his nose, then sighed heavily, "Yes, that was surprising. We've been looking into our procedures here to see what we can do to close up any holes for the staff stealing drugs. It's a problem in any hospital or medical center, but the higher-ups are looking into what needs to be done."

"Good," she exuded. "I have no doubt that the police and FBI are looking closely at the hospital to see if there was anyone else besides Mary who was involved.

His gaze jerked up to hers, a surprised, wide-eyed expression passing quickly over his face before settling. "Of course. I know they'll be looking at everything, but I'm sure Mary must have been acting on her own. I can't imagine there was anyone else. As a pharmacy tech, she had the access." He sucked in a deep breath and dropped his gaze back to his desk. "At least I hope she was working alone. Yes, I'm sure she was." He shook his head and replaced his glasses back onto his face.

"They were preppers and who knows what else she supplied them with." As soon as the words left her mouth, she glanced over to the table at the side of his office, noting there were no boxes. Just as quickly, her gaze shot back to his, finding him staring at her.

A strange sense of unease slithered through her. "Well, if there's nothing else, I need to head down to the nurses' station." She pushed off the doorframe, hesitated, then added, "I'll go ahead and tell you before you hear through the grapevine, but I plan on turning in my letter of resignation fairly soon. I'm going to be moving to another state and will start looking for a position there."

Eyes wide again, he leaned back in his chair. "I thought you were born and raised here."

"I was, but my family is all gone, and while I have friends here, I now have the opportunity to travel somewhere else with someone I care a great deal about."

"Well, I wish you the very best," he offered with a smile. "You'll be missed here."

Thanking him, she turned and left his office, heading to the nurses' station. An hour later, she walked into the cafeteria for an early lunch. After grabbing a chicken wrap, chips, and a drink, she looked around for a seat, her gaze landing on the booth in the back corner. Grinning as she walked over to it, she thought of the week before when Tate slid into the booth seat with her, effectively trapping her in place. She began eating but now felt the loneliness of not having Tate at her side.

Her phone vibrated and she glanced at the screen, seeing Tate's number. Connecting, she greeted, "Hey, sweetheart."

"I didn't think you'd be able to answer, babe, but I'm glad to hear your voice."

"I'm taking an early lunch, and guess where I'm sitting?" Not giving him a chance to reply, she continued, "I'm sitting in the corner booth where we were a week ago."

Chuckling, he said, "I'm surprised you didn't kick me out of there, but honest to God, Nora, it was the only way I could get you to talk to me."

"I'm glad you did. I'm glad you didn't give up on me."

"Never again," he vowed.

They were silent for just a moment, then she asked, "Are you finished with your job?"

"Yes. The job was a pain in the ass and I'm glad it's over."

"Is it super-secret?"

Chuckling again, he said, "Nah, but I'll tell you about it when I see you. I know today was your first day back and that's why I wanted to check and see how you were doing."

"That's sweet, but I'm really fine. I thought it might be strange to walk into the hospital considering the way I was taken out the last time, but it's almost as though that didn't happen."

"Is everyone being cool with you?" he asked.

"There are questions, and I get the feeling some people are handling me with kid gloves, but overall, it's fine. It seems like most people are talking about Mary and her involvement in stealing drugs in the hospital."

"Yeah, that's bound to bring up questions."

"I did have a conversation with Dr. Hawkins." She hesitated, then sucked in a deep breath and blurted, "I let him know that I was going to turn in my letter of resignation sometime soon and would be moving."

"Oh, babe, you've got no idea how hearing those words make me feel! I want to be there right now to plant a kiss on you to let you know how grateful I am to have you back in my life." She was silent and he asked, "Are you okay? Do you regret telling him—"

"No, no regrets. I know it seems rushed, but I don't want to live without you one day more than I have to."

"Was he okay with your plans?"

"We didn't talk about it much. He was more interested in what happened at the cabin. I think the idea that a meth lab was there was shocking to him. He wanted to know what they had said to me, if I'd seen it—"

"What the hell, Nora? Was it just curiosity or was he digging for what you knew?"

"Uh... well, I'm sure that he was upset that someone from the hospital was caught stealing. He's the Senior Physician, so he feels responsible for what happens."

"Did it seem like more?"

She thought about Dr. Hawkins' expressions and the vibe she felt as his gaze searched hers. "Um…"

"Tell me."

In those two words, his tone changed completely, going from loving to concerned. "Well, it's probably nothing, but he seemed nervous when talking about Mary. It was as though he wanted to convince me that she worked alone and no one else was working with her. When I mentioned that the police and the FBI would be looking into who else could be involved, he got very fidgety." Tate was quiet, and she felt foolish for having said anything. "I know it's nothing, just a bit of an overactive imagination right now—"

"I'm calling Levi."

Blinking in surprise, she dropped her sandwich back to the plate. "Tate, there's no reason to go overboard—"

"I'm not going overboard, Nora. It's not like Levi is going to march in there and arrest him, but you're right about them looking into anyone else who might have had something to do with the thefts. The hospital is going to be looked at carefully anyway, and I'm just gonna let Levi know he needs to keep an eye on the man."

"Don't make me sorry that I talked to you, Tate."

"Babe, I've just gotten you back into my life and I don't want anything to fuck with that. Your name is not going to come up to Dr. Hawkins, but there's no reason not to let the investigators have all the information we can give them."

She agreed with what he was saying, but it still felt strange to have someone so protective looking out for her. Wanting to steer the conversation around to something easier, she asked, "So, when are you going to be coming back?"

"Since we finished early today, we were able to get Babs to get us an earlier flight."

"Babs?"

"She works at LSI and is now married to another Keeper, Drew. They're both good friends and I can't wait for you to meet them."

"I'm looking forward to that, too."

"That was the other reason I was calling—to let you know that I'll be heading there this afternoon. I think I'll drive directly to the ranch so I can go ahead and check on my parents and then be ready for you as soon as you get off work."

A smile spread across her face. "That is the best news you could have given me!" She glanced at her watch and said, "I've got to get back up to the floor. Have a safe flight, and I'll call you as soon as I get off work."

Disconnecting, she threw away her trash and headed back up to her floor, her heart full.

29

Nora changed her mind about waiting to talk to HR, stopping by their office on her way back up to her floor. Explaining to one of the administrators that she did not have long because she was due at her station, she told them that she needed to get information on the resignation process so that she would not lose her health insurance before finding another job. The administrator was helpful, giving her the forms and information she needed.

She could hardly wait to see Tate at the end of the day, letting him know that she had moved the process of her resignation up even more. *Hopefully, I won't have a problem getting a job in Maine!* Pushing that thought away, she decided to focus the time with Tate on enjoying his company. *After he leaves tomorrow, I can get online and start searching.*

Her afternoon shift was uneventful, and she was grateful that the other nurses on her floor were now used to seeing her and no longer talking about the kidnapping. The gossip about Mary and drug thefts was still going strong, though.

Near the end of her shift, she typed her patient notes and reports into a computer at the back of the nurses' station, where she had a little quiet and privacy. Seeing Dr. Hawkins' name on several prescriptions was not unusual and yet brought his jittery behavior back to mind. *Why would he be so insistent that Mary must have been working on her own? How would he know that? Is he simply trying to shine a better light on the rest of the hospital staff, or is he trying to deflect anyone looking at him?*

Peering around and seeing no one close by, she tapped through several screens on the computer, searching for his name on other prescription requests. Considering he was a doctor in a hospital, there were hundreds of prescriptions—not unusual and certainly not alarming. Wondering if there were any drugs he prescribed more than others, she immediately went to pseudoephedrine. It did not require a prescription, but at the medical center, all medications had to go through a prescriber.

What popped up on her screen was a long list of prescriptions for that drug, and when she clicked through the records, she found that almost all of them were filled at the pharmacy by Mary. Sucking in a quick breath, she looked around nervously to see if anyone was close by. Feeling foolish, she turned back to the computer screen. She considered trying to print the screens she was looking at but didn't want anyone to find out she was searching. Uncertain what to do, she slid her phone from her pocket and began taking pictures of each screen as she continued to click through the pharmaceutical orders between Dr. Hawkins and Mary.

Suddenly, the computer screen froze and did not move even when she continued to hit enter or backspace. *Somebody else must be on the same pages! Shit! Can they see that I'm in them also?* Fearful that it might be evident that someone else in the hospital was looking at these files, she did not have a chance to log off before the prescription screens went blank. *Are they being deleted? Can someone even do that?*

Her heart pounding, she quickly logged out. Standing, her eyes still pinned on the now-dark screen, she took a step backward from the computer as though the physical separation would erase the cyber connection. Breathing heavily, she tried to focus. She glanced around but there was no one watching her. The desire to get safely to Tate filled her mind, and she grabbed her purse and coat, and with quick goodbyes to the few other nurses around the station, she hurried out of the building.

Jumping into her car, she locked the doors and jammed the key into the ignition. Blowing out a deep breath, she closed her eyes for a moment, attempting to still her nerves. *It was probably nothing... I've got a crazy, overactive imagination.* Even as that thought moved through her mind, she couldn't wait to get to Tate.

Sucking in a deep breath before letting it out slowly, she started her car and pulled out of the hospital parking lot.

"Dad, I thought I'd let you know that Nora has decided to turn in her resignation." Tate and his father were standing outside the barn, enjoying the snow-covered vista of the ranch after the storm. Thomas had taken Clay inside the barn to show off the horses.

Frank turned his warm gaze upon him. "Son, I can't think of anything that makes me happier than knowing the two of you are going to be together. Your mom is going to be beside herself."

Shoving his hands into his pockets, he grimaced slightly. "I know she's been an important part of your life for a long time and now I'm taking her away."

"Tate, there's nothing that a parent wants more for their children than for them to be happy. It's been our pleasure to have Nora be part of our lives all these years, but we've known she hasn't been happy for a long time. And honestly, because she seemed like your other half, we couldn't imagine that you were completely happy either. So, if we only get to see her a couple of times a year now, it's worth it knowing that you're together and happy."

Tate turned and looked out over the horizon, the ranch as beautiful as he always remembered. The sunlight sparkled off the snow as the sun started to sink into the west. Hoping that Nora was almost at the ranch, he wanted to share that sunset with her.

His mom and Caroline stepped onto the wide front porch of the ranch house. "Dinner will be ready as soon as Nora gets here," his mom called out.

Looking back toward the barn, he watched as Clay and Thomas walked out, laughing and talking together. Smiling, he knew that he had it all. Good job, good family, good friends, and soon, the woman he loved would be at his side.

His phone vibrated in his pocket, and he looked down, seeing Nora's name. "Hey, babe. Are you almost here?"

"Tate! Somebody's following me!"

Immediately on alert, he signaled Clay and started jogging toward the house where the rental SUV was parked. "Talk to me!" He put her on speaker so that Clay, Thomas, and Frank could hear what was happening.

"I started doing some checking this afternoon and discovered that Dr. Hawkins has been sending a lot of prescriptions for pseudoephedrine with the direction that Mary fills them. I think there may be a connection between him and her when it comes to the drugs that were being stolen."

"Goddammit, Nora, who's following you?"

"I left the hospital, and I'm on Highway 23. There's an SUV that's been behind me ever since I pulled out of the hospital parking lot, and I can't tell, but I swear, I think it could be Dr. Hawkins. He keeps driving really close to my bumper."

"I'm on my way to you. Stay on the phone. I want you talking to me the whole time!" Turning, he looked at Clay and said, "Call Levi. Tell him that—"

"Already on it," Clay acknowledged, pulling out his phone and dialing.

"I'll call Billy," Thomas yelled, his actions mimicking Clay's.

Reaching the vehicles, Tate and Clay climbed into their rental SUV while Thomas and Frank climbed into one of the ranch trucks. Firing them up, they headed out.

Clay looked at him and said, "Your mom had already invited Levi to dinner since she knew you'd be here. He says he's on his way and should be close behind Nora."

"Nora, Levi is not too far behind you. Drive safely and keep telling me what's happening and what you see. I want you talking to me the whole time that you're driving."

"When I look in the rearview mirror, all I see is him right on my tail! I know how to drive on snow, but it's icy! He's too close and this road curves!"

"Babe, don't go too fast, just keep steady and drive as calmly as possible." Unable to take his own advice, he peeled down the snow-packed lane leading from the ranch house. He could not stand the silence, so he said, "Talk to me, sweetheart."

Cutting in, Clay said, "Levi thinks he has them in his sights."

"Levi is coming up behind you."

"Tate, I can't see anybody other than who's right behind me."

"Don't focus on anything other than the road in front of you," he gently ordered. Heart pounding, he took a curve too fast and started to skid. Correcting the vehicle, he slowed slightly.

"Man, don't wreck now. You're not helping her if you can't get to her safely," Clay said.

Fighting the urge to tell his friend to fuck off, he tightened his grip on the steering wheel. "Keep talking to me, Nora."

"I'm getting closer! I can see the ranch in the distance, and I know the Double T sign isn't far off."

A scream sounded through the phone, and Tate jolted. "What's happening?" The only answer was another scream. "Fuck!" He pounded the steering wheel, pressing harder on the accelerator. Looking ahead, he could see that he was nearing the road, the Double T sign just ahead.

"He's ramming me!" Nora screamed into the phone.

The sound of squealing tires and more screams were all that met his ears.

30

Nora knew how to drive in inclement weather and kept her small SUV in good condition, but her tires could not cling to the snow-packed roads while trying to evade the large SUV behind her. Her phone was clipped to the holder on the dashboard, and she was trying to draw strength from Tate's voice while letting him know what was happening.

The booming sound of the other vehicle hitting her from behind caused her to swerve while screaming in frustration and fear. Jerking on the steering wheel, she managed to stay on the road. Just ahead, she could see the tall wooden sign for the Double T Ranch and several trucks and SUVs coming down the lane. Screaming again, all she could think of was getting to Tate.

The gunning of an engine met her ears, and the SUV was pulling to the side of her. Before she could react, it clipped the back end of her vehicle and she began swerving around. Continuing to scream, she fought with the steering wheel but could not control her SUV from skidding off the road. Coming to a stop against a snowbank pointing downward, her heart pounded as the airbag forced her back against the seat before deflating.

Her hands were still clutching the steering wheel and her foot was still jammed onto the brake even as her door was wrenched open and Tate's ravaged face was just in front of her.

"Baby, are you hurt? Can you move?"

Before she had a chance to answer, she heard him yelling for an ambulance. Trying to catch her breath, she said, "No, no, I don't need one. I'm okay. Tate, I'm okay."

He grabbed her face in his hands, his gaze searching her eyes. Blinking, she nodded and repeated, "I'm okay."

He twisted his head and looked at her frozen posture. He gently pried her fingers from the steering wheel and leaned his body close to hers to unbuckle her seatbelt. Wrapping her arms around his neck, he lifted her up and out of her vehicle.

With her head resting on his shoulder, she saw Frank and Thomas climbing down the snowbank toward them. Frank grabbed her purse and phone while Thomas helped Tate maneuver up the incline.

Once up on the road, she gasped, seeing the dark SUV upside down on the other side of the road. Clay and Levi were trying to get the doors open. Sirens were sounding in the distance.

Tate's lips were pressed against her forehead as he murmured, "I've got you, sweetheart."

Clinging tighter, she shifted so that her lips met his. As she pulled back, she caught his wide-eyed expression. Blowing out her breath, she said, "I'm glad, Tate, because I'm all yours."

The ambulance came and checked her out while the firemen resorted to cutting off the door of the dark SUV. Inside was Dr. Hawkins... alive, but with a broken leg, broken arm, and several severe cuts and contusions. Billy had placed Dr. Hawkins under arrest and accompanied him to the hospital.

Tate carried her to his vehicle, allowing Clay to drive them up to the ranch house with Frank and Thomas following. Susan and Caroline waited anxiously on the porch, clucking and fussing over Nora as he carried her in.

She insisted that she could walk, but he hushed her with another kiss. "My heart is still pounding from hearing you scream," he said. "Right now, all I want is you in my arms."

Susan and Caroline prepared trays of food, setting them in the large den so that everyone could remain comfortable while eating.

Clay looked up and said, "Levi is coming over. He said the FBI has pulled the hospital and bank records from Dr. Hawkins, but he'd like to know what you found as well, Nora."

"Can't that wait?" Tate asked, hating that Nora was going to have to be questioned. He felt the soft touch on his arm and looked down, seeing her hand resting on him.

"It's okay. Honest."

Her gentle touch and words helped to soothe his frustration, but his anger was still at an all-time high. It didn't take long for Levi to arrive, Susan immediately plying him with coffee and food.

Nora explained the strange feeling she got from Dr. Hawkins and how she looked up his prescription records in the computer. She showed the screenshots from her phone and Levi had her send them to him.

"He may have thought he was deleting them, but we're able to go back and recapture everything," Levi said. "Even in the hospital, he was already beginning to talk. It seems that he and Mary have been working together for a while, both getting money from the meth productions. He wrote extra prescriptions when she was working, and she would always take more than was needed. Then they would simply change the records."

"It would've been very possible for Mary to have worked on her own," Nora surmised, "but I also knew that it would be very easy for someone else to be involved. I never dreamed it was Dr. Hawkins, but it was the strangest feeling that I got when talking to him. He seemed nervous, fidgety, and when I brought up Mary, he insisted he felt like she was working by herself. There would be no reason for him to know that or even think that."

Clay looked over at Tate and grinned. "Instead of being a nurse, maybe she should come work for Mace."

Growling once again, Tate said, "Don't give her any ideas!"

Laughing, she shook her head. "No, nursing is the career for me. But right now, I'll be very happy to take several weeks off before I find another job."

With his arm wrapped around her, Tate looked at her carefully. *Is she saying what I think she's saying?* Catching her smile, he asked, "And what will you be doing during your weeks off?"

"I hope I'll be with you in Maine."

He pulled her into his lap, kissing her soundly. She pulled back, blushing adorably as the others in the room grinned with enthusiasm.

"I have to see about getting out of my lease, but I don't think it will be any problem with HR at the hospital. I know you need to go back, and I need a little time here to get my affairs in order. But I think I'll very soon be ready to join you."

That night, after goodbyes were said to Levi, Clay was off in the guesthouse, and the rest of the family slept, Tate and Nora clung together in his room. With the moonlight illuminating off the snow casting a glow into the bedroom, they quietly made love. Cognizant of her earlier accident, he just wanted to hold her, but she insisted on sharing this night worshiping each other's bodies.

The next morning, the family piled in the SUVs and drove to the airport. Clay thanked Tate's family for their hospitality then walked over and kissed Nora on the forehead, whispering "Can't wait to have you part of our group, darlin'."

Tate had already said goodbye to his family, then gently wrapped her in a hug, sealing his lips over hers. "I'm counting down the days, babe."

"A week, maybe two at the tops. And then I'll be with you," she promised.

With another kiss goodbye, Tate and Clay climbed into the plane. Once more, Tate lifted the visor on his window and stared out over the flyover states. Snow-capped mountains and plains, houses and barns nestled among farms. Roads that weaved between small towns, connecting everyone below. As the plane flew east toward Maine, he smiled at the idea of Nora joining him. *They say home is where the heart is. As soon as she gets there, it'll be home.*

31

THREE MONTHS LATER

Nora moved through the kitchen, her mind focused on carefully placing each of the apple pies into the plastic pie container. She had made four, using Susan's prize-winning recipe, but only had three pie containers. Unable to come up with another solution, she decided one would sit on her lap as they drove to the LSI compound.

Casting her gaze around, she smiled at the updated countertops and floors. She had not wanted Tate to change his house for her, but he swore the kitchen and bathrooms needed updating when he bought the house but had never gotten around to doing so. She insisted on keeping the original wooden cabinets but loved the new granite countertops and tile floor. And since she enjoyed baking, Tate had surprised her with a new stove.

Tate's cottage-style saltbox home sported views of a cove that led to the ocean. Able to see the water from almost every room, she loved his house just as it was.

But the kitchen and bathrooms were not the only improvements he wanted to make. So, with fresh paint in the bedrooms and decorations she brought from Wyoming, they were making his house their own.

In the past months since moving to Maine, she'd found a job working for a small group of general practitioners. She had not found employment in a nearby hospital but discovered that having the opportunity to get to know entire families led to a sincere feeling of job satisfaction. That, plus being able to work days and have her evenings and weekends off made it even better.

She also loved getting to know the other Keepers and their significant others, becoming especially friendly with Julie, Helena, and Sara.

Now, with the pie containers stacked on top of each other and the single wrapped one on the counter, she called out, "I'm ready whenever you are!"

They were soon in his truck, driving to the LSI compound. Tate reached over, his hand pausing between them when he glanced to the side. "You made too many pies. You only have three pie containers."

"I didn't make too many pies. Quite the contrary, I'm hoping I have enough for everyone. The problem is I just don't have enough containers." Twisting around to look up at his smiling face, she asked, "Why are we talking about the number of pies I made?"

"Because one of my favorite things to do with you when you're sitting in my truck is to hold your hand, and I can't do it when you've got an extra pie sitting in your lap."

With her head tilted back, she held his gaze. "It won't

take as long to get there, and then I promise you can hold my hand."

"Have I told you lately that I love you?"

A giggle slipped out, and she nodded. "I believe this morning when we were making love I heard those words. And when we were in the shower. And when you passed through the kitchen earlier." She continued to stare as his face held an intense gaze, soft and warm as it focused on her.

"Nora, having you here with me means everything, sweetheart."

His words speared straight to the heart of her. From the moment she decided to be with him, she never looked back. "Quit making me want to leap over the console and kiss you right now because that would involve cinnamon apple goo-goodness landing all over your truck."

He chuckled, shaking his head. "Goo-goodness? Wouldn't want that, would we?"

An hour later, the fun was in full swing. Mace was a firm believer that the Keepers functioned better on the job when they spent time together building camaraderie off the job and made sure each Keeper felt part of the whole team. Tate was certain Mace had given no thought to the significant others of his employees considering they were all single when the company was developed. But so far, the ones with mates had found perfect matches for the individual Keepers as well as

LSI. Now, with Nora joining Helena, Sara, and Julie, their gatherings grew larger and more fun. He'd been pleased that Nora had become close to all the women, enjoying time with them even when the Keepers were not around.

By the time the pies had been consumed amongst moans of delight and promises from Nora that she would share Tate's mother's recipe, Mace stood to make an announcement. Not a man of many words, he stood with both Sylvie and David pressed to his side and beamed. "Looks like Sylvie's gonna increase our family."

With those simple words, the group erupted in congratulations. Tate was thrilled for his boss but shot a quick glance toward Nora. Her smile appeared genuine, but he could swear there was a specter of longing in her eyes. His arm was already resting on the back of her chair, and he curled his hand to her shoulder.

Rank stood, laughing, pulling Helena up with him. Placing his large hand on her still-flat stomach, he said, "Looks like it's in the water!" More cheers of congratulations followed, and Tate swore he heard a little sigh slip from Nora's lips.

Several hours later, Tate and Nora slipped away to the inside of the lighthouse and climbed the steps to get to the top. He had only brought her up here once when she first came to Maine but wanted to have the opportunity to share the sunset with her.

She stood with her hands on the railing, staring out at the water, and he wrapped his arms around either side of her. They stood for several long minutes watching the ever-changing colors of the sky painted above them.

Twisting her head around and up, she asked, "Do you remember all the sunsets we used to watch at the ranch years ago?"

He squeezed her middle and smiled. "Nora, I remember every one I shared with you."

"Even all those years we weren't together, the sunsets always made me think of you."

She stared up at him with her chin quivering slightly, and he continued, "I was a fuckin' idiot ten years ago, Nora, but I vow to spend the rest of my life making that up to you."

She swiped at the tear that had escaped and shook her head. "Life is life, Tate. We live it day to day, sometimes making mistakes and sometimes reveling in the fact that the stars align, and everything is perfect. And sometimes we have to go through the dark valleys before we can get to the mountaintop. Whatever brought us to right here, right now, today, is simply the path that we needed to take."

Hearing those words from her, he knew the time was right for the ring that he'd had carried in his pocket for the past week. Stepping around to her side, he dropped to one knee. Nervous, he grinned as her eyes widened and she gasped, her hand quickly moving to her mouth.

"If what you say is true, Nora, today is the path that we need to take. And I'd like it to be the start of forever with you." Holding out the ring, he took her shaking left hand and gently slid it on her finger.

Barely giving her a chance to say 'yes', he took to his feet and wrapped his arms around her, his mouth eagerly taking hers in a kiss that sealed their promise.

Two Months Later

Tate sat on his deck, reclined in an Adirondack chair with his feet propped up on the railing, one foot crossed over the other. He and Blake and Clay had spent a rare day off down by the water fishing off his little dock. After lunch, Blake left to pick up Sara, leaving Tate and Clay enjoying a beer in the afternoon sunshine. His phone vibrated in his pocket, and he glanced at the caller ID before answering. "Levi, how are you?"

"I'm good, but the real question is how is married life?"

Tate grinned. "Fuckin' fabulous," he replied. Deciding that too much time had been wasted, he and Nora had gotten married in a small ceremony a few weeks earlier. Tate's family flew to Maine, and with the help of the other Keepers and their wives, they had the wedding on the lawn of their property. The grass was green leading down to the water, flowers that Nora had planted blooming all around. They'd spoken their vows in the late afternoon and danced on their deck and patio as the sun set, painting the sky.

Levi chuckled and said, "Somehow, I knew you'd say that."

"So, what's the story? And, by the way, I just put you on speaker. Clay is here also."

"Today was my last day as an FBI agent."

Tate shared a glance with Clay. He had no doubt it was a bittersweet day for Levi. Levi had been in the military and an agent for the FBI and was now going to be the newest Keeper. "So, when are you heading here?"

"I'm finishing everything here in Wyoming, packing up the U-Haul, and I'll head out in a few days. I've decided to take a week to drive the 2300 miles. I'll do a little sightseeing along the way."

"Mace has the cabin near the lighthouse ready for you. You can move in as soon as you get here and stay until you find your own place."

"I appreciate that. Looking forward to being there and starting work for LSI."

"Be safe on the road. That's a long trip," Tate added.

Levi snorted. "After my Ranger and FBI career, being a tourist for a week will be a piece of cake."

They disconnected after saying goodbye, and Tate took another pull from his beer. Keeping his face toward the water, he grinned while asking, "Still looking for *no-drama*?"

Chuckling, Clay nodded. "Fuck, yeah. Just like what I told you. No drama, pretty, smart, and can cook."

"Tell you what, friend. You find someone like that, I'll celebrate with you. But, honest to God, I'm hoping you find one with just as much drama as the rest of us.

A woman like that will keep you on your toes and make every moment worth it."

The sound of tires on the gravel had them swing their heads around, seeing Nora parking just outside the house. Clay placed his boots on the deck with a thud and stood. "Looks like she's home early, so I'll let you enjoy the rest of your day." Tate stood as well, and the two men shook hands.

"Thanks for the fishing and the beer," Clay said. As Nora stepped up on the deck, he greeted her with a kiss on the cheek. Tossing a wave to both of them, he headed down to his truck.

"You're home early."

She walked straight into his arms and looked up, a sweet smile on her face. "I thought we could spend some time together, but I feel guilty having Clay leave so early."

"Don't worry about it, babe. He's got to pack for a trip. He'll be leaving tomorrow for another mission." Nora simply smiled, not peppering him with questions that he wouldn't be able to answer. Their lives had fit together so smoothly just like he always knew they would.

"I actually came home early because I need to talk to you."

Her voice had taken on a serious tone, and he pulled her close, his gaze moving about her face. "Babe, what's going on?"

She sucked in her lips for a few seconds before releasing a ragged breath. "I was at work today and had one of the doctors look at me—"

The bottom fell out of his stomach and he gasped. Grabbing her jaws with his large hands, he cupped her face, holding her close. "Oh, Jesus, Nora. What's wrong? Whatever it is, we can—"

She shushed him with her fingers over his lips and shook her head. "Nothing's wrong, Tate. Just unexpected... and well, unplanned."

He cocked his head to the side, his brow furrowed in confusion. Before he had a chance to ask further, she grinned.

"I'm pregnant."

His breath caught in his throat as his jaw dropped. Shaking his head slightly, he said, "But... but... I thought... you..."

She lifted her shoulders in a shrug. "The doctors said I *might* not be able to get pregnant. It looks like another little Frankie or Francine will be born in about six months."

He sucked in a quick breath. "You're already past the first three months?"

Nodding, she rushed to explain, "It wasn't that I was keeping it from you... well, not exactly. I must've gotten pregnant soon after moving here, and with all the changes in my life, I truthfully didn't notice I'd skipped a period. I've only been plagued by a little bit of morning sickness, so by the time I became suspicious that I might be pregnant, I was terrified to tell you. I was even terrified to admit it to myself."

"Because of the previous miscarriage?"

"Yes. It's almost as though I was afraid that I would jinx it. But when several more weeks went by and I still hadn't started my period, I decided to check with one of the doctors at work." Her smile widened and shot straight to his heart. "So, technically, I just found out today that we're going to have a baby."

With a whoop, he picked her up and whirled her around. With her feet still dangling above the deck, he held her tight and kissed her. His tongue thrust deep inside her mouth, tangling with hers, shooting bolts of electricity straight to his cock.

She wrapped her legs around his waist, pressing her hot core against his jean-clad erection, and laughed. "So, you want to go upstairs and celebrate?"

Stalking into the house, he grinned. "Oh, hell yeah." Once in the bedroom, he carefully lowered her feet to the floor and slowly peeled her clothes from her body. When she was standing naked in front of him, he dropped to his knees and pressed his lips against her still-flat belly.

Her fingers moved through his hair, and he turned his head slightly, pressing his cheek to her soft skin, closing his eyes, revering the moment.

Later, their bodies sated from lovemaking, they lay naked in bed, their arms encircling each other and legs tangled together. Her head had been resting on his chest, but she shifted and lifted her gaze to his. "I take it you're happy about the baby?"

Kissing her lightly, he replied, "Having you back in my life again was everything I ever wanted. Having a baby with you is a bonus I didn't expect, but an honor I'll always treasure." She smiled and settled her head on his shoulder so that their gazes stayed pinned on each other.

"I still remember what you said to me in the lighthouse when I asked you to marry me," he said. "Whatever brought us to right here, right now, today, is simply the path that we needed to take."

She held his gaze, warming his heart and she agreed. "This, Tate, is our path. Forever."

Don't miss the next Lighthouse Security Keeper's story!
Click here to pre-order Clay

For a bonus, Levi will be joining the Lighthouse Security Keepers in a free novella coming out in September 2020!
Join my reader group for the link when it goes live!
Maryann Jordan Alpha Fans

ALSO BY MARYANN JORDAN

Don't miss other Maryann Jordan books!

Lots more Baytown stories to enjoy and more to come!

Baytown Boys (small town, military romantic suspense)

Coming Home

Just One More Chance

Clues of the Heart

Finding Peace

Picking Up the Pieces

Sunset Flames

Waiting for Sunrise

Hear My Heart

Guarding Your Heart

Sweet Rose

Our Time

Count On Me

For all of Miss Ethel's boys:

Heroes at Heart (Military Romance)

Zander

Rafe

Cael

Jaxon

Jayden

Asher

Zeke

Cas

Lighthouse Security Investigations

Mace

Rank

Walker

Drew

Blake

Tate

Hope City (romantic suspense series co-developed

with Kris Michaels

Hope City Duet (Brock / Sean)

Carter

Brody by Kris Michaels

Kyle

Ryker by Kris Michaels

Saints Protection & Investigations

(an elite group, assigned to the cases no one else wants…or
can solve)

Serial Love

Healing Love

Revealing Love

Seeing Love

Honor Love

Sacrifice Love

Protecting Love

Remember Love

Discover Love

Surviving Love

Celebrating Love

Follow the exciting spin-off series:

Alvarez Security (military romantic suspense)

Gabe

Tony

Vinny

Jobe

SEALs

Thin Ice (Sleeper SEAL)

SEAL Together (Silver SEAL)

Letters From Home (military romance)

Class of Love

Freedom of Love

Bond of Love

The Love's Series (detectives)

Love's Taming

Love's Tempting

Love's Trusting

The Fairfield Series (small town detectives)

Emma's Home

Laurie's Time

Carol's Image

Fireworks Over Fairfield

Please take the time to leave a review of this book. Feel free to contact me, especially if you enjoyed my book. I love to hear from readers!

Facebook

Email

Website

ABOUT THE AUTHOR

I am an avid reader of romance novels, often joking that I cut my teeth on the historical romances. I have been reading and reviewing for years. In 2013, I finally gave into the characters in my head, screaming for their story to be told. From these musings, my first novel, Emma's Home, The Fairfield Series was born.

I was a high school counselor having worked in education for thirty years. I live in Virginia, having also lived in four states and two foreign countries. I have been married to a wonderfully patient man for thirty-five years. When writing, my dog or one of my four cats can generally be found in the same room if not on my lap.

Please take the time to leave a review of this book. Feel free to contact me, especially if you enjoyed my book. I love to hear from readers!

Facebook
Email
Website

Made in the USA
Coppell, TX
18 February 2022

73772774R00194